BLAIR DENHOLM
COLD SHOT

By Blair Denholm

The Fighting Detective

Fighting Dirty
Kill Shot
Shot Clock
Trick Shot
Shot to the Heart
Drop Shot
Point Blank
Moving Target
Cold Shot

Vinci Books

vinci-books.com

Published by Vinci Books Ltd in 2026

1

Copyright © Blair Denholm 2024

The author has asserted their moral right to be identified as the author of this work in accordance with the Copyright, Designs and Patents Act 1988. This work is a work of fiction. Names, characters, places and incidents are the product of the author's imagination or are used fictitiously. Any resemblance to actual persons, living or dead, places and incidents is entirely coincidental.

All rights reserved. No part of this publication may be copied, reproduced, distributed, stored in any retrieval system, or transmitted in any form or by any means, including photocopying, recording, or other electronic or mechanical methods, nor used as a source for any form of machine learning including AI datasets, without the prior written permission of the publisher.

The publisher and the author have made every effort to obtain permissions for any third party material used in this book and to comply with copyright law. Any queries in this respect should be brought to the attention of the publisher and any omissions will be corrected in future editions.

A CIP catalogue record for this book is available from the British Library.

Paperback ISBN: 9781036708306

The EU GPSR authorised representative is Logos Europe, 9 rue Nicolas Poussion, 17000 La Rochelle, France
contact@logoseurope.eu

Prologue

IN THE FADING light of the late afternoon, the world outside sweated in jungle-green lushness. Amongst the tropical foliage that framed both sides of the road, signs advertising tonight's exhibition ice hockey match hung from light poles. As the Melbourne Mavericks' team bus ferried the players to the newly built Yorkville Entertainment Arena, Jonas Eriksson stared out of the window. A massive billboard showing a collage of players from both teams loomed ahead. He should have been pleased to see it up there; only three representatives from each franchise had been chosen for the promotional photoshoot. Still, a grunt of displeasure escaped from under his breath. They'd spent all day at the photographer's inner-Melbourne studio, and for what? You could barely make out Eriksson's face, pushed to the back of the collage with the younger, more attractive men at the front.

Wounded vanity aside, he was pumped for tonight's match. Whatever life's circumstances, the game was everything to him. If anyone lived and breathed hockey, it was Jonas Eriksson.

Tonight's opening match would be the first of three encounters with the Glacier City Hawks, an outfit of try-hards from a flyblown province no one outside of Canada could even find on a map. His own team, the Mavericks, comprised roughly half Australians and half imports. They stood a good chance against the Canadians; beating them would give Eriksson immense pleasure. He'd played in a Swedish youth team that nearly won the World Junior Championship – scored a hat trick – only to be narrowly beaten by Canada in the final match in a penalty shootout.

The coach had spent thirty minutes at the hotel giving the team a rousing pep talk, working himself into a lather in the process. There would be more of the same in the change-rooms once they got to the arena. That type of thing had little impact on Eriksson, no matter how stirring the speech. He was practically impervious to manufactured hype. The thought of beating the Canucks at their own game was motivation enough.

As the bus rolled around a sweeping bend in the road, there was no conversation among the players. Coach Raff had his scarred, bald head firmly stuck in one of those political biographies he liked to read; his teammates were either glued to the screens of their mobiles or listening to music through earbuds. Eriksson did neither; instead he visualised himself scoring goals and slamming the opposition into the boards. In his mind's eye, the Mavs had thrashed the opposition 10 to zip, the Canucks left to lick their wounds. The toot of a car horn yanked him out of his dreaming.

He stretched and yawned, body stiff from sleeping on a too-hard hotel bed. Or maybe it was age catching up with him. The average retirement age of hockey players was 36, and he was already 38.

He absently rubbed away a light coating of his condensed breath from the window glass. It looked like rain was coming. Clouds grey and menacing. The rain would be heavy, maybe a tropical storm. It would be a welcome relief from the oppressive heat they had endured the last couple of days in Yorkville. Made a change from Melbourne's miserable summer, but only a madman would settle in these steamy parts voluntarily.

In many ways Far North Queensland reminded him of Florida. Hot, humid, coastal. He remembered playing a couple of forgettable matches in the southern American state, against the Panthers and the Lightning. It wasn't long after the last game against the Panthers in 2011 that a horrific shoulder injury sent him crashing out of the National Hockey League.

Only after a year of tortuous rehab was he able to put the skates back on and hit the ice. But he'd lost much of his once mighty mojo; despite herculean efforts, he was unable to get back to his best form. Always in the back of his mind lurked the fear of reinjuring the shoulder, so he stopped playing like a man given days to live. He got all cautious and, if he was going to be completely honest with himself – timid.

The Boston Bruins dropped him, and the other franchises wouldn't touch him. All that was left to do was to scratch out a living as a journeyman player in the Euro leagues. It wasn't the worst option in the world for a Swedish guy. Then, after a long slump, none of the European teams wanted him either.

Now, here he was, in Australia, where ice hockey ranked marginally above competitive marbles as a serious sporting pursuit. On the positive side, a genius sports psychologist in Melbourne had helped him reacquire his mojo. Over the last year, his former fearlessness had come back, but he was smart enough to know that returning to the big league of the NHL was a pipe dream.

Another sign caught his eye, illuminated brightly by lights as the storm clouds gathered and dusk loomed. A simple warning: don't swim at the town's beaches unless you want to end up as a saltwater crocodile's lunch. The words were repeated in a number of languages. His mind drifted back to Florida again, the Everglades. Swap out crocs for alligators, southern drawl for Australian twang, and you could almost wake up in one place and think you were in the other.

His mobile buzzed. He didn't want to look at the message, but his eyes were drawn to the screen. The bus was a tourer, big enough for the players to have two seats to themselves if they wanted privacy. Eriksson wasn't much of a socialiser, so he almost always had an empty seat next to him. Not that any of his teammates wanted to share his company anyway. And that was fine by him.

Another glance at his phone. His heart nearly leapt out of his mouth. An American phone number, just like the previous one. His – *or her, or their* – demand had quadrupled. Because now it wasn't just a vague threat. The hard evidence had been produced.

Sixty-thousand US dollars by the end of the week or the photo would be released all over the internet. The details of how to make the payment would be sent tomorrow exactly 24 hours from now.

Shit.

He didn't have anywhere near that kind of money saved up. There was one chance to borrow it, but that was a long shot. Dammit, his life would be ruined beyond all repair if the image was made public.

The aircon in the bus was set to Siberian chill, but sweat dripped under his shirt. Heart thudding, he re-read the message, which ended with the instruction to open the picture file. In case he had any doubt about how serious the extortionists were. But there was no need to open it. He could already see in preview mode what it was. Jonas Eriksson, ten years ago, in Prague, shirtless, and with a joint hanging out of his mouth.

He wasn't alone. The other person in the photo wasn't wearing a shirt either. He was holding aloft a can of beer.

But there was more.

Both of them were surrounded by blocks of compressed heroin with a street value of over a million dollars. Money Eriksson never got his share of. As if that mattered now.

One thing puzzled him deeply. He had a pretty good memory, but he was stoned out of his head when the picture was taken, couldn't remember it happening. Was the other person in the photo being blackmailed, too? Eriksson imagined he must be. He'd try and contact him on the quiet, but it wouldn't be that simple. There had been no contact between them for years. Most puzzling of all, who took the damned photo?

He closed the message, switched off his phone, shut his eyes and took a deep breath.

Win the match first, deal with this shitstorm later.

Chapter One

THE TEAMS STOOD in straight lines either side of centre ice, dancing coloured spotlights creating a kaleidoscope for the spectators. A skinny, acne-faced young man belted out the national anthems of Australia and Canada in an off-key falsetto. The fact he had a tin ear and completely lost control of his upper register, where the notes wandered around like a drunk trying to cross a busy highway, had no bearing on the fellow's enthusiasm. Loud and proud and painful to listen to. As the last note of "O Canada" faded into silence, the crowd roared its approval of his raucous performance.

Skye Lisbon stretched her body around to speak into her father's ear as frenetic organ music burst out across the arena. 'He's the worst singer I've ever heard in my life.'

Detective Sergeant Jack Lisbon nodded sagely. 'Terrible, I agree.'

'But why did they clap for him?' She pursed her lips critically. 'I would have booed the guy off the rink.'

'I think he's got some kind of rare illness. He was in the

papers last week. A charity's been set up for him. Apparently he loves to sing, even if the talent doesn't match the passion.'

Skye's face crumpled at the news and she slunk back into her seat. 'Oh no! I feel terrible now.'

Jack squeezed her hand. 'You weren't to know, love.' He smiled warmly. 'I'll make a donation to the family on your behalf if it'll make you feel better.'

Hope lit up her face. 'Please do. Lots of money!'

'Of course.' He was about to add something, but a sharp, shrill whistle from centre ice and a voice to his left cut him off.

'Guys. Enough talking. Pay attention. It's about to start.' Detective Claudia Taylor's eyes burned with excitement as the referee dropped the puck onto the ice. Sticks flashed in a blur, one of them connecting with the puck and sending it to the opposite side of the rink.

Soon, just under 4,000 spectators were screaming for the Melbourne Mavericks. Everyone in Australia loves an underdog, and the Aussies were at long odds to beat the visitors. There were some fans wearing Hawks gear sprinkled about the stands, but they were clearly in the minority.

For a couple of minutes the action seesawed across the ice, with both teams taking shots but missing the mark. Each attempt was met with shrieks from the audience. Jack could barely contain himself, stamping his feet and applauding like he was back in his youth at a Clash concert. What little ice hockey he'd seen previously on the TV was nothing compared to the real thing. For starters, the game was faster than any sport he'd watched before. And you could also see the puck a lot more clearly. Blink at the wrong moment, though, and you could miss something. But even better than that was the physicality of the game. The men slammed into each other with ferocity; each thumping body check and crash into the boards brought a smile to the old boxer's craggy face.

With five minutes elapsed in the first period, the stadium erupted when a burly forward from the Mavericks directed the puck into the opposition's goal with a perfectly timed slap shot.

As the excitement subsided, Skye pulled out a program and a pen. 'Did you get the number of the player who scored?'

'Number 11,' said Jack. He pointed to the centre-hung scoreboard that offered a view to spectators in all sections of the stands. 'There's a replay.' They both paused to watch the slo-mo.

'Jonas Eriksson,' said Skye. She twisted her mouth and, with a flourish, made a mark on the program.

'What are you doing, defacing an important document?' Jack laughed. 'I'm sure there's a statute against that.'

'Don't be a wally.' Skye shook her head, thick curls bouncing. 'It's a souvenir, innit.'

Jack guffawed. 'Please don't talk like me.' Despite the words, his heart ached for the kid. She'd slotted into her new life in Australia better than he could have hoped for. He'd been a fish out of water when he arrived in a strange land with a suitcase full of secrets, which, touch wood, still remained buried. It wasn't easy finding his feet, but for Skye it had been a cinch. A bit of teasing about her British accent was all she had to put up with. She'd already been to a couple of sleepovers and was now begging Jack to allow her to host one. So far, he'd held out. The thought of a bunch of teenage girls running amok in his house sent his heart rate into overdrive.

Play resumed quickly after the first goal. The coaches

made some reshuffling decisions; players leaped over barriers to replace their teammates like sheep going over a fence. Things were happening so fast, Jack had no time to figure out what was what, but he couldn't care less. It was all about the experience for the town, and, like everyone else, he was lapping it up. Skye's small hand grabbed his wrist as she pointed at the rink with her other hand. 'Look, Dad! A fight.'

Now we're talking, Jack thought. A bit of fisticuffs. The entire crowd stood and yelled their approval as two players threw wild haymakers at each other. One tried to pull the other's jersey over his head to get the guy off balance. Their sticks remained on the ice, drawing a pursed-lipped nod of appreciation from Jack. A fair fight is a good fight. Whatever the players' disagreement, it ended with both sitting on the bench, cooling their heels a while.

The first period came to an end with a couple of blistering waves of attack on both goals, the Hawks managing to slot away a pair, taking a 2:1 lead into the break.

Taylor offered to brave the crowds, headed down the steep narrow stairway to grab hot chips and drinks for everyone, leaving Jack and Skye to dissect the spectacle they'd watched thus far.

'Claudia's getting right into it,' said Skye, popping the lid back on the pen, which she stowed away in her down jacket pocket. It was the first time she'd worn it since arriving in Far North Queensland in the middle of a summer that was exceeding the long-term averages in both heat and humidity. Jack, too, had to search high and low for a jumper to wear tonight. He finally found a sweater in his suitcase, still folded up from his last trip to England. Winter apparel wasn't a priority living in the tropics.

'I know. Very surprising. She normally has little interest

in sports.' He scratched his chin, trying to remember if there was a sport she followed. 'Actually, correction. No interest whatsoever. Except for jogging along the Esplanade and swimming laps at the pool, but that's just exercise and doesn't count.'

'Just between you and me, I think she's having heaps of fun tonight.'

'I think you're right, sunshine. Never seen her get so het up over entertainment. She can't sit still.'

Skye flashed a lopsided grin. 'Or maybe it's because she's out on a date with you?' The observation came with a small, pointy elbow jabbing him in the ribs. 'I know she likes you, Dad. Why don't you two just—'

'Give over!' He protested, feeling the temperature rise in his cheeks and a prickling sensation under his scalp. 'She's only here because Aden Trevarthen couldn't make it because he had to look after his sick kid.'

'That's two "becauses" in one sentence. Anyway, you knew that before you got the tickets, Dad.'

Jack popped a pellet of gum, gave it a good mashing, then said, 'Look, she's happy because she's enjoying the show, that's all.' He decided to push another line to steer the conversation into safer waters. 'You know, I think secretly she likes boxing, but ain't gonna admit it to me because she thinks watching it's not ladylike.'

A slow shake of the head. 'Don't be disingenuous, Dad.'

'Bleedin' heck. What does that even mean?'

'It means that, ah…'

'What are you two chatting about?' said Taylor, handing over two steaming buckets of hot chips and a couple of oversized drinks. She kicked her protruding handbag further under the collapsible chair before resuming her seat. 'Why is your face red, Jack? Not feeling well?'

'I'm perfectly fine, thanks. It's a reaction to the cold in here. I think you're a tad flushed, too.' He turned around to face his daughter. 'Isn't she, Skye?'

A shake of the head. 'No. She looks perfectly fine.'

No time for more chat as the players filed out onto the ice, again to the accompaniment of organ music. The announcer revved up the crowd with appeals to cheer as loudly as they could for the Aussie outfit, and the request was met with instant uproar. The teams quickly got into position and it was on again.

Jack's phone buzzed in his pants pocket. He ignored it, focusing on the match. He'd not had a night out in weeks, and he wouldn't let anything interrupt tonight's entertainment. The phone rang out, then the sound signifying a message had been left. Then it rang again. Out of the corner of his eye, he saw Taylor rifling through her handbag. She pulled out her mobile, the sound of its ringtone barely audible over the crowd noise.

Something's up, Jack thought, as Taylor pressed a hand over one ear and listened intently, her facial muscles tense. A look at the screen of his own mobile confirmed the calls had come from the Yorkville station. Then another from Constable Ben Wilson's personal number.

'What is it, Dad?' Skye's lips were drawn taut in concern. She glanced at Taylor to her left, then back to Jack. 'Why don't you answer your phone?'

'We're out enjoying ourselves, innit.'

'I dunno. Could be something serious.'

Taylor ended the call, reached across to Jack, tapped him on the wrist. 'There's some serious shit...' she blinked hard, then looked at Skye. 'I mean there's an incident in the outer suburbs. Home invasion, residents terrified. Uniforms are combing the area for the suspects. Inspector Batista wants a detective there.' She thrust her phone back into her bag. 'I'll go.'

'No.' Jack shook his head. 'Despite you apparently not being able to speak without swearing in front of a child.' He smiled at Skye, who rolled her eyes; she was used to hearing much worse from him, in the school playground for that matter. 'I'd like you to look after her for a while. I'm gonna take it.'

Taylor squinted. 'Why the enthusiasm now? You didn't even want to answer Wilson's call.'

He ran a hand through his short-cropped hair. 'I've been getting nothing but spam calls for weeks now. Crooks in the Philippines trying to rip me off with offers to buy solar panels or some such nonsense. They've been calling at this time of night.' He stood, drawing the ire of a woman in the row behind who screamed at Jack to sit down. He turned, glared at her, flashed his Queensland Police Service badge and she quickly shut up. Turning back to Taylor he said, 'Anyway, I'm pulling rank. You're staying to look after the kid. Ring me when the game's over.' As he descended the stairs, the crowd erupted. He looked up at the big screen. The Mavs had scored to level up at 2 apiece. In the car park he dialled Wilson and got the details. He hated to miss the match, but he hated missing the opportunity to nab violent offenders even more.

Chapter Two

HE STEPPED CAREFULLY over and around the fragments of shattered glass. The sliding door from the balcony had been smashed in, presumably with the handle of the garden spade which was now lying in the centre of the living area. Jack knew this address; he and Taylor had interviewed one of the residents in relation to the murder of a pool hall owner. Her testimony and co-operation had helped seal a conviction.

'Over here, Detective Lisbon,' called Constable Kylie Smith, standing beside a seated woman with a slim, athletic build. Jack recognised the victim in an instant. Local independent sex worker Michelle "Misty" Roach. Thirty-eight years old, of Indigenous heritage, and highly popular with the local male population.

'What happened here, love?' said Jack in his best sympathetic tone, the one he reserved for vulnerable females. 'You can't stay out of mischief, can you?'

Head hung low, the woman, exposed shoulders bathed

in a sheen of sweat, muttered something incomprehensible under her breath. 'I didn't catch that.' Jack flicked her softly under the chin, a feather-light touch. Misty looked up, blinking away tears. Out of the corner of his eye he saw Constable Smith compress her lips and shake her head slightly. It was frowned upon to touch people without a reason. Yes, he could have said something to get the woman's attention, but the action was instinctive and brought no reproving words, just a blank look.

'Three men broke into the house, threatened to beat up my customer just as he was putting his pants back on. One of them landed a vicious punch on him when he started to protest. Sat him on his bum and shut him up quick smart. Then they robbed him of his wallet and phone, took my money, too.' She waited a couple of beats. 'Well, some of it. Look, do I have to go over this again?' She flicked her large brown eyes towards Smith. 'I already told her everything.'

Smith nodded, placed a hand on Misty's back. 'You may have to repeat the facts several times, Ms Roach. Now, please tell Detective Lisbon what you told me. And add anything you might have forgotten and since remembered.'

'Take your time,' Jack encouraged. 'What you tell us while everything's fresh in your mind will help us catch them quicker.'

She shrugged her shoulders quickly. '*If* you catch them. Listen, I need a cigarette. There's a packet in the kitchen.' Misty folded bony arms across a voluptuous chest that defied gravity.

'You need a doctor after what you've been through, sunshine,' said Jack. He reached for his mobile. 'I'm going to call the paramedics, OK?'

She puffed out her cheeks and shook her head. 'Does

doctor sound the same as cigarette? I'm fine. They didn't touch me. Just let me fetch my smokes.'

'I'll get them', said Smith just as her mobile phone chirped in her pocket. She made an excuse-me face and ducked into the kitchen. She gave "uh huh" responses to the other party, a moment later brought a packet of cigarettes, plastic lighter and glass ashtray, then disappeared again.

'I don't think bringing punters back to your place is such a good idea. When did you start doing that?'

A tear formed in the corner of her eye behind a curtain of blue smoke. 'Since mum passed away.'

Jack swallowed hard. He remembered Betty-Lou Roach as a kind-hearted woman. 'I'm sorry to hear that.'

Misty brushed specks of ash from her lemon-yellow sun frock. 'Well, that's breast cancer for you.' She sucked in a lungful, expelled a cloud. 'So, there's no need for me to skulk around hotels 'n that. Mum knew what I did, of course. Never approved, but she loved me all the same.'

Fighting off the urge to hug the woman, with his own ex-wife recently succumbing to the big "C", Jack focused on the task at hand. 'Please, Michelle. Time's of the essence. Can you think of anyone who would target you?'

'Ha! Just about half the crims in town. People know I'm a cash-based business. Shit's getting worse with break-ins in Yorkville. Getting to be as bad as Cairns. These arseholes think they can do whatever they like without having to face punishment. I'm just grateful we weren't stabbed or bashed to death…this time!'

Jack nodded. He could get into a discussion with her about the causes of the QPS's lack of resources, the upsurge in crime. How the leniency of the courts was to blame, soft-on-crime politicians, kids getting their jollies by running rampant and uploading videos to social media to get likes. But what would be the point?

'What can you tell me about the attackers?'

'Young, I reckon. Probably teenagers. Dressed in jeans, dark t-shirts. And they all wore those bloody bala-whatcha-callits.'

'Balaclavas,' Jack prompted.

'Yeah, them.' She paused for a moment, eyes widening. 'My client won't need to speak to you, will he? I mean, I gotta protect his privacy. I'm valued in this town for my discretion.'

Jack scratched the back of his head and pulled out a small notebook. 'Give me his name, Michelle. Another witness won't hurt our case when we take the perpetrators to court.'

'Ha,' she scoffed. 'As if he told me his real name. He was going to pay me an extra bonus, too, before he was robbed.'

'We're getting off track.' His sympathy was dipping and he had to check the edge creeping into his voice. In any event, they could trace the client later via phone records if necessary. 'Was there anything familiar about the offenders?'

She tapped ash furiously into the ashtray. 'I was too scared to pay much attention. They were big – at least they seemed big. Didn't say much. One of them barked orders at us, the others seemed to be doing what he said. The leader threatened to tie us up and give us a hiding if we resisted. Like I said, my bloke had already copped a punch, so he did as he was told like a good 'un.'

'Could you see any part of their bodies? Skin tone? Tattoos?'

'Could have been Indigenous or white. It was pretty

dark, I just had candles going. Don't remember any tattoos on their arms. Again, like I said, it was dark.' She closed one eye as she concentrated. 'Geez, I'm not much help, am I?'

'Sorry to interrupt.' Smith appeared with an apologetic frown. 'Just had Wilson on the phone, sir. Constable Semmens called it in. He thinks he's found them.'

Jack stood to his full height. 'Thinks?'

'Three lads in a stolen late-model Camry tried to rob a service station out on Pramberg Road. They fit the description Ms Roach gave us. Still wearing their balaclavas, too. In this heat, can you imagine! Anyway, the manager was able to lock the front door, trapping the robbers inside the servo. He's hiding in a secure storeroom in the back, waiting for us to rescue him. He reckons he's safe there for now, but still scared out of his wits.'

'What's Semmens doing?'

'Waiting for backup. In other words – you and me. Trevarthen's home with his kid while his wife's working nightshift at the hospital. And Wilson's on comms duty.'

'No time to dawdle then.' Jack pocketed the notebook. 'Did Wilson say if there are customers stuck inside with these thugs?'

'Apparently not. At least he didn't mention it.'

'Which service station? There's two on Pramberg Road.'

'He didn't say.'

'Call him back, get him to ring me in…one minute. You stay here with Ms Roach.'

'I don't need babysitting now you've got them,' said Misty, reaching for her cigarettes. 'Call me when you've caught the bastards.'

Jack grinned. 'We don't know for sure it's the same perpetrators.'

'Of course it's the same boys!'

Jack shook his head. 'On the face of it, yes. But I've been around long enough to know not to make assumptions. I want someone here with you until it's confirmed a hundred percent.' He shot her his best disarming smile. 'Besides, Kylie makes a great cup of tea.'

'In that case,' Misty sighed and turned to Smith. 'I'll show you where everything is.'

Chapter Three

DRINKING SO MUCH WAS A MISTAKE, he realised. Should have eaten more to soak up the scotch. If only Australian bar snacks weren't so horrible. Those so-called meat pies were unfit for human consumption. Now, after imbibing so freely, mainly to mask his social insecurities and to make the event more bearable, he regretted not sticking with his initial decision of drinking only mineral water. Too late now. Just be careful not to fall and break a leg.

This late-night meeting out on the rink wasn't his idea. He liked the symbolism of it, though, so he'd readily agreed. He took careful, slow steps across the smooth ice. Funny how much harder it was to walk on it compared to skating, even on one leg zooming around the goal net chasing a puck. The mirror-like ice gleamed under the dull overhead lighting. Refreshed after the Zamboni treatment, the arena was primed and preened, ready for game two on Sunday night. Thank God it wasn't scheduled for tomorrow; the looming hangover for a non-seasoned drinker like him was sure to be a doozy.

He craned his neck up at the electronic scoreboard, now blank and lifeless. Just hours ago, his name had flashed in bright lights after he turned a certain draw into a breathtaking victory. The crowd had screamed his name. JO-NAS, JO-NAS! A boost to any man's ego, even for a man with the threat of being exposed as party to a massive drug deal hanging over his head. Didn't matter that it was years ago; the force of the law was sure to rain down hard upon his head. Interpol, that was it. They'd throw the book at him.

The photo he'd been sent was time stamped: nine and a half years ago. He'd looked up the statute of limitations for hard-drugs crimes committed in the Czech Republic. Ten to 15 years, depending on the scale. And the scale of his felony was huge. That meant no escape clause due to the passage of time. It would take a clever lawyer indeed to save his arse. He couldn't afford lawyers, let alone clever ones. As luck would have it, an extradition treaty had just been signed between Australia and the Czech Republic. He couldn't hide behind his Swedish passport, either, because there was also an extradition agreement between Sweden and the Czech Republic. The best option was just to pay the demand. Problem was, how?

Perhaps he could stall for time. He had a rich second cousin who lived in the city of Jönköping. Ulrika was married to an heir to the Husqvarna company. She'd be drowning in cash: sadly, he'd never met her and, even if he could talk her around, she had a reputation for being careful with her money. He'd be willing to take a bribe to sway an ice hockey match, but there wasn't a market for this sport in Australia worth bothering about. Nickel and dime stuff, as the Americans would say.

He took a deep breath and glanced at the phone's screen. Another two minutes to wait.

A look around at the stands. Empty, the lighting in the litter-strewn aisles just enough for the cleaners to see what they were doing when they finally got around to tidying up.

He sighed, again regretting his drinking tonight. So many thoughts tumbled around in his brain, none of them too coherent. A metallic scraping sound made him look over his shoulder. Nothing, just the usual creaking of a large, empty building. As if amplifying the eerie mood, low rumbling thunder echoed under the steel roof.

He tugged at the ribbon around his neck, held the cheaply made medal up for a better look. Player of the Match. They promised his name would be engraved on it at the end of the tournament. Hilarious! There was also a bonus $500 check to go with that piece of plastic. Whoop-de-doo. Not enough to pay off the blackmailers. *But you know what?* he said to himself. *Fuck those bastards. I'll deny every-thing. Say it's AI and I'm not in the photos at all.*

He squared his shoulders and thrust out his chin. Life had thrown some lemons at him, but he'd survived, hadn't he? A broken marriage, people hating on him for his intro-version, which they mistook for arrogance, an illustrious career gone begging.

But, to paraphrase Elton John, he was still standing. He could handle anything the fates chucked at him, just like he handled tonight's match with aplomb. In his mind's eye, seeing things a little out of focus thanks to the whisky he'd consumed, he relived the last minute of the contest.

A loose puck flipped in the air after an opposition player mishandled. Suddenly, the little black disc fell at Eriksson's feet. The Mavs were down a man in the power-play, which made his deed that more heroic. Deftly, he swept past two defenders like they were standing still, blasted the puck past the goalie's right ear like he was a frickin' brass statue. The siren to end the match brought the crowd to its feet.

What happened after that was a blur. Short interviews with some local and syndicated TV stations, the ceremony where he got the medal. His curt response of three words. "Thank you, everyone." Then lots of hand-shaking, platitudes about how keen he was to promote the sport in Australia. Finally, showered, changed, and then – partying. An introvert's version of partying, anyway. And too many drinks, which led to his agreement to meet on centre ice for a "chat" after everyone had left the facility. To bury the hatchet. Why not?

'Hey, Jonas!' came the cheery voice from over his shoulder. 'So pleased you could make it.'

Eriksson turned, ready to do or say whatever it would take to make this latest of his life's long list of annoying problems go away.

Instead, something long and shiny was held aloft, an object he recognised in an instant. It was hard and heavy and in a nanosecond it smashed him in the nose with incredible force. His once-lauded lightning reflexes were not what they used to be. His hands began to rise up to defend himself from the surprise onslaught, but they were too slow. The object slammed into his mouth like a log swing, dislodging a couple of his remaining real teeth. Blinding pain arced through every nerve of his being. His ears were still ringing from the thumping bass-heavy music the band had played at the function, but he clearly heard the accompanying vile abuse being hurled at him.

'Please, stop. What…'

'Shut up.' Another blow struck him behind the ear, spun him around 180 degrees. He couldn't understand how, impaired by alcohol, he managed to remain standing after the savage blows. Perhaps it was survival instinct: once you hit the floor, you were more vulnerable than if you kept on your feet. Or maybe it was the muscle memory of a lifetime spent balancing on two narrow strips of steel while moving at speeds nearing 35 kph.

With his attacker now behind him and consciousness fading fast, his legs began to wobble and then to give way. His spine turned to jelly. Eriksson blinked twice, blood swirling in his eyeballs. His brain was no longer capable of thought. The hard object hit him in the head again.

He sensed himself falling towards the ice, the glossy surface rushing up to meet him. His hands thrust forward, fingers splayed, to brace against the impact of the fall. On the way down he was struck once more, harder than ever.

Jonas Eriksson was dead before his body hit the ice.

Chapter Four

JACK SCREECHED to a halt in a parking bay at the front of the Caltex service station. New tyres on the Hilux, too. Never mind, it was less than a millimetre of rubber. Next to him, Semmens sitting in the patrol car. They nodded to each other, alighted and strode to the reinforced glass doors. The glass was crazed from futile escape attempts made with snack food stands and whatever else the offenders could lay their hands on.

Jack cupped his hand to the glass. 'Have you seen them in there?'

'Yeah,' Semmens chuckled. 'They went at it like wildcats for about five minutes before realising there was no getting out. They're sitting beside the ice-cream refrigerator in the far right corner.'

'Yep. I see them.' The offenders sat among piles of debris, evidence of their rampage. One was even eating from a packet of potato chips. Insurance should cover the damages, Jack figured. Highly unlikely the young perpetrators would be paying for it. 'You got the code from the manager for us to get inside? Time to introduce ourselves.'

Semmens nodded, consulted his mobile and punched a sequence of numbers into a keypad. The officers took a step back to get in line with the sensor and the doors opened. Crossing the threshold with his Glock clutched in outstretched hands, Semmens at his shoulder in the same pose, Jack roared, 'All of you thieving pricks, stand up, hands behind your backs!'

In contrast to the teens' one-night violent crime wave, they surrendered in peace. No resistance, hands meekly folded behind their backs as commanded.

Stepping closer, it was clear none of the male offenders, balaclavas now off, was older than seventeen. Faces like babies, yet to feel a razor. Two of European background, one, contrary to Misty's guess, of Aboriginal descent. Not that it mattered: there would be no APB, no door-to-door search, physical descriptions now unnecessary. Jack clenched his teeth. This was, ironically, a bad result: they'd be dealt with by the juvenile justice system. A slap on the wrist, maybe some community work. He'd not seen any of them before in his five years working at Yorkville CIB. Which meant, as newbies to the courts, all they'd get would be a warning. Free to roam the streets again, terrorise people like Misty Roach and small business owners. Of course, they could be opportunists from out of town, hopefully with criminal records and hence more likely to get a custodial sentence. Time would tell.

Cuffed and subdued, they marched out in single file and into the back of the Land Cruiser, fitted out with a secure compartment to transport detainees. Jack slammed the door closed on them after Semmens had read them their rights.

He then turned on his heel to attend to the rattled service station manager, waiting by the coffee machine with a paper cup shaking in his hands.

Chapter Five

WELL PAST MIDNIGHT, the air still muggy and sticky, Jack clambered up the old wooden stairs. At the top was a broad balcony that fully wrapped around his old farmhouse. In need of some major repairs, he'd bought the property for a song two years ago at an auction. The house was part of a deceased estate, with the heirs keen to sell fast and pocket the cash. It was built in the early 1900s by a man who owned vast tracts of sugar cane fields and made a fortune in the boom times. The rambling house, paint peeling in spots under the eaves, was Jack's pride and joy. He'd vowed to restore it to its former glory if it took him the rest of his working life. At the rate he was going, it probably would.

He wiped his shoes on the rubber doormat, removing damp grass clippings from this morning's mow. Seeing much of the grass still adhered to his boots, he flicked them off with a mutter, shoved his manky black socks inside them and stepped into his castle. Taylor gave an uninterested "hi" without turning around; she was engrossed in an action movie on the TV. The volume was turned down so low he wondered she could hear it at all. Then he noticed the teletext subtitles flashing across the bottom of the screen. Skye lay beside her on the couch, curled up asleep, covered only by a thin sheet. A couple of ceiling fans whirred overhead, struggling to keep the prickling heat at bay. Born and raised in the deep north, Taylor coped with the conditions better than he did. The aircon in the living area had packed it in a week ago, and an urgent fix was required. Thankfully, it still worked in his and Skye's bedrooms.

Jack gave a nod of greeting as Taylor finally turned her head towards him. He grabbed a can of soft drink from the fridge, then tiptoed across the polished wooden floor boards, sat in his favourite armchair next to the couch.

'You going to leave her like that?' Taylor gestured at the sleeping girl. 'I'd have taken her myself, but she looked so peaceful sleeping I didn't want to wake her.'

'In a minute.' He ran a hand across his scalp. 'I just need a minute to pull myself together.' He drained half the can and placed a knuckle against his lips as he stifled a burp.

Taylor picked up the remote and turned off the television as the final credits rolled. 'You've been gone a long time. What's up?'

'The usual. Villains doing bad things.'

'Can you be more specific?'

Jack described what had transpired at Misty Roach's place, the arrest of the very same offenders at the service station.

'You got a break when they decided to push their luck,' said Taylor, taking off a yellow scrunchie and shaking her hair loose. Jack's eyes narrowed: she looked a million bucks with her hair cascading around her shoulders.

'They were cocky, like most teen offenders. We carried

out a short interview – a waste of time since they clammed up on the advice of the dickhead lawyer from Legal Aid. Called the parents: not even interested in showing up, can you believe it? Then we charged them, took photographs, fingerprints, all the bells and whistles. Considering the seriousness of the crimes, I was all for sending them for a stint in the youth detention centre until trial, but here's where "the usual" applies.'

Taylor nodded slowly. 'Let me guess. Inspector Batista vetoed it.'

'Spot on. I don't get what's come over him lately. Getting all soft the closer he is to retirement.'

'That's at least ten years away, Jack.'

'Really?' He rubbed a hand over his face. 'What a pity. He's turned into a bleeding heart when it comes to these young crims. All this molly-coddling isn't the way. The stats tell the story. What they need is a firm hand.' He clenched his fist and held it in the air. 'There has to be proper consequences for criminal actions.'

'You're preaching to the converted, Jack.' She offered a sympathetic smile. 'All we can do about it is what we're paid to do. Enforce the law. After that, it's out of our hands.'

'Rumour has it the new magistrate's of the same stripe as Batista.' He sighed deeply. 'You know, even if we did detain them, it would've only been an overnighter. There'd have been an early morning bail hearing with the young thugs walking free until a trial at the youth justice court, which would also be a complete waste of time.'

'I disagree,' she countered. 'The magistrate will see sense. These crimes are very serious. If all the victims testify they were scared for their lives, then–'

'They bleedin' were!'

'For sure they'll get handed a custodial sentence. Mark my words.'

'Wish I could share your optimism.' He leaned back, fingers interlocked behind his head. 'I fear for this society unless some changes are made. Big changes.'

Taylor said, 'I know being a cop's a thankless task, but,' she nodded at Skye, a line of drool at the side of the girl's mouth, 'at least you've got her in your life now, right?'

'True,' he replied flatly. 'No point lamenting about things I can't control. She matters more than anything in the world to me now.' He scooped Skye up in his arms, carried her to bed with a waddling stride. Two minutes later he returned to the lounge room. In the kitchen, the kettle whistled as it came to the boil. 'Not sure coffee's a good idea at this time of night. I'm ready to crash. The kid and I were planning on going fishing in the morning.'

'I'm making herbal tea. It'll help you relax and sleep better. I always carry a few sachets.' She ordered him to sit while she got them each a drink. Too exhausted to object, he mouthed a thank you.

A minute later Taylor had brought the drinks. 'You're welcome to stay the night if you want.' Jack sipped his tea, eyes closed as if the offer was a flippant remark rather than one he dearly wanted her to agree to. 'It's,' he checked his watch, 'getting on for 2:00am. Maybe you'd like to come fishing too?'

'I'd love to say yes, Jack. To both kind offers. Only I promised to drive down to Innisfail to visit my sister, Annie. You remember her, don't you?'

Before he could process her disappointing answer, Jack's phone exploded with the trademark "London Calling" ringtone. Constable Ben Wilson in a flap. 'Detective Lisbon, I'm so sorry to bother you at this late hour.'

'Don't apologise, you pillock. It's your job to bother me.' Rather disingenuous, he admitted to himself, since he'd ignored the urgent calls he'd received at the ice hockey match. He took another sip of the tea, frowning at the floral taste that was getting stronger with the bag left in the cup. 'I was just about to go to bed, so this better be important.'

He listened intently for a couple of minutes, brain spinning with the startling information received. Disconnecting the call, he turned to Taylor and said, 'The request to stay here tonight is now an order.'

Taylor sat up straight, confusion knitting her brow. 'Please explain?'

'Do you know where Skye kept the match program she was writing on?'

'It's there, right in front of you on the coffee table.' He reached down and grabbed it. 'Please, Jack, what on earth is going?'

'I need to quickly bone up on these guys. One of them might be a murderer.'

Chapter Six

ONE HAND on the steering wheel, Jack drank from the opening of the gleaming steel thermos. Using the screw-on plastic cup was out of the question when driving at breakneck speed. He savoured the last drop of his home-brewed extra-strong coffee, tossed the bottle over his shoulder onto the back seat. Pulling into the stadium parking lot, he turned to Taylor and said, 'I hope that tea you gave me doesn't have a...whaddaya call that effect of something that puts you to sleep?'

'Soporific?'

He closed one eye tight. 'I was thinking more like tranquillising, but I'll take your word for it.'

'Looks like everyone's here,' said Taylor. 'Except Kylie Smith.' She smiled, pleased with herself for suggesting the option of Smith doing babysitting duty so Taylor wouldn't miss out on the action. This was the biggest crime to hit Yorkville since Jack returned from Portugal six months ago.

'Looks like it,' said Jack. He took in the small gathering of vehicles. The pathologist's van occupied a position in a drop-off zone near the main entrance to the arena. Next to it, the Ford Territory Semmens had arrived in, and next to that Inspector Batista's personal vehicle, a two-year-old EV. It was a recent acquisition that Jack considered impractical for the rugged local conditions; he harboured the thought the boss had purchased the damn thing purely as a virtue-signalling exercise. The car was constantly playing up, needing something fixed, but Batista would only praise it as the pinnacle of automotive achievement. Bollocks. Jack would take a reliable diesel-powered Hilux any day of the week.

The two detectives were greeted by Constable Noah Semmens at the front entrance. 'Didn't expect to be seeing you again so soon, sir,' he said, fiddling with one of the straps of his kit.

'Me neither,' said Jack. 'Sounds like a juicy one. It's gonna be the talk of the town in no time. What do you know?'

Semmens quickly explained how a cleaner had discovered the lifeless body of Jonas Eriksson in the middle of the rink at around 01:15. 'The hysterical man rang the stadium manager, who happened to still be on site. Fell asleep in the executive box, apparently. No answer, so the cleaner searched high and low until he found him and was able to wake him up. The manager, in turn, called us. Also on the verge of hysterics, as you can imagine.'

'They both still here?' said Taylor.

A nod. 'Batista's upstairs with the manager and the cleaner now.' Semmens looked at Jack. 'He didn't want to let them go until they'd been spoken to by you, sir. They're up on the top level in one of the executive boxes. Want me to take you there?'

'We'll find it. Who else is here? Any of the other players, coaches, staff?'

'No, sir. They're at a hotel downtown. Presumably tucked up and sound asleep.'

'Has Batista officially informed anyone of the crime?'

'Don't know, sir. You'll have to ask him yourself.'

Jack frowned. Considering the lateness of the hour and the scale of the exhibition tournament, the Inspector would be wrestling with all kinds of decisions on how to proceed. Jack didn't envy him on that score. He touched Semmens on the shoulder. 'Hopefully, we can get the preliminary work done quickly and you can go home and get some rest.'

'I'm looking on the bright side.' His smile was a thin line. 'Plenty of overtime for Yorkville's finest, hey?'

'That's not the way to look at it, Noah,' said Jack, shaking his head. 'It's not all about money, is it? Is that why you joined the Queensland Police Service?'

'Ah...no, sir.' Semmens stared at his boots.

'Glad to hear it. Are the entrances secure?'

'Damien Wells is stationed at the door on the opposite side to us, just in case, but there's no way anyone's getting in here. It's a boutique arena with just two ways in and out.'

'Don't give anyone access through this door unless a senior officer gives the go-ahead.'

'Of course, sir.'

Jack and Taylor exchanged a glance that said *good luck* and made their way inside.

Chapter Seven

THE BODY, covered in a white sheet, lay on a gurney inside the home team's changeroom. 'We couldn't leave him out there on the ice to examine him,' said pathologist Margaret Proctor. 'Totally impractical.'

'I've walked on ice before; a frozen lake in Scotland,' said Jack, hitching thumbs into his belt loops. 'It's easy enough if you've got the right shoes for the job and you don't charge about like a billy goat.'

'I disagree,' said Proctor. 'Those disposable Tyvek shoe coverings we wear at crime scenes? They're useless on the ice. We'd need non-slip overshoes designed for icy conditions, cleats, something like that. None of those items are in our inventory. We have to work with what we've got.'

'How'd you get him off there, then?'

'Very slowly.' She nodded towards her assistant, Clara Littlejohn, watching on but keeping silent. 'The two of us, plus Constable Wells, picked him up – Wells under the shoulders, Clara and I had hold of a leg each. The victim is...*was*...a healthy 90-kilo specimen, but once we got him on the gurney we managed to wheel him in here with no one slipping over and breaking any bones.'

'So what about evidence out on the ice?' said Taylor. 'Surely it'll melt or…'

'It could theoretically melt if the power went out.' Proctor smiled in a way that was almost condescending, but not quite. 'And although unlikely, it could happen. That's why we had to move quickly. You would have seen a couple of yellow markers in the middle of the rink on your way here?'

Jack and Taylor nodded.

'That's where the cleaner found him. Before we brought the victim inside, we carried out a preliminary examination of the scene and the body *in situ*. Of course, there's a lot more work to be done.'

'Wouldn't there have been tracks left by the players?' said Jack.

'No.' Taylor chipped in. 'You missed it when you left to attend the home invasion. After breaks in play a big machine came out and smoothed over the surface. It's called a Zambonis.'

'Zamboni,' corrected Proctor with her trademark air of superiority. 'It scrapes off a thin layer of ice then drops some water, which quickly freezes, making the surface nice and smooth again. So all the tracks left by the players are gone.'

'That's good, isn't it?' said Jack. 'I'm assuming the machine was used at the end of the match too?'

'Yes,' said Proctor. 'That will definitely help us identify any faint footprints.'

'Photos?' said Taylor.

'Plenty.' Proctor tugged on her rubber gloves absently. 'The photographer took shots from many angles. Clara and

I collected samples from the surface around the immediate area of the body. His bloody clothes will be examined in the laboratory. The cold conditions out on the rink should preserve anything we've missed until we do a secondary sweep. Or until the site is no longer classified as a crime scene, and,' she paused, 'as long as no one turns off the refrigeration switch. However, I'm confident we've got enough to make a good start.'

'Was he still wearing his uniform?' said Jack. 'Did he have skates on?'

'No,' said Proctor, reaching for the top of the sheet. 'The victim was in a pair of blue jeans, a collared shirt with a cardigan, and a pair of rubber-soled shoes, not his playing uniform. Apparently there was a function in the top-tier box after the game. Now,' she paused for a moment, 'are you ready to have a look at this fellow, or do you want to wait until we get to the mortuary?' She adjusted her thick, black-framed glasses, glanced at Taylor. 'It's not pretty, and that's an understatement. I recall you can get rather squeamish at the sight of gore?'

'Go ahead,' said Taylor, stepping closer to the side of the gurney, still half a stride behind Jack, eyes agog and eager to see the damage. 'I've undergone a course of desensitisation therapy. I can handle it.'

The sheet slid back and Taylor gasped, her hand shot to her mouth. Jack reacted in an almost identical fashion, without the gagging sounds. Eriksson's featureless face was a mess of red and purple pulp. Taylor blurted, 'On second thoughts, perhaps I'd be more useful assisting the Inspector.'

Jack missed what Taylor said, transfixed by the horrific sight before him. A deep breath and a swallow, he craned his neck forward for a better look.

'Did you hear me?' said Taylor.

'Sorry?' He turned his head, frowning.

'I said I'll help the Inspector.'

'Sure, sure. I'll be with you shortly.'

With Taylor gone, Proctor summarised her initial conclusions and theories. 'Pending an autopsy to rule out other scenarios, on the face of it – excuse the turn of phrase – the cause of death is severe blunt force trauma to the head. Front, back and both sides. I've never seen a person's head beaten to such an extent.'

'Me neither. And I've seen plenty.' Jack swore under his breath. 'His face is so…destroyed…how can we be sure it's Eriksson?'

'There's just enough of his face intact that matches his driving licence for me to be certain. The shape of his ears, for example, is a perfect match. Of course, we can confirm through dental records and other means if necessary. It's a shame they removed "height" from licences, but even without that parameter, I guarantee it's him.'

'This was next-level brutal. Any idea what he was hit with?'

'Not fists, unless it was Mike Tyson using weighted gloves. Obviously something heavy. The physical damage is colossal. The samples we scraped off the ice will contain fragments of skull and brain tissue.'

Jack's mind rewound to his first murder case in Yorkville, when an MMA fighter was killed with a kettlebell swung in anger. He voiced the theory that something similar had been used this time.

Proctor compressed her lips tightly for a second. 'Probably. There are no signs of any defensive wounds or signs of a struggle, so I'd say the victim's been taken by surprise.'

'Which indicated he may have known the killer.'

'Yes, that would be my guess.'

'Time of death?'

'This is a fresh kill. Due to the cold conditions in the arena, rigor mortis hasn't even begun to set in. With that in mind, I'd estimate TOD as within the last three to four hours.'

Jack did a quick mental calculation. 'Cleaner found him at 01:15, it's now,' a glance at his watch, '03:17. Which means he could've found the body very soon after the murder was committed. He himself could, in theory, be a suspect.'

Proctor quirked one of her thick eyebrows. 'Indeed.'

'Was he murdered where he was found, or somewhere else and brought onto the ice?'

'Unless the killer had levitational powers, then the fellow was definitely slain on centre ice.'

'How so?'

'No blood trail from the side of the rink. You saw the face. All the blood was where the body lay, in an arc around the head. It was coagulated and partly frozen. The fact there are no bloody footprints left by the killer is very interesting. It tells me the weapon, whatever it was, was able to be wielded at some distance from the victim.'

'An ice hockey stick?'

Proctor shook her head. 'I'm no expert in the weights of hockey sticks, but I'd say something heavier was used here.'

'Cricket bat?'

'More plausible. The blows were hard enough that fragments could have broken off the murder weapon and ended up in the victim's skull or our ice samples.'

'Bloody footprints would have been mighty handy,' Jack mused, his eyes still riveted to the victim's disfigured face.

'Don't count it out. I'm hopeful the photos will reveal footprints that are invisible to the naked eye.'

'We might find soil or other contaminants – shoe polish, for example – in the samples we took,' said Littlejohn, startling Jack since she'd been silent until now. 'Maybe hair or skin flakes. Once you've got some suspects, that evidence could link to them.'

Proctor nodded. 'We grabbed a number of ice samples within a circle around the body with a radius of 20 metres, and in metre-wide bands running back to the edge of the rink.'

'Makes sense,' said Jack. 'With the victim in the middle of the ice and no obvious footprints, you can't be sure which direction either he or the perpetrator came from.'

'We can take educated guesses. There are two gates the teams use to enter the arena. Another where the Zamboni comes from. Most likely they came from those directions. The perspex barrier would be rather difficult to climb over.'

'Although not impossible?'

'Possible,' she conceded. 'With a ladder. It's about two and a half metres high at the goal ends, and one and a half along the sides. In reality,' she tightened her cheek muscles, 'not likely.'

'Did he have a mobile phone on him? Other devices?'

'No.'

Jack's immediate thought – the victim's phone had been taken by the killer. Which meant it could contain incriminating evidence. 'Any personal items on him?'

'A wallet with $260 in cash and the usual assortment of cards. That's it. Oh, and a medal around his neck with the words "Player of the Match" etched into it.'

Jack took possession of the bagged up wallet and medal. He'd log them at the station when he got there – whenever the hell that was going to be.

'Annoying about the lack of a phone. Fingers crossed he

just left it somewhere and the offender didn't take it and destroy it.'

'Telcos keep the metadata, don't they?'

'Yeah, but rarely the content if it gets deleted.' He gestured with his eyes towards the ceiling. 'In an arena like this, there's bound to be plenty of CCTV coverage. Maybe that will come to our rescue.' He smiled a humourless smile. 'Your work might end up being of secondary importance if the crime was caught on video.'

'I don't have a clue about that, Detective Lisbon.' Proctor's eyes widened. 'And I take issue with you insinuating our work is of secondary importance. On the contrary, it's more likely to result in a conviction than a video, which can be blurry or of dubious quality. It can be tampered with, altered. People can conceal their appearance if they know they're going to be filmed.' She held up a finger demonstrably. 'DNA and physical evidence, on the contrary, are—'

'Yes, yes. No offence intended, Margaret. I'm just hoping for an easy case. It's effin' late and I'm tired. It's already been the longest day I can remember and I've got a feeling it's far from over.'

Before she could comment further, Jack effusively thanked Proctor and Littlejohn for their efforts, said he'd catch up with them later at the mortuary, and exited the changeroom. He strode around the lower walkway, looking up. He quickly spotted an illuminated rectangular window at the top of the stands on the western side of the arena, shadows of figures moving about. He took the concrete steps two at a time, found his way to the first of the trio of executive boxes.

Inside, half-empty glasses, plates, wicker baskets and used cutlery lay on tables spread around the room. Seemed the cleaning crew hadn't got to this area yet. Possibly a good thing: Proctor and Littlejohn might find something useful up here.

Four people were clustered about a table – clean compared to the others – close to the door. Inspector Batista and Taylor were standing; two others sat in white plastic chairs. One was a visibly shaken man in his mid-sixties, the other was a younger man, early-forties, fidgeting like his nerves were about to snap. The tense lines in Batista's face relaxed a little when Jack finger-tapped on the side of the door frame. 'Come in. I've delayed this longer than I should have.'

'Sorry, boss. I had some questions for Proctor.' He took up a position at Batista's right shoulder. He nodded at the older man, dressed in grey overalls with a yellow shammy cloth poking out of his front pocket. 'You the cleaner?'

'Yes.'

'Can you confirm for me you're the one who found the victim out on the rink?'

'I already spoke to him, Jack,' interrupted Taylor. 'I took lots of notes. No need to put him through it again at this stage. You can see he's not up for it.'

'Agreed.' It was plain she was right: the man wasn't far from entering delayed shock. Jack made the quick call to Proctor. 'I've got a highly distressed witness here. Can you send Clara up to tend to him while we call an ambulance?' He ended the call, turned to the younger man. Before he could speak, the cleaner went to stand on wobbly legs; Jack stayed him with a motion of his hand. 'Whoa! Please, don't get up. Somone's coming to make sure you're OK.' Jack put in the call to the paramedics as the man collapsed back into his seat.

Taylor retrieved a bottle of spring water from a bar fridge, poured some into a plastic cup and handed it to the man. He took it in shaking hands, drank greedily, spilling drops onto the floor.

'I just want to go home to my wife. She's worried sick. I called her, but I wasn't allowed to tell her what had happened.' The man looked up, tears welling in his eyes. 'Please…'

Littlejohn appeared at the door, made a beeline for the cleaner. 'What's your name, sir?' she said, kneeling and reaching for his wrist as she subtlety took a pulse.

'Ravi Kapur.'

'Can you come with me, Mr Kapur? Let's wait downstairs for the ambos to have a look at you, hey? They'll drive you home.'

As she gently led him out of the room, Jack sighed with relief. Although loathe to let a red-hot witness off the hook, Ravi's presence would be a negative at this point. The other man, although highly nervous, looked like he was in a fitter state to be interviewed.

Batista suggested they all take a seat and received no objections.

'Jack, this is Ned Campbell,' said Batista with a sweeping hand gesture. 'He tells me he's the manager of the facility. Luckily, he was present in the arena when Mr Kapur found the body. I'm sure he'll offer us his complete cooperation. Unfortunately, I have a Zoom call with Assistant Commissioner Landacre at 9:00am and I need at least a couple hours sleep if I'm to stay awake for it.' He turned to Campbell. 'I'll leave you in the capable hands of my two best detectives.'

Jack smiled. They were his *only* detectives, but the chief somehow made the compliment sound genuine. Depending on the complexity of the case, other investigators might be seconded from Cairns, even Brisbane. He hoped it wouldn't come to that. 'Who's been informed of the murder so far?'

'No one knows about it apart from us, forensics and the paramedics who declared the victim dead. I'd like you to call the coach of the Mavericks at the Yorkville Grand Hotel and let him know one of his star players won't be coming back. Warn him to keep it under his hat until we've made an official announcement. Find out who the next of kin is, then get on the blower to them. I feel a shitstorm brewing over this.'

'It's effin' late, sir.' Jack recalled the name of the coach from the program. Gordon Raff. 'What if he doesn't answer?'

'Then you and Claudia will have to pay him a visit, won't you? In fact...' he paused like it was a lightbulb moment, '...I insist you go there in person tonight, or this morning, or whatever the hell it is. I repeat, I want the next of kin found and notified ASAP. I don't want them finding out over the bloody Internet.'

'Jesus, sir. Can't someone else do it?'

'There is no one else, Jack. This is little old Yorkville, remember? I can easily request backup from Cairns if you're not up to the task. They've got a couple of detectives twiddling their thumbs, I'm sure.'

'No need, sir,' said Jack tetchily. 'We've got it.'

At the door Batista turned around. 'Claudia? I'll need you to prepare a press statement about this, fire it off once the NOK matter's been resolved.'

'I was writing it out in my head, sir.'

'No alarmist language. Brief and to the point. Say the man died in suspicious circumstances and that inquiries are ongoing. The standard thing.'

'Sir.'

With Batista gone and Taylor at another table scribbling a draft on her notebook, Jack directed his attention to the manager. 'Now, Mr Campbell. Any idea what the hell went down here tonight?'

'Yeah.' The man's shoulders slumped. 'A friggin' disaster.'

Chapter Eight

'WHY WOULD you describe it as a "disaster"?' said Jack, taking the lid off a pen with his teeth and flipping open his notebook. 'A strange word choice in my opinion.'

The manager opened his mouth as if to speak, closed it again and screwed up his eyes. Weighing his words, not wanting to say the wrong thing. Understandable. This was a shocking situation. Nevertheless, Jack instinctively formulated a negative impression of the man. Campbell, muscles twitching and tensing, looked like the type who'd be more concerned about the fallout from the incident than the fate of the dead man, the feelings of his relatives and friends. It was often the way: people first see their own inconvenience when misfortune strikes.

A prompt was in order. 'Did you hear me?'

'Yes, I heard you,' came the raspy reply. Jack smelled stale alcohol on his breath. 'Of course it's a disaster. How else would you describe it?'

'A tragedy, maybe. A heinous crime. A disaster? That's a bushfire, a flood, a plane crash.'

Campbell shrugged. 'Well, that's how I choose to see it. Free country, isn't it? A man's been killed at the first important event held in this brand-new arena. It's totally fucked up.'

Jack needed details, not opinions on semantics. He pressed on. 'Tell me about the circumstances as you know them. What happened immediately after the match?'

'The place went nuts when the Mavericks won it 6-5 with 30 seconds on the clock. Ironically, it was Jonas Eriksson who scored the decider.' Campbell wrung his hands. 'Poor bugger. From hero to dead man in one night.'

'Then what?' Taylor had earlier told Jack the result of the match, including that Eriksson played a crucial role in the win and how the crowd went wild. It could be important that the victim was the one to sink the opposition. Perhaps that last-gasp victory pissed someone off, lost them a lot of money. Jack was no newcomer to murders where sports betting was a major factor. 'Why was the victim here so late at night and not tucked up in his bed?'

'Same reason I'm here, I guess.' Campbell puffed out his cheeks before pouting. 'There was a private function for the two teams and a number of invited guests. The company that built the stadium put on the show.'

'The show?'

He rocked back, then forward again, face contorting with the effort of recollection. 'Look, can we do this in the morning? I'm totally shattered...' He stifled a yawn.

'No!' Jack thundered, slapping a hand on the table. 'A man's been murdered!'

'Everything OK?' said Taylor, twisting around in her chair.

'Hunky dory, Detective Taylor. Sorry to interrupt you.'

She nodded understandingly and went back to writing in her notebook.

Jack refocused on Campbell. 'Listen, pal. Time is not our friend and I need answers quickly. Of course, the tournament will have to be cancelled now, so the sooner we get moving with this investigation, the better.'

'We can't cancel it!' Campbell jumped to his feet. 'A delay, maybe, while you run your inquiries, but you can't cancel it.'

'Sit down,' Jack growled.

Back in his seat, the colour began to drain from Campbell's face. As it did, Jack noticed the slightly bulbous nose, the way the red and purple capillaries throbbed against the paler skin of his cheeks. The man was a seasoned drinker. 'Why do we have to stop the tournament? I've got money invested in this.'

'Really?' Jack's initial gut feeling proved correct. It was all about *him*. 'I thought you were just the arena manager?'

He hissed through gritted teeth. 'Well, now you know different. I've got a massive stake in this endeavour. I can't let it fail.'

'That might not be up to you.' He reached in his jacket and plucked out a packet of gum. Campbell declined the offer to take a piece. 'So, who and what are you, exactly? Yorkville's a small place and, no disrespect, I've never heard of you.'

The man's frown flipped around to a half smile, lips pulled back from his teeth. 'I only arrived here recently from Victoria. Been renting a nice place on the Esplanade for a month, helping prepare for the tournament, learning how everything runs inside the stadium. Once things are going smoothly, a local person will take over and I'll go back to Victoria. I've taken leave from my job.'

'What do you normally do for a living?'

'I'm an electrical engineer by trade. These days I do consulting work mostly.'

'Why you, though? Why not a local person from the outset?'

'I've been involved in the ice hockey scene most of my life. Played until my mid-thirties, off and on. Then I got involved in the administration side of things.'

'When you said you've got your own money invested, how much?'

He sighed; a shadow crossed his face, like he regretted having said what he had. 'I've taken out a second mortgage on my house, tipped funds into a company that's going to set up a hockey super league, kind of like World Series Cricket back in the day. '

'I see.' Jack recalled the breakaway competition that revolutionised cricket around the globe, gave it more appeal to a younger audience. 'But cricket's the national sport in Australia. It was already popular. You've got your work cut out with ice hockey, pal.'

'True. But we believe we can build support over time. The crowd loved it tonight. Especially with the Mavs winning. Now…it's all going to be for nothing.'

Jack decided now was the time to ask the standard murder enquiry questions. 'Did you know the victim personally?'

Campbell's eyes narrowed before he inclined his head forward a fraction. 'I know all the players in the Mavericks, if only by name. I wouldn't call any of them friends, or even acquaintances.'

'Know why anyone would want to kill Eriksson?'

A slow shrug. 'No idea. They say he's a surly character. Keeps to himself pretty much. Had a rough trot in his life with injuries and the like. Failed marriage. Listen, you're going to get better answers from his teammates. And his coach, I reckon.'

'Don't worry. I'll be talking to them as soon as I'm done with you.' Jack hunched forward and said, 'Where can I see some CCTV footage?'

'Follow me.' Campbell almost sighed with relief at being let off the hook with questions. He led Jack down a set of internal stairs into an office on the ground floor. Like the rest of the place, it reeked of newness. The smell of fresh paint and carpets made Jack crinkle his nose. Campbell took a seat behind a white laminate desk and fired up two large monitors. Nine squares were arranged on them: two showed vision in real time, the others were blank. Each showed the current time and date and other parameters in white text.

'What's the set up?' said Jack.

'I've just turned on the feed running from two cameras in the car park.' He pointed at the night vision. Palms swaying in the breeze, puddles of water on the asphalt created by yesterday's late thunderstorm. A couple of cane toads hopping about. 'The footage is stored on a digital video recorder. There's also a camera installed just outside each main entrance, the two inside are only intended to run when there's an event on. They're installed high up, pointing back at the stands to catch any mischief going on in the crowd, for example. Then there's one in the foyer and a couple in the main stairwells. That's it.'

This didn't sound promising. 'Are the internal cameras still recording now, or did they stop when the match ended and the crowd had gone?'

'Sorry Detective...' He turned his tired face up to Jack

and held his palms open. 'They all turn on automatically at 6:00am and off at midnight.'

'Are they monitored somewhere by a security firm when they're running?'

'Nope. It's a passive system right now. We talked about setting up an active system down the track, but until the arena proves itself economically, the cost to pay people to sit and watch the monitors is simply too great. I'm of the view that what we have is more than adequate. In fact we've got more cameras than most other venues around town. At the end of the day, this is Yorkville, not New York Cityht?'

'And yet a horrible murder was committed under our noses,' Jack retorted sarcastically. He thought for a moment. 'Surely there are cameras pointing at the rink itself?'

'No. The cameras under the ceiling don't capture the playing area. We figured the TV cameras would take care of that. Besides, every second person's filming away on their damned mobile phones these days. If something sensational happened on the ice, the world would see it within minutes.'

Campbell was correct. No doubt social media was flooded with photos and video from tonight's game, all uploaded by members of the public. Jack pulled a 2-terabyte USB drive from his pocket and flung it at Campbell. 'I'm assuming you know how to transfer the files? Give me whatever can fit over the last day or two.'

'Does it mean I can go home to bed?'

'You've co-operated well, mate. I don't see why not. Just a couple more questions. Then I'm gonna need you to lock up the executive box area before we leave.'

'Sure.'

'And give us the keys to the palace.'

'Why?'

'This is a crime scene.'

'The entire stadium? You must be joking!'

'Not joking.' Jack nodded at the monitor. 'How are you going with downloading that lot?'

'Just a couple more minutes.' While Campbell clicked around with his mouse, Jack buzzed Taylor. 'We're almost done. Stay where you are. I'll pick you up on the way out.'

On the way back to the manager's office to fetch the keys, Jack dropped the official tone as he continued to probe for answers.

'Why ice hockey in the tropics? Doesn't make much sense to me. Sure, the action was right up my alley, but it's so foreign to Aussies. I'm not sure over the long term they're gonna go for it.'

Campbell replied as if he'd taken personal offence, like he was defending a loved one from slander. 'I don't know if you're aware, Detective, but since the last winter Olympics, the sport's been gaining popularity.'

'Really?' Jack decided to let the bloke get rid of his nervous energy by talking. Which he seemed to enjoy doing. 'I hadn't noticed. Tell me all about it.'

'It's still basically an amateur league. You could call it semi-professional if you were going to be generous. Most of the players have 9-to-5 jobs. They do it for the love of the game. The best of the imports get paid, but it's not a lot. Not yet, anyway. They look at a stint Down Under like a holiday where they get to keep their skills up.'

Jack scratched his head. Something didn't make sense. 'That all seems odd to me. The spectacle I watched from the stands until I got called away would have cost a ton of money to put on. Hundreds of thousands of dollars. How can that be? Who'd spend that kind of coin on a bunch of amateurs?'

'Ever heard of Herbert Jubb?'

'No,' Jack lied. Everyone north of the Tropic of Capricorn had heard of Jubb. 'Should I have?'

'He's a billionaire who lives in Cairns. Promotes Far North Queensland at every opportunity. He's an Aussie, but he lived a while in the USA and fell in love with ice hockey. Sees himself as a pioneer who's going to make the sport mainstream in this country.'

Jack knew Jubb was a property developer but nothing else about him. 'How will he succeed where others have clearly failed?'

'Ambition.' Campbell rubbed his fingers together. 'And a shit-ton of money, including mine. He's got visions of creating a new competition, bringing top players from overseas. Tonight's match was a wonderful advertisement for the game. But now...'

'Why in sleepy Yorkville and not Cairns?'

'Jubb wanted to base it there – bigger population, international airport. But he got stonewalled. Couldn't get planning permission from the local council. There's a rumour he seriously pissed off the lady mayor with some chauvinistic remarks at a council meeting. Yorkville said yes to the stadium, and here we are.'

'Obviously, you share Jubb's vision?'

Campbell nodded. 'Me and a couple of backers decided to toss our savings into the ring with him, borrow some money and see if we could get things happening in other parts of the country.'

'You said he's rich. Why does he need your money?'

Campbell barked a laugh. 'How do rich people *get* rich, Detective? By using other people's money wherever possible. Mitigate their own risk.'

Jack nodded. 'In Far North Queensland, though? No

offence intended, sunshine, but it sounds like a fast track to losing your money.'

'Why not? If they can have a team in the league as far away as Perth, why not here?'

'Apart from your financial contribution, what's your role here at the arena? You seem to know your way around the CCTV system OK.'

'General dog's body, really.'

'You're not tempted to stay here for the long haul?'

'No. Too hot and sticky for my liking.' Campbell proceeded to talk at length about the background to the arena build, much of which Jack already had a grasp of, apart from who was paying for it. The media had only mentioned a company's name – Ambrosia Development Group – in their stories about the arena. Jubb had done well to keep his own role in the venture buried in the complexity of corporate structure. Jack would set up a meeting with Jubb if he couldn't crack the case quickly. For now, he decided to put a stop to Campbell's rambling.

'Please, Mr Campbell. Let's get back to the basics.'

'Basics, yeah, sure.' Campbell chose a route to his office that took them via the executive box. It soon became apparent why. 'Can I get a drink?' There was a hopeful gleam in the man's eyes. 'I'm still in shock.'

Taylor, still working on the press release, acknowledged them with a nod. Jack fetched a bottle of water and placed it in front of Campbell, who had sat down again. The manager said with a hint of disappointment, 'I was hoping for something stronger.'

'I ain't making you a coffee.'

'I was thinking more along the lines of a scotch.'

'I know what you were thinking. I used to be an alcoholic like you...no need to make a face. You'd be better off dealing with it. But I'm not an effin' therapist. Where's your apartment?'

Campbell gave Jack the address.

'How convenient. Not far from where we're going. We'll drop you there.'

'But...my car's here.'

'Get a taxi back to pick it up once you've had a good rest. I've got a couple more things I wanna ask you on the way. Tell me what I need to know, and I'll leave you alone for a while. Deal?'

A nod and a whispered, 'Deal.'

Chapter Nine

TAYLOR AGREED to take the wheel, to give Jack the chance to fully concentrate on what Campbell had to say. She'd never driven the Hilux before. Jack was protective of his car, obsessive almost. For him to hand over the reins took her by surprise. Taylor's own car was an unnoteworthy Camry sedan that had automatic transmission, as did the CIB's Kia Stinger she got to drive on rare occasions. Even though out of practice with manual cars, from deep in the recesses of muscle memory she tapped into old skills, managed the clutch and gearstick like she did it every day. As she drove through the dark, deserted streets of central Yorkville, she eavesdropped on the conversation between the two men in the back seat. Now and then she glanced in the rear vision mirror to check the body language.

'Who was at the function and when did it finish?' said Jack curtly. 'Tell me anything unusual you heard or saw. The tiniest detail could be more important than you think.'

'Everything seemed normal to me. Just a bunch of

people enjoying themselves. All the players and coaching staff from both teams attended.'

'No one missing from the Mavericks or the Hawks?'

'The guys had showers and got changed here; nobody went back to the hotel as far as I know. In fact, it was mandatory for them to be at the event. Part of the PR requirements.'

'How was the mood?'

'Upbeat. Everyone seemed happy to be there. At least no one seemed unhappy. Even the defeated Hawks were in party mode; it's a friendly exhibition tournament after all.'

Taylor recalled the non-stop, brutal action on the ice; it didn't look all that friendly to her.

Campbell continued. 'The party started about 8:45 and was scheduled to end at 11:30.'

'Who else was there besides the players and coaching staff?'

As they passed under a yellow streetlight, Taylor observed Campbell nodding his head. 'Let's see. Some invited guests, local personalities. I don't know who they are. Apart from Herbert Jubb, of course.'

'Can you provide a list of local attendees?'

Campbell paused for a moment. Taylor could hear his breathing; not laboured, but not free and easy either. 'The invitations were of the "plus one" variety. A number of attendees would have brought their wives and girlfriends, for example – but they're not on the guest list. Whether everyone who was invited actually showed up, I can't say. We didn't check them off; it was a casual, laid-back affair.'

'Never mind,' said Jack, a touch of irritation in his voice.

'No one expected a murder, you know?'

'No, of course not. Did any of the players bring friends or relatives with them to Yorkville?'

'I don't know. That's down to the individual teams. I'm pretty sure if any extras travelled here, it would have been at their own expense.'

'OK,' said Jack, tiredness croaking his voice. 'We'll find out eventually; we always do.' After a few seconds he said, 'This is very important. How did Jonas Eriksson seem to you? Worried, anxious?'

'Like I told you before, they say he's a lone wolf. From what I recall of the evening – which isn't a lot – he spent a lot of time sitting on his own on a couch with a blank look on his face.'

'Odd. He scored the winning goal in a close match. Surely people would have been swarming him, trying to get close to the hero?'

'At first, yes. A couple of female guests, in particular. But after a while, they must have realised he wasn't up for a party and they left him alone.'

'He didn't argue with anyone?'

'No. But I can't vouch for what happened after I fell asleep.'

'Anyone else there I should know about?'

'Five or so wait staff. Oh, and a local rock band. Three-piece outfit. Like The Police. Not you, ha ha. I mean the band, with Sting.'

'I get it. Tell me about the band that played at the arena.'

'They're called "Cover Up". It was eighties and nineties music. I found them on the Internet. They've got great reviews and didn't charge much for the gig. They played one set, for about an hour. Good stuff, too. The crowd got right into it.'

'But not Eriksson.'

'No.'

'It's a lucky break for us that you fell asleep, hey? We didn't have to go chasing after you.'

'Yes,' came the sheepish reply.

'Are you prone to falling asleep in the middle of social events?'

'No. It's never happened before.'

'But, and don't take offence, we've established your fondness for the drink. Did you have more than usual tonight?'

'What? Listen, that *was* rather offensive. You've already called me an alcoholic. Is that the normal way Yorkville Police behave?'

'No, it's not!' said Taylor, lowering her head towards the steering wheel to hide the grin. 'Apologise, DS Lisbon.'

'Yeah, sorry 'n that. We're all knackered. Now, answer the question. Did you overindulge?'

'As it happens, I only had two small beers all night.'

'Honest?'

'OK. And a rum and coke. But I swear, that was all. It must have been exhaustion that knocked me out.'

'Hmmm, sure,' Jack relented. 'Do you remember what time it was when you fell asleep?'

'I can't be precise. Maybe 11:00? The band had stopped playing, I know that much. Packing up and ready to go. People were still here, milling about, getting ready to leave, party on at the nightclubs on the Esplanade. I dunno, this sudden wave of tiredness came over me. I retreated to my office, sat in an armchair and started to flick through my phone. I must've dozed off then, and it was lights out until Ravi woke me up to tell me what he'd…Oh my God, I can't believe this has actually happened. Maybe I'm still asleep in the armchair and this is a bad dream.'

'Want me to pinch you?' said Jack, drawing another smile from Taylor. And then, like a lightbulb was switched on, he added, 'So, if you were asleep when everyone had supposedly gone home, who locked the place up?'

'Ah... no one.'

'Meaning the joint was wide open for anyone to stroll in off the street. Perhaps with the intent of murdering Jonas Eriksson?'

'Oh shit...' came the almost inaudible reply. 'I didn't mean to...'

'Perhaps you *accidentally* dozed off so the killer could stroll in and do their thing?'

'No...what are you...?'

'Claudia, pull over and let Mr Campbell out. This is his apartment block. I'll escort him back to his flat.'

Taylor waited five minutes for Jack to return to the vehicle. 'Why did you go with him?'

'To make sure he really lived there.'

'You didn't think he gave you a fake address, did you?'

Jack puffed out his cheeks. 'I don't trust him. He talked a lot but he's holding something back. Him falling asleep, the person responsible for locking up the building, was way too convenient.'

'But if he inadvertently let the killer in, then he might have also let the victim in. Or maybe both were still in the venue and hadn't gone anywhere?'

'Listen,' Jack jammed the keys in the ignition. 'Go and bang on Campbell's door.'

'What for?' Taylor narrowed her eyes. 'He's probably in la-la land by now. The bloke was exhausted.'

'As am I, sunshine. His apartment is No. 203, second floor. There's internal stairs, turn left at the top.'

'What am I going to say to him?'

'Tell him to prepare for a blood test.'

'What?'

'I think he might've had his drink spiked by the killer.'

'You reckon?'

'It's possible.' Jack smacked a palm on the steering wheel. 'Perhaps the perpetrator lured the victim onto the ice after everyone went home? And so they made sure old Ned Campbell was off with the fairies at the time.'

Taylor opened the car door, stepped out into the dark humid morning. 'I'll call you when I'm inside.'

'Don't let him eat or drink anything. I'll see if Littlejohn can get here and take his blood.'

'What if Campbell refuses to cooperate?'

'If he's got nothing to do with the murder, he won't refuse. If he kicks up a fuss, arrest his arse.'

Two minutes later Taylor called, said Campbell was tetchy but willing to spill a little blood if it would prove he'd been drugged and the result would put him in the clear.

'Littlejohn readily agreed to do it', said Jack. 'She was delighted to be asked to assist.' He smiled: the young woman was the perfect apprentice for Proctor. Lived and breathed her job.

'What do I do after we've taken the blood sample?'

'Go home, Claudia. At least one of us should get some rest.' He added the caveat. 'I may need you soon, depending on how things develop. Sleep with your clothes on and one eye open.'

Chapter Ten

A BLEARY-EYED BALD man with a rugged, pitted face answered the door. An unattractive bloke by most standards. A head like a robber's dog, as Jack recalled the colourful Australian idiom. Despite that, there was kindness in his tired face.

Other bleary-eyed hotel guests peered around the corners of their doors, curious to know what the racket was all about. One was more than curious, he was livid.

'It's five in the morning, dickhead!' roared the flabby-jowled man. 'Keep the bloody noise down, for heaven's sake.' Hairy, white flesh poked through a wide gap in a terry-towelling dressing gown that failed to encompass a barrel of a waist. Jack brandished his ID and told the aggrieved guest to get back inside or he'd be arrested for indecent exposure. The fellow's head disappeared like a rabbit retreating into its hole. Jack offered Gordon Raff a smile that was no more than a straight line and briefly introduced himself.

'What do you want?' Gordon Raff asked in a rasping voice. He stood in a pair of black-and-yellow silk boxer shorts, sporting a six-pack most men his age could only dream of.

'May I come in? It's rather urgent.'

'Have I done something wrong, officer?' All politeness from the American-born coach. Raff's diaphragm rose and fell rapidly as he blinked, searching for comprehension at the early hour. 'Something amiss with my visa?'

'Nothing like that, sir.' No point waiting for Raff to move aside before entering the room; clearly he wasn't fully awake. Jack shoved his way past, drawing incoherent noises of token protest. 'It's bad, I'm afraid, Mr Raff.' He gestured towards a plush wingback chair with, presumably, Raff's going-out clothes from last night draped across it. 'You need to be sitting down to hear this.'

Three minutes later, after Jack had delivered the news, not holding back on the brutality of the murder but without giving away crucial details, the tough-guy coach was cradling his head in his hands. His body rocked back and forth as he let out soft, whimpering sobs that belied his ogrish physical appearance. Jack stood back, gave the man time to cry, to come to terms with what he'd just been told. He used the opportunity to duck into the small kitchenette and put in a call to Taylor.

'Has Littlejohn taken a sample of Campbell's blood yet?'

'No. She's still ten minutes away.'

'Get over to the Grand as soon as you can when she's done. And tell Campbell not to go anywhere until I say so.'

'I thought I could go home and rest. You said–'

'Yeah, well, I hadn't thought that through. I'm gonna need you and all the other hands on deck. We've got to question the players and staff staying here ASAP. While they're conveniently all in the same building. They're gonna want to go home after they hear what's happened, and we can't hold them without grounds until we can dredge up some suspects.'

A couple of deep sighs before Taylor said, 'You've got to be kidding, right? We're all barely standing on our feet.'

'We need to push on, Claudia. This isn't some murder at a lonely farmhouse with the perpetrator holding a smoking effin' gun. We've got people by the bucketload we need to talk to.' He took a peak at Raff, head between his knees, body still heaving. If this man, overcome with raw emotion, was the murderer, Jack would cook up his police badge and eat it. Then again, many criminals were supreme actors. 'Listen, I'm pissed off that the Inspector's more worried about his Zoom call with Assistant Commissioner Landacre than solving this murder. He should be here at the hotel with me or making other bleedin' enquiries. Working out a plan of action.'

'Not fair, Jack. He'd scheduled that meeting with the Assistant Commissioner weeks ahead, and besides—'

'I don't care! A murder inquiry trumps everything. And you're right. We're all exhausted. Much as I hate to admit it, this one's got way too many moving parts for us at Yorkville to handle it on our own. I'm going over Batista's head and calling in Cairns CIB. At least to help us with the evidence gathering.'

'Leave it, Jack. Is it worth your job?'

He clenched his teeth; anyone but Taylor and he would've let rip. 'Is it worth *Batista's* job? The media could flay him alive when they find out he's shirked his responsibility, preferred to have a chinwag with Jennifer Landacre instead of looking for a murderer. You know how much I respect the man, but lately...I dunno. He's lost the plot.'

'I wouldn't advise doing that, Jack. At least wait a couple of hours. I'm sure you can convince the boss to make the call to Sheridan Street after he's done with Landacre.'

'Sure.' Jack ended the call, agonising over the question of calling Inspector Andrews in Cairns or letting it slide like Taylor insisted. Problem was, would Batista act with the required urgency? The sound of a toilet flushing and a door closing snapped Jack out of his thoughts.

'What happens now?' mumbled Raff, wiping his face with a fluffy hand towel. His eyes were still red from the flood of tears. He'd slipped on a pair of jeans and a polo shirt, a pair of lace-up leather shoes.

'There was no need to get dressed for me, sunshine,' said Jack.

'I thought maybe you were going to ask me to answer questions at the station.' His voice barely rose above a whisper.

'You offering yourself up as a suspect?'

'Ah...no...it's just...'

'I'm happy to chat here, where it's more comfortable for you.'

'Suits me.'

The men sat at a small round table. Jack wasted no time. 'You asked what happens next? First up, the tournament is obviously going to be cancelled. The organisers will have to refund people who bought tickets. The citizens of Yorkville won't take too kindly to being out of pocket, tragic homicide notwithstanding.'

In contrast to Campbell's histrionics, Raff merely nodded understandingly. 'Of course. It would be...insensitive to proceed.'

'Clearly. And the arena remains a crime scene until the police say otherwise.'

'I get it.'

'We'll have to talk to everyone we can who's connected with Jonas and see if we can find someone with motive and means. In a moment, I'd like you to knock on the doors of all your people and tell them to gather in the conference room downstairs in one hour. Can you do that?'

'I can't believe it's someone in the ice hockey community. Perhaps it was an outsider? A random crime?'

Jack shook his head. 'I can't get into the details, Mr Raff, but from what we've been able to work out so far, we think Jonas knew the killer.'

Raff wiped his face again with the towel he'd brought from the bathroom. 'Jesus. I can't believe it.' His shoulders seemed to relax for a moment, at ease with Jack leveraging his "good cop" demeanour. 'Tell me how I can help.'

'Before getting into the uncomfortable part, we need to deal with next of kin.' Jack had his notepad and pen at the ready. 'Who do we call?'

'I'm not sure. He's got an ex-wife in Melbourne. Emily. She followed him out from Sweden a couple of years ago. They grew apart, but as far as I know, they remained friends after the split. He showed me some pictures once. She's a real looker.'

'Ex's don't really count, unfortunately.' Jack scratched behind his ear with the pen. 'Or fortunately, depending on how you look at it. Any kids?'

'No kids. Jonas thought he had undiagnosed autism, didn't want to pass it on.' Raff's shaking hand reached for a water bottle. 'He didn't, of course. Just an introvert who struggled in the company of others. Except on the ice. On the ice, he was in control. You know, if a few things had gone the other way in his life, he could have achieved so much.' Raff forced a smile, then blinked hard.

'Surely he's got a mother, father, brother, sister?'

'You mean here or in Sweden?' He bent his head as if in prayer and said softly, 'Why would someone do this to Jonas of all people? He was a good guy.'

'Let's work out his next of kin first, then we can rack our brains trying to figure out who had it in for him, OK? And it doesn't matter where they live,' said Jack curtly, fighting to keep his temper down. Raff's confusion was understandable in the circumstances; slack needed to be cut. 'I just need to contact them. Quickly.'

'His mother, I guess.'

'Right. Now we're getting somewhere. Know her name?'

A blank stare.

'Please, Mr Raff. Think. This is an important step. We can't release information to the media or make an appeal to the public until we've told the closest family members about what's happened.'

'Why?' Genuine puzzlement raised Raff's bushy eyebrows.

'We need their consent. It's a legal requirement.'

'Right. I honestly can't tell you off the top of my head what his mom's name is. Like I said, Jonas kept pretty much to himself, didn't give too much away.'

'What about this ex-wife, Emily? She's bound to know. Do you have her number?'

'No.' Raff sucked in his lips, frustrated at his own lack of knowledge. 'But I think she's still living in Melbourne.'

The lack of sleep was affecting Jack's physiology: he sensed his heart rate was up even though he wasn't exerting himself. His exasperation at not getting the information he wanted didn't help. 'What's her last name?'

'Same as his, I think. Eriksson.'

On a hail Mary play, Jack googled the name. A couple of hits around the world, including a home-based beautician in the Melbourne suburb of Moonee Ponds. She had a Facebook business page, complete with a mobile number. The woman was the epitome of a Scandinavian beauty. He flipped the phone around and asked, 'That her?'

Raff donned a pair of reading glasses and squinted at the small screen. 'That's her, alright.'

Jack growled as the call went straight to voice mail. The words he almost barked were terse. *This is Detective Jack Lisbon of the Yorkville Police with a message for Emily Eriksson. Call back immediately in relation to an extremely urgent police matter.* No pleases, no beg-your-pardons.

Three minutes elapsed; no return call. He dialled again and left a similar message. Another couple of minutes passed in silence. Not surprising when it was pre-sunrise, 5:55am. No daylight savings in Queensland meant it was almost 7:00am in Melbourne, still early. And it was a Saturday. The woman was probably still in bed, like any normal person would be.

'What next, then?' said Raff when Jack pocketed his mobile. 'Gather the troops?'

'OK,' Jack stood and looked out of the floor-to-ceiling windows. A red crescent glow hovered on the horizon as the sun began its daily ascent in a blue vastness. The clouds and rain of recent days were gone, but they were never far away in the tropics. 'Get your guys ready to assemble in the conference room. And I'll need an introduction to the Hawks and their people. They need to be spoken to as well.'

'Of course.' Raff's face turned white. 'Hell, what do I

tell my boys?' he pleaded. 'What excuse can I give them for this sudden meeting?'

'Use your imagination.' There was no time to give more advice as Jack's phone burst into life. He didn't bother mucking around with pleasantries. 'Thanks for returning my call. Yes, it's Detective Lisbon, Yorkville CIB. It's about your husband...I mean ex-husband.'

'Oh shit. What has he done? Is he in trouble? Did he get into a fight? Do I need to bail him out?'

Jack rubbed his chin hard. 'No, I'm afraid something has happened to him.'

'It's a good thing I'm here, then, isn't it?'

'What do you mean, "here"?'

'I'm in Yorkville. I flew up to watch the tournament. Jonas doesn't know. I wanted to surprise him later today. Take him out to lunch. He's been doing it tough lately. You know his mental health can be rather...delicate.'

'Do you know how I can get in touch with his mother?'

'Why would you want to do that? She's an Alzheimer's patient in a facility in Gothenburg.'

Another wrinkle. He pinched the bridge of his nose. 'I've been informed he has no children. Can you confirm that?'

'Yes.' The sound of a cigarette lighter sparking came down the line, the deep inhalation of smoke. 'Now, what the hell's going on? You said it was urgent. Stop beating around the bush.'

Jack made the split-second decision that, in the circumstances, Emily was the closest thing to Jonas Eriksson's next of kin. 'You said you're in town?'

'Yes. I'm staying at an Airbnb off Oliphant Avenue.'

'What's the exact address, Emily?'

'Wait a minute,' she said. 'I'm not feeling comfortable here. You could be someone pranking me with ill intent.'

Jack gave the general number for the police station. 'Ring it, ask to be put through to Detective Jack Lisbon. I'll be waiting.'

While he waited for a return call, Raff paced the room, chewing a knuckle. Best to wrap things up with the ex-wife fast or this bloke would have a meltdown. Jack shot him a supportive smile. 'Don't worry. I'll be beside you all the way. Just let me deal with Emily first.'

The Clash's iconic song interrupted proceedings yet again. 'Emily?'

'No, it's Claudia. All done with Campbell. His blood's in a vial, on its way to the laboratory with Littlejohn.'

'Excellent.' One small item ticked off on a list that was bound to be long and growing over time. 'Are you on your way here?'

'Clara's dropping me off. Just turning into the entrance now.'

Jack ended the call; seconds later Emily Eriksson was back on the line. 'OK, you seem to check out. The young man on the desk who took my call sounded worried.'

Constable Stan Billington, whom his colleagues still called "the rookie" despite him being at the station a year now, would make a terrible poker player. 'I'm sorry to inform you that Jonas has...passed away.'

Only the sound of her breathing, then a sharp, 'Say that again. I don't believe you.'

'I'm going to send one of my officers around to speak with you. A woman. Please stay where you are for now, OK?'

'Can't you tell me what happened?' Jack was sure she was choking back tears on the other end. 'Was it an accident? I suspected him of taking too many steroids to mask the pain of his injuries. Was it an overdose?'

'Detective Constable Taylor will tell you everything when she gets there.'

'Please, can you just–?

'I'm sorry. Good-bye.' He disconnected the call and put his head in his hands. He loved his job, but this part was the worst.

Chapter Eleven

EVEN WITH CRIED-OUT eyeballs the colour of radishes, Emily Eriksson exuded elegance. A silk dressing gown with a Japanese print enveloped her voluptuous figure as she leaned over the railing. Long red fingernails contrasted starkly against the milky skin of her hands. Her face was blemish-free apart from a Marilyn Monroe mole at the right edge of her top lip. A walking advertisement for her beautician business, Taylor observed.

Emily opened her mouth, went to say something, then pulled herself up. She was gripping a cigarette between thumb and index finger like she was trying to squeeze the last ounce of nicotine from it. She sucked in a lungful and emitted smoke in twin jets from her nostrils. The fingers of her other hand combed through thick locks. She turned to Taylor and said in a monotone, 'I knew something like this would happen to him one day.'

'Surely not like this?' Taylor replied, then rested her hand on the balcony railing. The holiday flat Emily was renting sat atop a building about 500 metres from the beach, offering ocean glimpses between two carbon-copy structures on the opposite side of the broad, leafy avenue. A ribbon of golden light shimmered, lighting up a path from the horizon to the nearby shore as the sun slowly rose higher into the sky.

Emily Eriksson dabbed her eyes with a tissue. 'Not murdered, of course. Nobody expects that. But I knew in my gut he'd come to an untimely end before he had the chance to grow old. I've had premonitions about it. Dreams. Please,' she gestured at a small glass-topped table and two cane chairs, 'take a seat.'

The women sat, locked eyes for a moment before Emily gazed out at the ocean. 'You know that expression they use when someone's life ends at the scene of their profession, or hobby or whatever? "*He died doing what he loved*"?'

'Yes, I know it.' Taylor nodded.

'It's total bullshit, of course. Imagine a surfer out there,' she waved her cigarette over her shoulder, 'on a beautiful morning like this, waxing his board in the warm sun, then going for a surf and getting attacked and killed by a shark. Now, they might say he died doing what he loved. Surfing. But no.' She waggled her finger about rapidly. 'He died by being eaten by a fucking shark. He didn't *love* being attacked by sharks, did he? It wasn't the surfing that killed him, it was the shark!' Her face was glowing red with fury as she crushed the cigarette in the ashtray.

'Would you like me to make you a cup of tea?' said Taylor, wracking her brain as she tried to figure out how to deal with the woman. Before Emily could reply she added, 'Then I'd like to ask you some questions. Hopefully you can point us in the right direction, so we can quickly find whoever committed this barbaric crime.'

Emily lightly touched her on the wrist. 'Of course.

Sorry for the outburst. But make it a coffee; there's a machine on the bench. One of those detestable pod things, but it'll do. I'm Swedish, we drink more coffee than anyone.'

You haven't met Jack Lisbon, Taylor mused but held her tongue. 'Sure.'

'Black, no sugar.'

'Coming up.'

The temperature and humidity outside had jumped in the short space of time it took Taylor to make the coffee. Tiny droplets of perspiration clung to Emily's high forehead. She took a slug of the hot brew like it was iced water. 'Fire away.'

'Do you know anyone who would want to see Jonas dead?'

She shrugged. 'I can think of a few, actually.'

Taylor's fingers itched as she scrambled to get her notebook onto the table. Suspects. That's exactly what they needed. 'Let's start with who you think is the most likely.'

Emily sipped coffee, leaving a red lipstick mark, and excused herself for a moment. Taylor heard the woman talking to herself in Swedish, isolated sobs. Emily returned with her mobile phone in hand, sat and placed the device in the middle of the glass table, screen facing Taylor. 'Here's the person I'd put at the top of the list.' She tapped the tabletop with a manicured fingernail.

The detective picked the phone up, looked closely at the portrait-mode photograph taking up the entire screen, and said, 'Who's she?'

'Lena Holstrom.'

'Is she Swedish like you?'

A nod. 'Second-generation. Her father was a hockey player in Sweden some years ago. When he retired, he took a job in Australia at Swinburne University of Technology. Something to do with computers. Lena was born here but thinks she's more Swedish than Abba. Can hardly speak a sentence in Swedish. What a joke.' She laughed sarcastically.

'You seem to know a lot about her.' Taylor made sure to write down every detail.

'Ha! She's well known among the ex-pats and in the ice hockey community. Not much we don't know about each other.'

'Why do you have a photo of her on your phone?'

The question seemed to rattle Emily for a second. It seemed a little too convenient to Taylor that the woman was able to locate the photo so quickly, almost as if she'd prepared for this moment. Emily dispelled the suspicion in Taylor's mind with her next words. 'She applied for a job at my beauty salon.'

'I thought yours was a home-based business?'

Emily gave a knowing smile. 'It is, but I do employ a couple of casuals from time to time. Lena sent me the picture with her CV. I would never hire her, though. She's been charged with shoplifting before, not the sort of person I want in my home with cash lying around.'

'And why would this Lena want to murder your husband, I mean ex-husband?'

'It's alright, Detective Taylor. We're still technically married, even though we've been separated since 2019.'

Taylor's eyebrows lurched upwards. 'So you *are* his next of kin!'

Emily raised her ankles to the edge of her seat and hugged her knees to her chest. Taylor doubted she'd be flexible enough to pull off a move like that. 'I guess so. Never thought about it.' She stared off into space for a moment then refocused on Taylor. 'Getting back to Lena Holstrom. She fancies herself as a kind of hockey groupie. Dated some of the guys in the league. Hooks her claws into the imports, usually. Sleeps with one, then the other.'

Taylor drank water from a tumbler, then said, 'How old is Jonas?' She found it impossible to use the past tense when asking the age of a recently dead person.

'Thirty-eight.'

'This Lena doesn't look older than 21.'

'You guessed correctly, Detective. She's only 20. Studying vet science at college.' Emily fiddled with her packet of cigarettes, opened it, shut it again. 'Jonas complained to me about her just a couple of months ago. I think what she did was part payback for me rejecting her job application.'

'What did she do?'

'Jonas told me Lena was stalking him after he refused to go out with her.'

'You have proof of this?' Taylor knew one thing very well: ex's can get very jealous of their former partners' new love interests. Emily's behaviour, pointing the finger at another woman, matched that profile.

She shrugged. 'I'm sure there's evidence on Jonas's phone. He told me she sent him suggestive texts. And more. Photos of her breasts. Disgusting. I suggest you pay very close attention to Lena.'

Another look at the picture on the phone. Holstrom had a slight build. Taylor wasn't sure how much more to reveal about the murder, then decided to go for it. 'Jonas was beaten savagely. It would have taken a person of enormous physical strength to do the damage they did to him.'

Horror sucked the colour from her cheeks. 'Do you need me to identify the body? I will if I have to.'

Taylor shook her head. 'Not necessary. There are technical means to do that. We have no doubt the victim is Jonas. As next of kin, though, you'll have to think about funeral arrangements after the coroner says the body can be released into your care.' She took a deep breath. 'You know, this young woman you're showing me is as thin as a rake. She wouldn't be up to the job of murdering a man the size and strength of Jonas. I had the privilege of watching him play – he was a beast on the ice.'

Taylor's positive words produced a glint of pride in the woman's eyes. 'Yes, he was a beast.' She winked, but the accompanying words were forced. 'In more ways than one, if you know what I mean.'

Taylor smiled politely. The innuendo came off as a bizarre coping mechanism.

Emily dropped her voice to a whisper. 'Lena, too, is a beast. But like the one in the Bible. Evil. Of course, she would be too much of a coward to try and take someone on herself. She would have hired a hitman to kill Jonas.'

'Any ideas who that might be?'

'Maybe a local desperado?'

Taylor said, 'Do you know where we can find her?'

'She's here in Yorkville. I saw her at the match last night. If I had known what she was planning to do, I would've stopped the bitch. Don't waste time. If she's behind this, she won't hang around.' Emily gave Taylor the woman's phone number – not hard to do when it came on a job application. The rest of Emily's coffee went down with a double gulp before she dropped the cup on its saucer with a loud clatter. Shoulders hunched forward, she re-tied the bow of her dressing gown and almost ran inside in a flood of tears.

Taylor picked up the cups and saucers from the table on the balcony, stepped into the apartment and called out, 'Do you want someone to come and be with you? I'd stay, but I'm needed to run the investigation.'

From behind the bathroom door came a bird-like voice. 'That would be lovely.'

'I'll stay with you until my colleague gets here.'

'Thank you.' Those two short words conveyed more gratitude than an Oscars acceptance speech. Emily was taking the shocking news much worse than her masking behaviour was almost able to hide. 'I'll be out in a minute.'

While they waited on the balcony for Taylor's replacement to show up, something occurred to Taylor. 'You said before you could think of a few people who might want to kill Jonas. Who else apart from Lena Holstrom?'

'A man called Jari Aalto.' She looked towards the horizon, flicked her head slightly, as if the man she'd just mentioned wasn't far away. 'A hockey player from Finland.'

Taylor jotted the name down. 'I don't recall his name on the program from last night's match.'

'It wasn't. He's in Melbourne. Jari got cut from the Mavericks to make way for a new guy. It was a toss up between Jari and Jonas getting the chop.'

'How do you know this?'

'Jonas told me. Anyway, Jari wasn't happy about it, to say the least. I heard he's facing deportation because he's got no job now and he can't get a renewal on his visa.'

Two taps of the pen on Taylor's notebook. 'When you say he wasn't happy, what do you mean?'

'Look,' she said in a conspiratorial tone, leaning in closer. 'I never saw or heard anything first-hand, but according to Jonas, the man started drinking heavily. Not unusual for Finns, by the way.'

'Did Jonas say Jari made threats against him?'

A defeated look cast a shadow over Emily's face. 'No. But...'

Taylor decided the woman had taken enough questions for now. She advised Emily to rest for a while; she agreed and went to lay on the bed.

Twenty minutes later, a bleary-eyed Constable Kylie Smith arrived.

'Who's looking after Skye?' said Taylor, greeting her at the door.

'She's staying at a friend's place. They're having a pool party, apparently. The mother said Skye's welcome to stay the entire weekend if she likes. It's all been squared away with Detective Lisbon.'

Emily emerged from the bedroom, eyes still wet. Taylor shook her hand. 'Thanks for the leads. We'll be sure to follow them up. I'm so sorry for your loss.'

'What should I do now?' Genuine worry twisted her immaculately trimmed eyebrows.

'Constable Smith will guide you through what to expect next. Again, thank you.'

STANDING OUTSIDE THE BUILDING, she placed a call to Jack. 'I've got a couple of leads,' she said, watching about a dozen rainbow lorikeets squabbling over nectar in orange grevillea flowers. The garrulous birds amped up the volume of their argument, forcing her to clamp a hand over her free ear. 'How are you getting on?'

'We've got help from Cairns.'

She sighed. 'You went over Batista's head after all, huh?'

The sound of air being sucked through teeth came

down the line. 'I thought about it, but in the end I decided to heed your advice and ask Batista to do it.'

'Good. I'm glad you could see sense.'

'Good? The old geezer let fly at me. Told me I should've used my bleedin' initiative and called them myself.'

The word *oops* flashed like a neon sign in Taylor's head. 'When are they getting here?'

'Already arrived. They're taking care of the Hawks side of things, but I need you back here to help me with the Mavericks. I'd lay a lot of money on the killer being among his own teammates.'

'My leads are in another direction, Jack.'

'Get me up to speed when you arrive. I've already diverted Trevarthen to pick you up on his way here. He's finally able to get away from babysitting that useless son of his.'

'I can just as easily take a cab. It'll probably be quicker…OK cancel that. I can see him coming around the corner now.'

As Aden Trevarthen sped back to the Grand Hotel, Taylor dialled Lena Holstrom. Voice mail. She ended the terse message with a thinly veiled thread. *If you're still in Yorkville, Ms Holstrom, do not leave town without my permission to do so.*

Chapter Twelve

DETECTIVE INSPECTOR WILLIAM ERHARDT of Cairns CIB chewed absently on the end of his ballpoint pen. He'd been using this one for a week, generally the limit before the teeth marks in the plastic cap were too disgusting even for him to deal with. His partner for today's exercise, Detective Sergeant Kirsten Genk, stood by his side, hands on hips, surveying the room. The surly curl to her mouth came courtesy of a knife slash suffered at the hands of a would-be rapist. The offender had suffered more: she'd fought him off then killed him with a bullet to the stomach that delivered a slow and painful death. Acquitted of the charge of manslaughter at trial, she was a hero to members of the QPS in the deep north. With the public – a different story. The unfortunate disfigurement meant she had to work extra hard to gain people's sympathy and trust.

The plain-clothes officers were bookended by two uniforms, both hard-nosed constables known for their work ethic and attention to detail. The Cairns team was hand-picked by their station chief when Joe Batista put out the call for urgent assistance in a murder inquiry. In addition to the elite police officers, a support forensic unit had been dispatched. These men and women were currently scouring the interior of the Yorkville Entertainment Arena building and the adjacent car park under the supervision of Dr. Margaret Proctor.

Now, at 11:15 on a Saturday morning, the entire Glacier City Hawks touring party, comprising 23 people, sat on stackable plastic chairs spread about the floor of the hotel's spacious gym. Erhardt noted a number of those in attendance sported damp, pink eyes. Others wore blank expressions. Others still stared at the floor. To his surprise, none was holding a mobile phone. The mood among the Hawks could only be described as sombre.

Erhardt coughed into a fist. 'We don't want to take up too much of your time, everyone. I understand this is extremely difficult for all of you. We intend to speak with each of you individually.'

'What exactly happened to Jonas?' called out a burly red-headed man in his early twenties. 'All we know is he's dead. It's not good enough. We deserve to know.'

Erhardt, having spoken the matter through with Batista, let them have it without sugar coating. Graphic description over, he said, 'We are clearly dealing with a psychopath. I sincerely hope it's not one of you.'

'And if it is,' said Genk. 'You have absolutely zero chance of getting away with it.'

Erhardt scanned the room for guilty reactions. None of them flinched. That wasn't definitive, of course. Psychopaths can remain cool as cucumbers when your average person would crumble under the stress. 'Depending on decisions made by Yorkville CIB's detectives, we may have to requisition your devices and examine your personal belongings.' Batista had informed Erhardt that a heavy blunt object was the likely murder weapon: perhaps it was concealed in a sports bag or suitcase. A careful and clever murderer would have disposed of the weapon efficiently. In Erhardt's experience, though, many were careless and stupid. 'We will obtain warrants tomorrow and your playing equipment *will* be subject to thorough examination.'

Groans came from a number of the players. A couple of "what the hells".

Erhardt held up a hand to the assembly. 'Look, I understand the frustration. But a man has been murdered in horrible circumstances. What we do now is crucial to finding out who did it. If it's any comfort, the Mavericks will be under even greater scrutiny: it's far more likely the perpetrator is among them than among you.'

'Is all of this really necessary for my guys? Some of them are still in their teens, for goodness sake.' The man speaking was the Hawks' head coach, Reece Tabberer, through whom Erhardt had set up the meeting. With his slim build, sinewy arms and classic short back and sides hairdo, he cut an almost military figure. 'We've barely arrived in this country. None of us knows any of the members of the Mavericks.'

'At this point, we only have your word for it. I'm led to believe a couple of the Mavericks players enjoyed a degree of fame. Eriksson in particular. I'd be surprised if your squad isn't familiar with his story.'

'He was in his prime years ago,' said a woman sitting next to Tabberer. 'Different generation. Eriksson wasn't exactly "famous" among younger people.'

Erhardt's nostrils flared. 'And you are?'

'The team's physiotherapist. Mathilde Forest.'

'You look about the same age as the victim. Perhaps you knew him and had a motive?'

'Of course I didn't!' she shouted. 'None of us did. All of those people are strangers to us.'

'Still,' said Genk. 'We're obliged to make enquiries of everyone who had anything to do with the victim. To put that in perspective, the Yorkville police will also be interviewing the band members from the party, other guests and the bar staff. All unlikely to have had a motive. But,' she said with a finger pointing in the air, 'they may have seen something, heard something. Same goes for you guys. We're not necessarily looking at you as suspects. So please, relax.'

'I don't wanna hand my phone over to the cops,' said a ruddy-cheeked man from the back of the room. 'It's got personal stuff on it I don't want no one to see.'

'Nudes of his girlfriend,' said another.

'Or his boyfriend's pecker,' said yet another, drawing awkward laughs from some, tut-tutting from others.

'Despite what he said, I'm sure Glen's got nothing incriminating on his cell,' said Tabberer, a touch defensively. 'The boys all happily left their cell phones in their rooms so they wouldn't be distracted while you addressed them. I have 100-percent confidence in my players and staff. If they saw or heard anything odd, they won't hesitate to tell you.' He folded his arms demonstrably.

'I'm sure they won't.' Erhardt smiled to himself. Big respect to the coach, sticking up for his tribe. 'Speaking of your devices,' he continued, eyes scanning the room, 'I would encourage you not to delete anything from your phones – texts, photos, files of any kind.' He stared hard at the lad who had objected. 'It'll make you look bad if Yorkville CIB decides it wants to send them off for analysis.'

He paused, then said, 'Interviews will be at the temporary tables set up at the back. We all good to go?'

Moans of "yes" greeted his words. He gestured to Genk to say a few concluding remarks. She said, 'Once you've been interviewed, you are free to wander about the hotel: visit the bar, restaurant, whatever. However, do not return to your rooms until Detective Erhardt gives you the all clear.' She gripped a clipboard with a list of names, called out the first four in alphabetical order. 'One final thing. To avoid potential collaboration on your stories, do not speak to each other while you're waiting your turn.'

'What are we meant to do? Stare into space?' It was the objector again.

'That, yes. Or do squats, stretching exercises, pray, I don't care.' She turned and whispered to Erhardt. 'None of them will know a damn thing.'

He puffed out his cheeks and said to her out of the side of his mouth. 'Don't be too sure.' He nodded at the second man approaching the interview tables in the single file. 'I watched the game on TV last night. That's their goalie, Kirin Pascoe. Eriksson flattened him from behind and Pascoe started throwing punches. They had a running battle the rest of the match.'

'Interesting,' whispered back Genk. 'But is that enough to drive Pascoe to murder?' She looked back at the crowd of miserable faces. 'I've arranged for the hotel to make some sandwiches and drinks. All at the Queensland taxpayers' expense.' She smiled. 'Aren't we lucky?'

―――

TAYLOR STRODE into the conference room, tucking her blouse back into her skirt, a sweaty-faced Aden

Trevarthen on her heels. Jack waved them over to the trapezoid desk he and Taylor would be working from. On the table sat a silver laptop, spiral notepads and pens, and a small black device with an assortment of dials and outlets. Two other tables had the same set up with Yorkville uniforms seated at each station. Taylor nodded at the chunky black box. 'Where did that bad boy come from?'

'Cairns CIB had a stash of these digital recorders in their inventory. Latest thing, Erhardt tells me. Even in a crowded room like this, it's possible to conduct interviews without the ambient noise interfering with each recording.' As he spoke, the hubbub coming from the chattering people in the room was appreciable.

'It's a lot easier in interview room 2, Jack. More intimate. This looks like an evacuation centre when a tropical cyclone hits town.'

'Needs must. There're simply too many people to talk to on our little patch. With this gear, we can effectively record a conversation with multiple participants. Take a seat and I'll set you up, if I can remember how.' Taylor sat and Jack attached a lapel microphone to her jacket, made sure she was connected to an allocated channel.

'Impressive,' she said, as he checked his own connection.

Jack looked up at Trevarthen, patiently waiting for instructions. 'Sorry to leave you hanging, Aden. I've paired you up with Constable Wilson. He knows this tech stuff backwards. Semmens and Wells are on the end table. There's a list of questions printed out for both of you, but feel free to wing it if you think the conversation needs to go in a particular direction. Make sure they sign their statements. Be firm, but have some empathy at the same time. Can you do that?'

'Of course, sir.' Trevarthen made his way to the farthest table where Wilson was miking up one of the Mavs.

'Empathy?' said Taylor. 'That's not your style. Getting soft?'

He blushed a light shade of coral. 'I'm only hard on people when they deserve it. Besides, you can see how traumatised these lads are. Benefit of the doubt, innit?'

Taylor sighed. 'Whatever you say, DS Lisbon.'

'Wait a second while I brief them, and then call up contestants 1, 2 and 3.'

'How many are there altogether in this lot?'

'Twenty-five. With luck, we should process them in a couple of hours, tops. We gather the basics now, and if anyone stands out as a likely suspect or seems like they know more and are keeping mum about it, we focus on them in more familiar surroundings later.'

She puffed out her cheeks as Jack stood in front of the table, made a mini speech to the group of players and staff. The upshot of the exercise: each person would be questioned and voluntarily sign a statement. After that they would be free to do as they pleased until further notice. He repeated the words Erhardt had recommended about the witnesses not deleting anything from devices if they didn't want to arouse suspicion. *Smarter than he looks, that Erhardt,* Jack mused. In conclusion, he said, 'Your coach told me he'd booked and paid for a week's accommodation at the Yorkville Grand and that you will all remain here for that period even though the tournament has been cancelled. That's good news for you, because you can grieve and take stock without the hassle of a long flight back to Melbourne to deal with it. And it's good news for us, because,' he waved a hand around, 'I've got a hunch the murderer could very well be one of you lot.'

Gasps and muttering, a sob or two, gave Jack a moment to pause. He glanced at Taylor, rolling her eyes at him as he jettisoned the empathy he'd just said was important. 'If you've got nothing to do with this crime, you've nothing to worry about,' he continued. 'I must stress that no one here is a suspect at this point. I won't name names, but I can tell you we are chasing up a couple of leads already. Whether they later point to any of you guys remains to be seen.' He moved back to his position behind the table and said, 'If the guilty party is here, let me assure you our jails are stinking hot and the people in them mighty unpleasant.' He looked at his printout, cleared his throat. 'Would Braxton Burt please come and take a seat with me and DC Taylor? Also, Andrew Bolis and…let's see…equipment manager Gavin Dahlgren. Please take a seat where our officers are waiting to take your statements.

As the hulking Braxton Burt approached with an unsteady gait, Taylor whispered in Jack's ear, 'I'm going to get confused with all these names. Plus there's all the Hawks people the Cairns police are processing.'

He locked eyes with her. 'We'll eliminate nearly all of these as suspects in the next couple of hours, mark my words.'

'You sure?'

He shrugged and said with a frown, 'I bleedin' hope so.'

Chapter Thirteen

'YOU LOOK a lot happier behind your own desk,' said Jack, placing on her desk a steaming cup of tea he'd bought from the café next door. Prior to that he'd spent an hour with the Inspector and Taylor going over what they'd learned so far. In a nutshell: not much.

She logged onto her computer and brought up a number of databases. 'I'm surprised at how well that procedure went at the hotel, to tell you the truth.'

Jack took residence in his corner workstation, easily the messiest in the office. 'You looking into the leads from Eriksson's...should I call her a widow?'

Taylor nodded. 'Technically and...well...I think she carried a candle for the guy even though they'd split.'

Jack ran an Internet search for images of Jonas Eriksson. So far he'd seen him in the match program, through the visor of a hockey helmet, and then, the awful pulp that was his face. A couple of smiling portraits caught his eye among the action photos, some going back a decade and more. He called Taylor over. 'You reckon this fellow's handsome?'

She pursed her lips, put her head on an oblique. 'I'd say he's fairly good looking. Why do you ask?'

'It's just Emily's like a supermodel, yeah? And he's an average dude, and that's being generous. You heard the expression, batting out of his league? That's what this fella was doing.'

Hands placed on the back of his swivel chair, she bent low and said breathily, 'I don't know, Detective Lisbon. You've got a face like an old battered boot, but some people I know find you rather attractive.'

He nearly spat out the coffee he'd just taken into his mouth. Another signal? Before he could formulate a coherent response, the Inspector appeared from his aquarium of an office.

'Incident room, everybody. Now.'

BATISTA HEARTILY INTRODUCED DETECTIVES Erhardt and Genk to his officers, drawing a half smile from Jack. Everyone present, bar Kylie Smith and reception jockey Constable Stan Billington, had already shaken their hands and got acquainted at the end of the preliminary interviews. The Cairns uniforms who assisted in writing up statements were absent, having returned to Cairns in a hurry to attend a multi-vehicle fatal accident on the Bruce Highway. Seats were plentiful, yet half chose to stand. Jack, as usual, sat on a table, kicking his feet back and forth as Batista warmed the crowd. He mashed a wad of gum, going over in his mind the words he'd rehearsed for the briefing. Since he hadn't slept a wink in more than 38 hours, he had rough handwritten notes as backup in case his brain shut down. Batista finished by thanking everyone for going above and beyond at such short notice and handed over to Jack.

'Firstly, let's get the Hawks out of the way. Detective Erhardt and his crew don't think the killer's one of them. He—'

'Before you go any further,' interrupted Batista. 'Have you finished the press release, Claudia? I've had the Assistant Commissioner in my ear about getting something out there. She's telling me all sorts of rumours are circulating in the community. We have to take control.'

Taylor nodded. 'I finished it a long time ago, sir. Just waiting on your approval. I sent you an email.'

'You did?'

Jack side-eyed the boss. Definitely losing the plot, and he had a good night's sleep compared to us.

'Yes, sir.'

'Right. I trust you. Consider it approved. Hit the send button and get it out there.'

Two minutes later, with Taylor back in the room, Jack outlined the progress made by the Cairns delegation. A single potential suspect had been identified among the Canadians, with on-ice hostilities between goalie Kirin Pascoe and Eriksson a possible motive.

'There's nothing in that whatsoever,' said Taylor. 'I saw them fighting, but they shook hands and laughed together after the match. It may not have been captured on TV and Erhardt may have missed it.'

'Good point,' said Jack. 'In fact, Pascoe's own statement says more or less the same thing. Denied he was angry at Eriksson, said violence is part and parcel of the sport. Also, none of the Hawks can recall anything suspicious happening at the party after the match. They kept pretty much to themselves, with just a couple of the more outgoing players socialising. And not with the Mavs, but with a couple of young women among the invited guests. Detective Erhardt's advice after he read all the statements was for us to concentrate on the Mavs. He agrees with me that we ought to chase up the two leads DC Taylor got from Emily Eriksson as a priority, then tap on the shoulders of the rock band and the bar staff. I've still got my eye on Ned Campbell. Him falling asleep before the party ended was too convenient.' He squinted at the chief. 'With your permission, sir, I'd like to drop the entire Hawks touring party from our hands-on enquiries. They're a young bunch. If some of them are too traumatised and keen to return to Canada, I say let 'em go.'

Batista glanced up at a slowly rotating ceiling fan, then back to Jack. 'Agreed. Still,' he looked at Ben Wilson, 'until they depart the country, set up one of those social media alerts for tracking key words and account holders. You never know.'

Jack exchanged an optimistic smile with Taylor. The QPS had a range of technologies to automatically monitor social media. Perhaps the Inspector wasn't losing it after all. His next words removed all doubt. 'In fact, plug in the names of everyone in this ensemble cast. Work out the parameters – keywords and whatnot – with Jack and Claudia.'

Wilson grinned. 'Too easy, sir.'

'Claudia, tell us about the leads you got from Emily Eriksson.'

As she began to speak, Jack jumped off the table he was riding, grabbed a marker pen and wrote two names on the whiteboard. Lena Holstrom and Jari Aalto. Taylor outlined why Emily Eriksson thought they could have motive. 'I've left a number of messages on Holstrom's phone, which she hasn't returned.'

'Do we know where she's staying?' said Aden Trevarthen.

'Yes. The Grand.'

Constable Kylie Smith said, 'When I took over from DC Taylor, Emily Eriksson opened up about how she hated this Lena Holstrom. Called her a harlot and said that she'd want to be as close to the players as possible.'

'If she doesn't call back,' said Jack. 'Claudia and I will head to the hotel this evening, leave a message at the desk if she's not in her room.'

'Excellent.' Batista poured himself a glass of water from a carafe. 'I hope she hasn't flown the coop already.'

Jack made a *pfft* sound. 'She can't hide forever, boss.'

Batista flicked through a five-page report. 'Initial findings from Proctor. Stuff we already know. Time and cause of death. She'll get us the toxicology on him, and also… great work on this, Jack, by the way…Ned Campbell's blood test results should be available next week. Also the ice samples.'

'Did the second forensic sweep find anything?' said Semmens. 'Surely the killer left something behind.'

'We won't know for a couple of days. But Proctor's initial impression is it'll be a negative result on that score.' Batista drained half of his water in one chug and refilled the glass. He looked at Jack and said, 'What did Eriksson's teammates and the Mavs staff have to say?' Batista sounded like he needed to hear positive news from this one. 'Any of them blink when you grilled them?'

Jack puffed out his cheeks. 'To be honest, no. All of them said the victim was an introvert off the ice and they had very little to do with him. One, though, Martin

Kornilov, revealed he was the player who took his place in the side at the expense of,' he tapped the marker pen on the board, 'Jari Aalto. He's already been fingered by the widow as someone with a grudge. Kornilov wasn't as harsh; he just said the bloke was upset. As anyone would be, but not to the point where he'd kill someone over getting cut from the team's roster.'

'I got the same vibe when we spoke to Kornilov,' added Taylor. 'But I'd still be digging into it further.'

Batista nodded towards Wilson. 'After this briefing, get all the contact details you can on this Aalto character.'

'Sir,' said Wilson.

'And run checks on all the Mavericks players and staff through the National Police Reference System, Central Names Index, anything else you can think of. Trevarthen can help you; he's the only one of us who's had any time off lately.'

'Will do.' Wilson beamed as if he'd been told he'd won the lottery. Jack knew the team was lucky to have Wilson, who relished having more work thrown at him than most could handle.

Batista ran a hand through his sparse hair and said, 'That will do for this afternoon. Some of you desperately need to rest and come back to this task tomorrow refreshed.' He gave Jack, Taylor and Semmens their marching orders for the day. 'Wilson and I will trawl the CCTV footage we got from Ned Campbell, the rest of you – normal duties.'

'You're not going to see anything of the murder scene on the CCTV,' said Jack. 'No cameras pointing at the middle of the rink.'

'Never mind. How often has a security camera handed you the perpetrator on a plate?'

'Ah...never.'

'Exactly.'

'What about the social media tracker?' said Taylor.

'Tomorrow.' He scratched his chin. 'Actually, Constable Wilson can use his own initiative to create parameters. It's a start, at least. Now, bugger off you three. The rest of us have work to do.' Batista's phone buzzed in his pocket. He plucked it out, looked at the screen, and put it back in his pocket.

'The missus?' said Jack, knowing how the Inspector never took calls from his wife when other people were around.

'Worse. First call from the media in response to Claudia's press release.'

'Which vulture was it?' said Jack.

'Holly Maguire from Channel 11.' The phone chirped again, Batista ignored it.

'We do have to deal with them, you know,' said Jack. 'It's part of the unwritten social contract.'

Batista gave a grim smile. 'I'll call them all back shortly. Organise a press conference for tomorrow morning. 8:30am. I want you and Claudia either side of me.'

'Of course,' said Jack. 'But they'll be mad as hornets that you didn't call it today, you realise that? They'll say you're only half-hearted about finding the killer.'

Batista squared his shoulders. 'Let me deal with it. We're all way too tired to front a presser now. More likely to say something out of turn. They've got their press release, that's enough for now.'

An hour and forty minutes later and back in his own bed, Jack fell into a deep sleep. But not before setting the alarm for 7:00pm. That was the time he'd booked the restaurant, ostensibly to discuss the case. He'd decided to put Taylor on the spot, get her to expand on her remark that *some women* found Jack attractive.

Chapter Fourteen

'YOU DON'T LOOK like you've had any sleep at all, sunshine,' said Jack. He flipped over the laminated menu, running his fingers down the dinner options. He didn't know why he bothered looking: the bill of fare at the Pelican Pub hadn't changed since he arrived in Yorkville five years ago and he doubted it ever would. Its patrons liked it plain and simple, and that suited him fine.

'Neither do you,' said Taylor with a grin. 'To be honest, I didn't even try to get any sleep. I spent the last couple of hours scrolling mindlessly on the internet, then a shower and a cab here and suddenly...here we are.'

'I got in three solid hours' kip. Dreamless, like I was under general anaesthetic. If not for Daisy jumping on me and wiping her slobber all over my face, I'd have missed the alarm completely.'

'You'd miss a lot of important appointments without that dog.' She laughed as she swapped the salt and pepper shakers around. 'What would you do without her, huh?'

'I'd have to go on my morning runs by myself, for

starters. Skye's getting to that age where she wants to lie in every morning, so she's out of the equation as a running partner. But Daisy – she'll go with me wherever and whenever, no arguments. Best dog in the world.' He put the shakers back in their original positions, grinned, pointed at them and declared, 'I think you'll find that's check.'

'Huh?'

'A chess reference.'

'Oh, yes. I get it now.' She pushed her tongue into her cheek then said, 'You know, I could probably beat you at chess. I was rather good at it as a youngster. School champion in year 8.'

'Oh really? When was the last time you played?'

Taylor looked up and sideways, trying to summon the memory. 'I'd say about seven years ago. Against my sister. She's no dummy, and I wiped the floor with her.'

'Can you remind me. What's the piece called that looks like a horse?'

She chewed her lip for a moment. 'The mare? No...' She jabbed a finger at him. 'The stallion!'

Jack clicked his teeth then shook his head. 'Dear, oh dear...'

'Of course it's the knight, you oaf,' she blurted. 'No need to be so patronising, you know.' She crossed her arms high on her chest and leaned back in the chair.

He gulped as he felt the sting of heat prickles ascending his neck, creeping into his cheeks. 'Why did you do that to me?'

'What?'

'Lure me into a trap. I swear...'

She reached across and touched the back of his hand before retracting hers. 'Lighten up. Just playing you at your own game, that's all.'

He gave a deep sigh. 'Why is it I'd rather be facing down a gang of thugs in the street with only my fists to defend myself than get into these mind games with you?' He looked away like he'd been wounded to the quick, blinking at the giant TV screen on the wall. A replay of a classic boxing match. Mike Tyson vs Lennox Lewis. On his own, he'd have been riveted to the action. 'Seriously, I don't know if I can even...'

'Oh, Jack,' she said, her lips twisting into a knot. 'I didn't mean to—'

'Gotcha!' He spun his head around, a grin splitting his face. 'One all, and I think that's a fair result.'

'Speaking of scores, I think 5-5 would have been a fair result at the hockey last night.'

'You reckon Eriksson sealed his fate by scoring the winner at the end? Pissed off a gambler who lost a bundle and decided to kill the guy who ruined it for him?' Jack swirled his glass of rum and coke, the original chunky ice now tiny pearls. He pushed it aside, drank from a tall glass full of sparkling mineral water. The alcohol, as ever, would remain untouched.

She shook her head. 'Actually, no. I'd say Eriksson was doomed no matter what he did in the match. I think this was no opportunistic crime; the killer had it planned meticulously.' She toyed with the stem of her wine glass. 'That's why nothing's jumping out at us. No weapon, no obvious evidence or suspects. Eriksson's phone missing hurts us.'

'Let's see about that.' He'd been hoping to avoid talking about the case despite saying it was the reason for the dinner, but since the conversation had quickly gone down that path, he'd pursue it. Taylor, time and time again, had provided incredible insights that eluded him and the other officers. 'I've been wracking my brain thinking how the hell both the victim and the killer managed to find themselves alone in that stadium, with no one noticing their absence.'

'Absence from where, though, Jack?' She sipped chardonnay from a glass covered with condensation bubbles. 'There was no requirement for Eriksson to "be" somewhere. From all the statements we've taken, the players who took off to the Esplanade to hit the nightclubs were free to do as they pleased.' She steepled her fingers, then said, 'All the statements have the witnesses returning to the hotel between 2:00 and 8:00am. Wilson and Wells ran through the hotel's CCTV footage from the front door. It's picked up every single person staying there from both teams when they came back. Apart from Eriksson, of course.'

Jack swore under his breath. 'It's a pity the Grand's swipe card system's so antiquated. If the killer's among the Mavs or Hawks, one of them could've somehow snuck back to the hotel and avoided the cameras, grabbed a weapon, gone back to the arena and offed Eriksson. Then back to the nightclub and back to the hotel, making sure the CCTV at the front door has picked him up, giving a bleedin' alibi.' He sighed heavily. 'Most hotels with as many stars as the Grand's got log when the guests come and go.'

'They're not obliged to have a system like that. Why would they spend money they don't have to?'

'For enhanced bleedin' security, innit. To help the police out when one of their valued guests gets their head caved in.'

Taylor winced at the blunt choice of words, took another sip of wine. 'We can only deal with things as they are, not as we'd like them to be.'

'You're right, Madam Philosopher.' He took a deep breath, but he wasn't quite ready to drop the subject entirely. 'And the swipe card thing is probably irrelevant anyway. Like you said, they all claimed to have drifted back a couple of hours after the murder was committed. What's beyond dispute is that none of them saw Eriksson out on the town.' Jack tapped his finger on the table. 'So I can only come to the conclusion he remained at the arena, met with the killer on some pretext and got taken by surprise.'

'Sounds logical, but don't forget, they're all saying Eriksson was this lone wolf. Maybe he did hit the town, but on his own, then came back to the arena?'

Jack nodded. It was plausible. Back in his own dark, drinking days in South London he'd often go on benders with only his own sorry arse for company.

'Or,' continued Taylor, 'perhaps Eriksson was out with the killer, who knew the coast would be clear to return to the arena because he or she had knocked Campbell out cold?'

'We've gotta get the toxicology back before we speculate further about that. And what's with this "he or she" nonsense? Those vicious blows were landed by a man, an effin' strong one.'

A waiter loomed over Jack's shoulder. 'Ready to order, sir?'

'You new here?' he said, not recognising the lad.

'Yes, why?'

'The regular waiters call me Jack, not sir. And they know I always order the rump steak, medium rare, with chips and salad. Garlic bread on the side, and then sticky date pudding and a double espresso to finish.'

The kid scribbled on a small pad, looked at Taylor, laid on the charm, smiling with a pair of oversized brown eyes. 'And what do you always have?'

She gave a tiny shrug. 'I'll have the same as my partner tonight.'

Jack felt himself blushing to the roots of his hair. When the waiter had gone away with the order he said, 'Why did you say partner like that? Made us sound like a couple.'

She absently stroked the cylindrical salt shaker. 'Oh? Fancy that.'

He felt his pulse quicken. 'Accidental, was it?'

She winked and said, 'Checkmate.'

THE CONVERSATION over the rest of the dinner centred on mundane matters, but now and again gravitated back to the case, despite both of them promising a couple of times to drop it. Partly because it was still brand new, partly because it was simply the way they were wired.

They agreed on a couple of key matters. Firstly, they needed to get plenty of rest tonight in order to back up Batista at the early-morning press conference. Jack himself had received a number of texts and missed calls from journalists whose names came up on caller ID. Tomorrow, he knew, they'd be baying for blood. Secondly, Emily Eriksson's leads needed to be hit hard: not hearing back from Lena Holstrom had already lent that woman an aura of suspicion. Thirdly, Jack wanted to brainstorm with the team to flesh out plausible murder scenarios. If they could work out the how, that might lead them to the who.

When the bill came at 9:30pm, Jack held up his hand and insisted on taking care of it. He extracted his wallet from his back pocket and pulled out three 50-dollar notes. To his horror, a condom that had been nestling inside for over a year as he endured a period of abstinence decided to hitch a ride with the cash. It came loose as Jack held the notes, landed on the table. Right next to the proudly standing salt shaker.

'I hope that's for me, and not a tip for the waiter,' said Taylor huskily, glancing at the purple foil wrapper.

Jack thought his heart had stopped beating for a moment. 'What?'

'You heard. Is it for me?'

Be careful how you respond, sunshine. 'Do you want it to be?'

She tipped back the last of her third glass of wine, smacked her lips. 'I've wanted it – I mean I've wanted *you*, not that condom – since the day you walked into the Yorkville CIB.'

His hands trembled as he retrieved the prophylactic and shoved it in his pocket. He locked eyes with her. 'You sure that's not the alcohol talking?'

'I've only had three little wines over two hours. Based on experience, that would give me an approximate blood-alcohol level of 0.03%. Fit to drive, fit to fu–'

'Right,' said Jack, grinning like an idiot. 'I believe you.'

Heart racing and unable to think about anything except how he was going to explain away Taylor's sleeping over to Skye, he drove the streets with knuckles white on the steering wheel. He relaxed a fraction as he remembered the kid was at a friend's house for the night. Neither of them said much on the forty-seven minute drive to his farmhouse, content to listen to a classical music CD. When Jack pulled up on the gravel drive next to the front steps, the last notes of Chopin's nocturne op. 9 no. 2 fading, he turned to look at Taylor. Her eyes were closed, soft snores, barely audible, fluttered her lips.

'Why didn't you get some sleep before?' he said. He exhaled all the air from his lungs and glanced at her with longing. 'Now it ain't gonna happen, dammit.'

One eye sprang open. 'Gotcha.'

'Damn you, Claudia.'

'You might have to carry me inside, big guy. I'm not sure I've got the strength to walk.'

Although her words were said in jest, Jack took up the challenge, raced around to the passenger side and scooped her up in his arms. Daisy hared around the corner of the veranda and leaped up on both of them. The three went inside, and Jack kicked the door closed with the back of his heel.

Taylor excused herself to attend a call of nature. She made good use of a spare toothbrush, came back and flopped on his couch. Jack squeezed her hand, headed up the corridor to freshen up. When he returned to guide her to his bed, she was lying perfectly still on one side, her eyes closed, the epitome of serenity. He double checked to make sure it wasn't another gotcha moment. Light shoulder shaking and whispers in her ear failed to rouse Taylor from her deep slumber. He tucked a cushion under her head, draped a cotton sheet over her and placed a glass of water on a side table. Satisfied she was comfortable, he wandered back to his lair, flicking off lights as he went. The dog trotted in at Jack's heels; he bent down and gave her a pat.

One thought stuck in his brain as he climbed into bed.

There's always another day.

Chapter Fifteen

THE PRESS CONFERENCE was well attended, with all the local media outlets represented. Familiar faces in the crowd. A couple Jack liked, others he tolerated, others he hated. In addition, the big guns – national newspaper, radio and television networks – had dispatched a couple of well-known celebrity reporters to cover the sensational story. Tables had been set up end to end at the front of the room. The usual practice was for the police to stand at a lectern, providing them with an elevated platform that looked over the journalists, thus, symbolically at least, reinforcing the authority of the law. For some reason Batista insisted on sitting down for this one. Jack suspected it had something to do with the chief's dodgy back.

Sitting to the left of Batista, he was having the devil of a job concentrating on proceedings. The momentous events of the night before pushed everything to the side.

It had come as a total shock. Taylor, naked and warm and glorious, sliding her way under the sheet. She made her move about half an hour after he'd tucked her in on the couch. *I thought you were asleep?* he'd said, heart pounding like a freight train. *I woke up and found myself in a strange place and I got scared*, she said. *Will you protect me, Jack? Put your arms around me?*

And so he had.

And a lot more besides.

Driving with Taylor to the station for the press conference, they barely spoke, just like last night on the drive back from the pub. No music this time, just warm air flowing through the open windows. They were suddenly like shy teenagers who had "done the deed" and now were unsure what to do next. Only they weren't teenagers; they were adults. She in her late 30s, he was...what...46 this year. Which meant that between them they had enough life experience to be able to figure it all out. In theory, anyway.

His mind rewound to this morning, the sun peaking through the window as dawn broke. His own body clock woke him this time – no need for an alarm or Daisy. His heart had skipped a beat when he turned his head on the pillow, to realise he hadn't been dreaming. He really was lying with the woman he'd desired for five long years.

Then came the awkwardness over coffee in his kitchen. Not knowing what to say to each other, where to look, or how to behave. But that was OK. Predictable. Their relationship had just taken a sudden and giant leap from professional and platonic to something altogether different. Jack felt his heart thrumming, adrenaline surging through his body, as he contemplated what life might have in store next for him. A future with her? Would it be at the level of friends with benefits? Would it develop into something deeper, with Taylor moving in at some point? And most important of all: how would Skye deal with it? The kid loved Taylor, but the recent death of her mother in the UK was still fresh in her mind. Skye had often joked about him and Taylor getting together, but now that it was a reality, she might think differently. These were questions he desperately wanted answers to, but it would all have to wait.

A vague yet annoyingly familiar voice echoed in his head, bounced around like an elusive blowfly he wanted to swat. A question of some kind, but he missed the meat and potatoes of it. He felt a sharp nudge in the side. Batista's bony elbow. The Inspector turned his head and whispered harshly, 'Answer her, man! She wants to know why we didn't brief the media yesterday. You know what to say.'

Jack managed to glare at Holly Maguire from Channel 11, sitting in the middle of the journalists, while simultaneously smiling amiably. It was a skill he'd honed over many press conferences. The atmosphere in the room was charged, like there was an electrical storm brewing.

He glanced over his shoulder at the Queensland flag for inspiration, cleared his throat and said in a measured tone, 'Yes, Holly. I heard your question, and I thank you for it.'

She pursed her lips as she thrust her head forward, demanding he respond.

'I want to be careful with my reply, which I was just about to give if you'd bothered to wait another ten seconds.' He frowned as he looked at a sheet of paper containing a bullet-pointed list of the facts they'd agreed to talk about.

Murmurs bubbled among the crowd, perhaps excited by the prospect of an argument between Detective Lisbon and the local journo. It was no secret they weren't on each other's Christmas card lists.

'You've had long enough to prepare for this press conference, Detective Lisbon,' Maguire goaded. 'I would have expected a more professional approach.'

He inclined his body towards the microphone, opened his mouth to reply, but she cut him off.

'We've had to wait over 30 hours from the time the victim was found for this conference to be called. I repeat: 30 hours! Yes, we got a press release, but it was scant on detail. Why is Yorkville CIB dragging its feet on this? The murder victim was a guest of our town, we've had an important entertainment event cancelled. The public wants and deserves answers.'

He took a deep breath, told himself not to rise to the bait, to stay cool and calm. There was no guarantee he'd be able to manage it. Maguire was able to push his buttons like no one else. Taylor had promised to jump in if his Mr Hyde personality decided to make an unwelcome appearance. 'We appreciate your concern. Let me just reassure—'

'Then what's the answer?' She blurted. 'Stop talking in circles.' He grimaced as he watched her, sitting cross-legged in her pencil skirt, flicking her hair from side to side for no apparent reason. How Jack despised the woman.

Batista quickly stepped into the breach, perhaps anticipating a meltdown from his top investigator. 'Our detectives have been working this case non-stop from the moment Jonas Eriksson's body was discovered in the early hours of Saturday morning. The number of people we need to interview in relation to this homicide exceeds anything we've ever had to deal with before. Yorkville police have worked long hours with no respite and they are utterly exhausted. Now, we've finally got the opportunity to catch our collective breath and share what we know so far with you good people.'

Jack smiled as the chief's beautifully chosen words wiped the smug look from Maguire's heavily made-up face.

'Indeed,' Batista continued, 'we're still working through

our list.' He paused for a moment, took a sip of water. No one dared interrupt him. 'Even with assistance from colleagues in Cairns, we have finite resources to work with.' He smiled and added, 'If only we could sell advertising space like you lot in the media, we might be able to afford to put more officers on the payroll.'

The gaggle of media laughed; even Maguire's sour face reluctantly broke into a grin.

'Still,' said Johnno Peroni, a sports journalist who doubled up as a general reporter for Channel 3 in times of need. 'Do you have any suspects in custody? Is our community in danger?'

Jack felt his fists clench under the table. He wanted to shout out: *Yes. They are in bloody danger. Every day. From violent street thugs, crack addicts and home invaders.* But he remained silent as Taylor, probably also prompted by a nudge from Batista, took up the cudgels.

'The victim is not a local, most of the people we are speaking with are not local. In our opinion, whoever did this, on probability, does not present a danger to the community.'

'You answered the second of his questions first,' noted a squat, bearded man in a bow tie. Jack recognised him as Hamish Wendt, a famous reporter from one of the national networks. 'Which suggests to me you avoided the first one because you haven't arrested anyone and you have no idea what to do next.'

Jack frowned. Maybe there was a journalist more worthy of loathing than Maguire.

Taylor responded flatly. 'I can tell you that we have identified a number of persons of interest and are pursuing several promising leads. Our priority is to maintain the integrity of the investigation. We'll be working hand-in-hand with our outstanding forensic unit to make sure the culprit is brought to justice.'

The crowd murmured, not entirely satisfied with the stock answers. But there was nothing in Taylor's words that the hacks could object to. To top it off, Taylor's delivery was smooth and reassuring. Jack mentally applauded her performance.

'If past experience is anything to go by,' she continued, 'Detective Lisbon and his team will be making an arrest in the foreseeable future. We're proud of our unblemished, 100-percent clear-up rate in this little town.' She scanned the room, smiled with her large eyes. 'There's no reason to expect otherwise in this case.'

Jack nodded slowly as she put the jackals in their place. She was only telling the truth: he and his colleagues had solved every murder committed on this patch since he arrived.

'He even had a hand in cracking a murder case in Portugal late last year, as most of you will be aware. Have no doubt, we will catch this person.'

'Tell us about the devastating consequences for this much-vaunted ice hockey tournament?' The question came from a wizened woman, Fiona Wagstaff, a seasoned columnist from the *Yorkville Times*. She could have retired on a pension years ago, but no one was able to get her to leave.

Jack decided to field this one: he liked Wagstaff, a genuine old-school scribe. 'It's, of course, unfortunate, as you so rightly put it, Fiona. But it's not a tragedy.' He thumped the table and a burst of camera flashes lit up the small media room. 'The tragedy is the death of Jonas Eriksson. And we won't rest until we find his killer.' He rocked back in his seat. 'I think we're nearly done here, unless there are any more pertinent questions.'

A couple of seconds after Jack finished speaking, Hamish Wendt barked: 'The victim. Tell us about him. Was he a foreign national or an Australian citizen?'

'He was a Swedish citizen living in Australia on a permanent residency visa,' said Batista in his most authoritative tone. 'As required by law, we've notified his next of kin, who has the same status.'

'How was he killed?' sparked up Maguire. 'Surely you can tell us that without compromising your investigation?'

'No, we cannot reveal that at this stage,' said Jack. 'The circumstances are unusual, although it was a violent murder. The killer is no shrinking violet, let's put it that way.'

'Any truth in the rumour the murder is connected with sports betting?' said Peroni. 'We've had a similar murder in this town before.'

Jack twisted his lips to one side. 'Aren't you a sports journalist, sunshine?'

'Yes, I am, as you know very well. However—'

'No, Johnno. There's no truth in that rumour.' Jack ran a hand over his face, traces of stubble left after shaving in a hurry. 'You know, I wouldn't be surprised if that so-called rumour originated in your imaginative brain.'

Peroni, undeterred, tossed out another one. 'Motive? If it's not related to gambling, why would someone want to kill this guy? I've done my research on him, and he doesn't seem to have any enemies.'

'Research, Mr Peroni?' said Jack, unable to hide his irritation. 'Perhaps you'd like to come and assist us? Perhaps you think your resources at Channel 3 are superior to the numerous proprietary databases at the disposal of the police? Better than the cooperative arrangements we have with the Federal Police, governments at all levels, Inter-bleedin'-pol!'

Cold Shot

Jack groaned softly as the boss's sharp elbow struck its mark once more. Inspector Batista had clearly decided it was time to end the show. He rose to his feet and said, 'Thank you, ladies and gentlemen. You will be provided with updates as and when we have information that we are able to share. Meantime, I'd like to appeal to any members of the public who may have attended the ice hockey match on Friday night and heard or saw something suspicious, to please come forward.' He gave out the phone numbers for Crime Stoppers and the direct line to the Yorkville station.

Outside on the back landing, the three officers breathed in the humid, salty air blowing in from the Pacific Ocean. Batista spoiled the atmosphere by lighting up a cigarette and inhaled deeply. 'I thought you'd given up?' said Jack.

'I have. I found these in the back of my drawer. I'd forgotten all about them. Must've been there for over a year!' He looked at the glowing end, took another drag and said, 'I should have tossed them away, but I had one earlier and I enjoyed it.'

'Don't get hooked again, sir.' Jack nevertheless inhaled a wisp of second-hand smoke. He himself quit the habit a long time ago, but often he found the scent irresistible.

'I won't, don't worry. There's only two left after this. Then, finito.' He turned to Taylor, thanked her for keeping a cool head when a certain somebody was unable to.

'Thanks, sir,' she said, shielding her eyes from the glare of the sun bouncing of a neighbouring building. 'Someone has to tame the wild beast.'

Jack felt himself blushing, the extra heat pushing out droplets of sweat all over his face.

'You alright, mate?' said Batista. 'You look like your blood pressure's through the roof.'

'All good, boss. Missed my morning run for the first time in months. Body's protesting, I guess.'

'Hey,' said Taylor. 'Want some good news?'

'The murderer walked into the nick and confessed?' said Jack.

'Not quite. Lena Holstrom's finally replied to my messages. Sent me a text.' She held up her mobile for the men to see.

Jack read the words aloud. *'Happy to meet you to talk about poor Jonas. My flight leaves at 11:00am. I'll be waiting in the hotel bar in the Grand.'*

'Both of you go,' said Batista, crushing the cigarette out under his boot. 'This is the most promising break we've had. I'm off to get a massage for my aching back.'

Chapter Sixteen

'YOU THINK ANYONE SUSPECTS?' said Taylor, unbuckling her seatbelt as he parked in a no-standing zone next to the hotel's main entrance.

He shook his head. 'I don't think so. Why would they? We were the epitome of discretion this morning. But it's gonna be hard to keep it a secret.'

'We don't have to keep it a secret. It's not against the QPS rules. It's OK for us to be in a relationship. '

'Is that what this is? A relationship? We've had sex once.' He instantly regretted his phrasing, almost like it was no big deal. She'll think it meant little to him when the exact opposite was the case.

'Do you think that's all it will ever be?' she pouted.

'Oh...no...it's just...oh, man.' He felt sweat forming under his arms. This type of chat was not his thing, never had been. Last of the great romantics.

She rested her hand lightly on his wrist, the merest touch sending a surge of excitement through his body. 'Listen,' she said. 'We're a couple of mature adults. Let's play it by ear for now, OK? If it develops further, we tell the boss and everyone else what's going on.'

'I know...but it'd be weird. People would treat us differently if we were a...' he made air quotes...'couple.'

'They'd learn to live with it,' she said rapidly. Before he could answer, she pulled a pink scrunchie out of her shoulder bag and dangled it in front of Jack's bulging eyes.

'What are you playing at?' he said, genuinely puzzled.

'I bought this five years ago.'

'And?'

'It was Batista's words that reminded me. How he left the packet of smokes in the back of the drawer and forgot all about them. This was in the back of *my* drawer. Have you ever seen me with a pink scrunchie in my hair?'

'No,' he admitted, wondering where on earth this was going. She favoured a small range of colours, in particular yellow, but pink was definitely not one of them.

Her lips formed a half-smile. 'You're going to think I'm silly, but I swore to myself I'd never wear this until Jack Lisbon took me to bed and proved to me there was more to him than meets the eye.'

'You're kidding me, right?'

'Yeah, I am. It was white before I washed it with a couple of new red towels.' She opened the car door. 'Let's go and talk to this Nordic groupie.'

LENA HOLSTROM WASN'T ALONE. She sat in a booth seat, pressing a handsome and athletic young man into the wall with her body. A medium-sized hard-shell suitcase sat on the floor. She was ready to depart Yorkville, but not before getting close and personal with one of the players.

'I recognise you,' said Jack, extending a hand across Holstrom as if she wasn't there. The man shook Jack's hand, a bewildered look on his face.

'You do?'

'Sure. Kirin Pascoe, the Hawks' goalie.' Jack had only seen the man's uncovered face in the printed program, not in the flesh.

'I'm surprised, because the goalie mask makes me pretty anonymous to the spectators. Except for our own fans, of course.'

'Can we join you?' said Taylor, laying her ID on the table. 'You've been expecting us, haven't you, Lena?'

'What's this about?' said Kirin, his lips twisting to accompany the raised eyebrows. 'You in trouble? Have you got something to do with the murder?' He stood, placed his palms on the table. 'If you have…'

Jack shook his head. 'It's fine, Kirin. Lena here just wants to help us out with our enquiries. Would you mind giving us a little privacy?'

'Sure.' He gave Holstrom a withering look.

'But don't go too far. We might like to speak to you again. Depending on what Lena tells us.' He pointed at the bar. 'Perch yourself over there and don't move until I tell you.'

Pascoe squared his shoulders. 'Look. I've already told the other cops everything. They know about the fight with Jonas.'

Jack nodded. 'So does everyone. Please, just humour me, OK?'

Pascoe shrugged, went to the bar and ordered a beer. Jack called out, 'Good lad. Don't get drunk.'

Holstrom, thick blonde hair framing an elfin face, bent her head and sucked a fruity drink through a straw. She looked up, eyes darting from Taylor to Jack, and said, 'I can bet who put you onto me. Emily Eriksson, correct? She's got it in for me, the bitch.'

Taylor ignored the question, dropped her notepad on the table and said, 'You've gotten out of this lightly.' She gestured towards Pascoe, who was talking amiably to a dreadlocked barman. 'Him and his mates had to give signed statements, had their interviews recorded digitally.'

Jack said, 'Voluntarily of course.' He nestled his backside into the soft leather bench seat. 'We won't put you through that, if you do the right thing, that is.'

Her eyes crinkled as she squinted. 'I have to check in at the airport in an hour. I booked my return flight in advance with no flexibility. If I miss it, there's no refund and I can't afford to buy another ticket. You can't hold me here.'

'We can if we arrest you,' said Taylor. Jack noted the colour slipping from Holstrom's face.

'Arrest me?' She lowered her voice and pointed at the broad back of Kirin Pascoe. 'I spent the night with him.'

'I don't believe you,' said Jack. 'He just said to you...*got something to do with the murder?* If you'd spent the night with him, why would he say that?'

She sighed defeatedly. 'OK. I wasn't with him. It's rather a delicate matter. I'm not sure I want to say.'

'Look.' Jack tapped a finger on the table, the sound echoing in the booth. 'We know you were stalking Jonas Eriksson. We have every reason to suspect you of being involved.'

'That Emily is lying!'

'I think not,' said Taylor. 'You were prepared to drop Kirin Pascoe in it, just to provide an alibi. Then you crumbled when we easily got you to retract that lie.' She shook her head. 'You just don't come across as an honest person.'

'Tell us the truth, Lena,' said Jack. 'Can you account for your whereabouts after the party at the arena?'

'Yes. This is the delicate part. I was with Herbert Jubb.'

'Say again?' said Jack, scratching behind his ear with a pen. 'Then why did you say you were with Pascoe? Trying to protect the old bloke's reputation?'

'Something like that.' She sighed. 'He's married, you know. Had the same wife for thirty years. He told me his sick wife's been in hospital for many months. Herbert told me she might not have long to live.'

'When you say you were "with him",' said Taylor. 'What exactly do you mean?'

'I went back to his house just after midnight, got a cab back here at 8:00am or so. The hotel's CCTV will probably show me stumbling in a little the worse for wear.'

'Did you sleep with him? Some people might interpret you being "with him" to mean exactly that.'

'None of your bloody business!' She took a long sip of her cocktail. 'Does it have anything to do with a man getting murdered whether or not I sleep with someone? Geez, give me a break.'

Jack grinned. 'We'll be corroborating your story with Mr. Jubb.'

'Go ahead.' She waved her hand around. 'He'll vouch for me.'

'You sure about that?'

She shrugged. 'I don't care if he does or not, to be honest. I can prove I was there.' She scrolled through her phone, gave a satisfied grin and turned the device around. On the screen was a selfie of Holstrom making a peace sign in front of high metal gates attached to white stucco walls. 'That's me in front of his mansion. There's other pics on my phone of me inside the house if you want to see them.'

She offered a smug smile and looked at Jack. 'It's possible to tell what time a photo was taken, isn't it?'

Jack nodded. 'It's in the metadata.'

She tucked a loose strand of hair behind her ear and laughed. 'I knew it.'

'Any shots of you and Jubb in the frame together?'

'Of course not! I don't want to make trouble for him. That's not the kind of person I am.' Jack realised this 20-year-old woman might be a lot of things, but she was no fool.

'It would only be trouble for him if you chose to release such photos, maybe post about it somewhere,' said Taylor. 'Keep them to yourself and there's no harm, right?'

She waggled a finger. 'Uh-uh. Someone else could set me up. Phones can get stolen, can't they? Or even hacked. So no, there's no pictures of us together at his house. He's a lovely gentleman and I have no intention of exploiting him for my gain.' She pulled the phone back towards herself, tapped the screen and returned it to her handbag. 'Listen. Time's marching on. Can you please hurry things along?'

'We've been advised that you stalked the victim,' said Jack, inching his face closer to Holstrom. 'Because he didn't respond to your advances and you were upset. Very upset. How do you react to that accusation?'

'It's bullshit.' She toyed with a swizzle stick. 'As a Mavericks fan, of course I admired him and…give me a moment please.' She closed her eyes tight, nostrils flared, and began to breathe in and out deeply, almost to hyperventilate.

'You OK, Lena?' said Taylor, a touch of anxiousness in her voice.

Jack looked on, unsure if the woman was acting or not.

'Yes,' she shook her head a couple of times. 'Whoa. The reality of this is starting to hit home.' She looked up for a couple of seconds, then back to the detectives. 'Emily hates me on suspicion, but she's totally wrong if she thinks I had something going on with Jonas. Or that I was interested in him, you know, sexually. She believed all the baseless rumours about me.'

'Baseless?' said Jack. 'How long have you known *him*?' He gestured towards Pascoe's back. 'Looked like you were getting rather romantic with young Kirin when we showed up. Then there's Mr. Jubb. Seems to me there's plenty of grounds for people to draw certain conclusions about you.'

'I pick and choose very carefully. I don't go after every guy. And Jonas, God rest his soul, well, he just didn't do it for me. And he's Swedish like me. Too much same-same, if you know what I mean.'

'Emily says you sent him suggestive texts,' said Taylor. 'Intimate photos of yourself.'

Her eyes expanded. 'What!' Then a burst of laughter. 'She's off her rocker. I've never sent a nude to anyone, and I never will. If you check on his phone, you'll find nothing like that. At least not from me.'

'Conveniently, the phone is missing,' said Jack.

Holstrom pouted. 'When it turns up, you'll see I was telling the truth.' She plucked her phone out of her bag, brandished it in her outstretched arm. 'Wanna scroll through my phone? See if there are any spicy selfies in there?'

'That won't be necessary,' said Taylor. 'Any more questions from you, Jack?'

He narrowed one eye. 'Yes. Why did you apply for a job with Emily Eriksson if there's so much animosity between you? That makes absolutely no sense to me.'

'I did it for a laugh. To wind her up. If you took the time to read my application, you'll see I wasn't serious.'

'No?' said Taylor.

'Ask Emily to show you the cover letter. I wrote in it that my expectation was $100 an hour. The top rate for experienced people wouldn't be more than $30. It was a piss take, detectives.'

'We'll be verifying your claim, Ms Holstrom,' said Jack. He exchanged a look of disappointment with Taylor. His gut told him Holstrom was a mischief-maker with a huge opinion of herself but was a long shot as a legitimate suspect in this case. 'We won't detain you much longer. One more question. Do you know anyone who had it in for Jonas?'

'Well.' A shake of her hair. 'Finally, a question I can help you with. If you want my advice, take a close look at David Quinn.'

Taylor scribbled as Jack sucked in a breath, remembering the name from the program. A teammate, still in town, no tracking down required.

'Tell me why Quinn would want to murder Jonas?'

'Tell you? I can show you!'

After they'd watched the two-minute-long video, recorded clandestinely on Holstrom's phone, the young woman agreed to make a copy of the clip available to the police by uploading it to a cloud drive. The detectives insisted on watching it a second time, transcribing what dialogue they could decipher. Holstrom grabbed her suitcase and hustled out the door to the waiting line of taxis.

'Why do you think she waited so long to show us that video?' said Jack. 'Would have saved her a lot of angst if she'd been up front from the start.'

'I can answer that in two words, my dear,' said Taylor. 'Drama queen.'

Jack put in a call to Gordon Raff, asked him to track

down his gargantuan defenceman David Quinn and dispatch him to the lobby bar.

'I don't trust Holstrom,' said Jack. 'Remember she said she had a plane ticket that couldn't be changed?'

'Yes.'

'That's a lie. She didn't fly all the way up here from Melbourne to watch one match and then go home again. She would've stayed for the entire tournament.'

'You can't be sure of that.'

'No. But we can check.' He stood. 'I'll ask at reception.'

Back at the booth, he wore a frown. 'Damn receptionist was a stickler for privacy. Wouldn't tell me anything without a warrant. Can you believe it? The old Lisbon charm's starting to fail me, sunshine.'

'All good. I've already confirmed your hunch was right. I remembered Emily telling me about Lena's dad being a professor at Swinburne University of Technology. I buzzed Wilson; he dredged up the man's mobile number off the database.'

'And?'

'I asked him if I could speak to Lena. He said she'd be in Yorkville for the entire week.'

'Had he spoken to her?'

'Yes. She said she was shaken by the murder but was thinking about staying for the rest of the week anyway. Her studies don't resume for a month, so there's nowhere she has to be.'

'Then why did she lie about her plane ticket?' Jack cradled his chin between thumb and forefinger. 'There was no need for it.'

Taylor smiled and tapped the side of her nose. 'Like I said. Drama queen.'

Chapter Seventeen

THEY DIDN'T HAVE to wait long for David Quinn to arrive. Perhaps his coach didn't trust him to front for questioning because Gordon Raff was right beside his player. Quinn struck an imposing figure: boxy shoulders, narrow waist on a frame that stretched to 6'3". His ears and jaw were angular and he had a nose which seemed to be set slightly on the left side of his face. Like boxing, ice hockey wasn't a sport to take up if you wanted to preserve your looks.

'David's nervous,' said Raff. 'Wants me to sit in on this with him. That alright with you two officers?' The coach's eyes flicked between Jack and Taylor.

'I'm OK with it,' said Taylor. 'What about you, DS Lisbon?'

Jack spread his hands expansively. 'The more the merrier.' He gestured for them to take the seat so recently vacated by Holstrom that the leather was probably still warm.

'I already told the other cops everything I know,' said Quinn in what Jack figured to be a New York accent. 'They had uniforms on, I can't remember their names.'

Jack cleared his throat and scribbled a couple of meaningless lines in his notebook. 'First of all, thanks for your co-operation. Much appreciated.'

Quinn smiled, beatific relief relaxing his face muscles. 'You're welcome.'

'I've read all the statements from the Mavs players and staff,' said Jack, an almost weary note in his voice. 'And, to be honest, they were a little light on detail. Yours included.'

'What do you mean?' said Quinn. 'I was asked a bunch of questions, and I answered them honestly.'

'Oh, I don't doubt that for a second. But the information is the minimum we could get away with and process everyone quickly. Now, using that basic information, we've been able to narrow things down a little. Not as far as I'd like, but we've settled on a number of people who we think could help us...' he made an exaggerated hand gesture as he emphasised the next word... '*flesh* out our understanding of what's going on.'

'And you,' added Taylor, as if congratulating him on winning a raffle, 'are one of those people.'

Quinn's chest rose and fell; his blink rate picked up. 'What...am I a suspect?'

'I wouldn't go that far, Mr Quinn,' said Jack. 'Not yet, at any rate.' He gave a throaty chuckle. 'However I'd like to know a little about a very heated argument you had with Jonas Eriksson at your home rink on...when was it DC Taylor?'

'November 19th, according to the witness.'

Now Quinn was blinking so fast the effect was strobe-like. 'What witness?'

'Interesting you said *what witness*, and not *what argument*,' said Taylor. 'Do you concede that there was such an argument?'

'Yeah.' Quinn turned up his palms. 'I've had several arguments with Jonas over the years. We've kinda known each other since…geez…2006, I think. We were both just 20 years old then. He'd just come over to America from Sweden; we played a couple seasons in the ECHL before…'

'What's the ECHL?' said Jack. 'Please remember, we're clueless about ice hockey.'

'Sorry. The East Coast Hockey League. Two rungs down from the NHL. Anyways, Jonas and I played in that league for three years.'

'Were you teammates?' said Taylor.

'In the first two seasons we played against each other, maybe six times. Our clashes were always on the ice, heat-of-the-battle kind of thing.'

'I get it,' said Jack. 'I used to be a boxer. A man gets physical with another, throws punches; at the end of the day, no hard feelings. There's nothing personal in these things, right?'

'Yeah,' Quinn nodded and grinned. 'You get it man.'

'What about the third season?' said Taylor.

'Somehow for half a season we ended up in another franchise together, the River City Blizzards. After that, he went to the NHL.'

'So you weren't bitter when Jonas moved across to the big time?'

His eyebrows formed a steep V-shape. 'No way! Lots of guys made that move to the NHL. Me and Jonas weren't friends, and we weren't rivals; more like competitors who respected each other.'

'Did you follow his career?' said Taylor.

'Nope. Why would I? I heard about him getting recruited to the Boston Bruins at the start of 2011. Before that he played a couple of seasons in the second-tier competition, the American Hockey League. Getting into the NHL was bittersweet for him, 'cos he got that real bad shoulder injury before he had a chance to make his mark and it fucked him up mentally.' He widened his eyes, nodded to Taylor and apologised for swearing.

'Why aren't you apologising to me, too?' said Jack. 'I'm a very religious man.'

'Oh,' muttered Quinn. 'I didn't mean...I'm sorry.'

'Don't sweat it, sunshine.' He doodled something on his pad, then said, 'So, we've established these arguments in the ECHL days were your normal, everyday sporting fights. Nothing more to it.'

'Exactly.'

'Then why were you yelling and screaming at each other on the 19th of November at the Mavericks' rink?'

He shrugged. 'I honestly can't remember.'

'Let me remind you. I'm quoting what DC Taylor and I heard on a video secretly recorded by one of your fans who was attending the training session. The place had emptied out, but the two of you remained out on the ice. She – this fan – ducked down behind a seat and held the camera up like a periscope to catch your interaction.' He turned to Taylor and said, 'You be Eriksson, and I'll be Mr Quinn here. Ready?'

'Yes, I'm ready.' She looked at Quinn with a tilt of the head. 'Sorry in advance for the profanity.'

Gordon Raff said, 'What kind of goddamn circus is this? David, you don't have to–'

'Please!' said Jack, glaring at the coach. 'One could be forgiven for assuming you aren't interested in catching who killed Jonas.' He swung his head around towards Taylor again. 'OK, sunshine. You first.'

'Right. I told you I'd pay you back the fucking money. Just give me until next week.'

'What the hell happens next week, asshole?' Jack hammered it up, busting out an appalling version of an American accent. 'We get paid at the same time. And it ain't next fucking week. It's the week after!'

Taylor said, 'In the video, the men get closer to each other. There's only a couple of inches between their noses, their chests are touching and bumping. Then Eriksson backs away and says to you, Mr Quinn: *A friend is going to lend me the money. You'll get it. Just shut up about it, alright!*'

Jack said, '*You'd damn well better get it to me or I'll fucking end you. One more week. No more excuses!*' He looked up from his notes. 'That's where the video stops.'

'I don't believe there is a video,' said Raff, arms folded across his chest. 'These are nothing but intimidatory tactics. Bluff. If there is, why can't you show us now?'

'Because we don't have a copy. We only just witnessed it ourselves. I'm confident the clip will be uploaded to our secure cloud storage by the end of the day. Believe me, Mr Raff, I don't have the imagination to dream up a fake video like that. It's real, and it's incriminating. Mr Quinn's words – *I'll fucking end you* – sound like a threat that's been realised.' He turned to Quinn. 'I'm sure DC Taylor and I can make a solid case to the prosecutor to proceed with a trial should we choose to arrest you. You are a giant of a man. Bigger than Jonas. He was killed by brutal blunt force trauma to the head. You could have done it without raising a sweat.'

'For fuck's sake!' said Quinn. 'As if I'd kill a man over a couple of grand. Yes, I threatened him, but it was an empty threat.'

'Prove it.'

'One second.' Quinn scrolled around on his mobile phone for two minutes, cursing as he made a mistake with a password. Then, 'Here, this is my banking app. On the 26th of November a deposit was made into my account by Jonas Eriksson to the tune of $2,000, exactly a week after our... chat.'

'I guess that friend came good,' said Taylor. 'And in so doing, they may have saved you from being arrested. People have been convicted of murder based on weaker circumstantial evidence than this. You're a very lucky man.' She exchanged a look with Jack. 'Shall we let him go?'

'Shortly. I'm curious, Mr Quinn. What was the money for?'

'A pair of skates, believe it or not. Someone stole his favourite pair and he was desperate to get replacements.' He paused, a look of pain shrinking his eyes. 'Poor bastard only got to wear them a couple of times.'

'Two grand for a pair of skates?' said Taylor. 'Are you kidding me?'

'You can pay even more for the very best.'

'Why did he ask *you* for the money?'

'He didn't. I felt sorry for him, knew he was short of cash, so I offered to lend it to him. But he was taking so long to pay me back, I thought he'd taken me for a ride. I don't like it when people try to stiff me.'

'Fair enough,' said Taylor. 'Do you stick by the story that you left the party at 11:30pm, attended Regine's nightclub until chucking-out time and came home at 7:30am?'

'Yes,' he blurted, eyebrows knotting.

Jack nodded. However he wasn't quite ready to end the conversation just yet. 'If it wasn't you who killed him, Mr Quinn, then who was it?'

'The other officers asked me the same thing. I honestly can't even begin to imagine.'

'The name of a former Mavs player, Jari Aalto, has

been mentioned to us by another witness. They reckon he was bitter about being cut from the team to make way for Martin Kornilov. Eriksson was also in the firing line to get the chop, but he hung on by the skin of his teeth. Either of you gentleman care to comment on that?'

Raff's arms finally uncrossed and dropped loosely to his side. 'Aari's a good man. Very unlucky to get cut from the team. It was a close call, but Jonas was more consistent, had a better attitude towards training. Jari has more natural talent, by a mile, but he's got an issue with alcohol.'

'I was told the same thing,' said Taylor, nodding.

'I liked Jari more than Jonas,' admitted Quinn. 'Jari likes to joke around, but coach Raff is right. He partied too hard, and it affected him on the ice. Well, in all aspects of his life really. I'm worried he'll do something stupid with his visa about to run out.'

'Like hurting someone?'

He shook his head hard. 'No. Like hurting himself.'

Taylor tapped her pen on the table. 'Have either of you seen Jari in Yorkville?'

'I certainly haven't,' said Quinn.

'Me either,' said Raff. 'As far as I know, he's barely got enough money to buy his favourite chilli-flavoured vodka, let alone pay for a flight and hotel. And you know what? If he was going to kill someone for getting dropped from the team, it wouldn't be Jonas.'

'Who would it be?' said Jack.

'Me.' Raff pointed at his chest. Tears welled in his eyes. 'If I'd dropped Jonas instead of Jari, he'd probably still be alive.'

'You can't know that for sure,' said Jack. 'You can't blame yourself for this. If the killer was motivated enough, they would have struck anywhere.'

Jack's own words got him wondering: why here and why now? Was there some weird symbolism for the murderer in the choices he made?

'I agree with coach Raff about Jari being a good guy,' said Quinn. 'If you check up, he's probably sitting in a bar in Melbourne somewhere, crying his eyes out about what happened. I was reading about people called "empaths". Jari's one of them. Not a killer.'

'OK, thanks,' said Jack, gathering his notepad and car keys. Nothing else for it but to hit the databases and make some phone calls. The band and the bar staff were currently being spoken to by Trevarthen, Semmens, Smith and Wells.

'Just before you go, something's just gone off in the back of my brain. Don't know if it could mean anything...'

'What?' said Jack. 'Remember something from the night of the murder?'

He shook his head. 'No, but it could be a motive, maybe. I said before, I couldn't imagine anyone would want to kill Jonas.' He bunched his lips, as if trying to reconcile suspicions with reality, his heart with his head. 'Nah, it couldn't be...'

'What?' said Taylor. 'We won't mention you if you give us a name.'

'Riley Kane.' The words came out reluctantly, as if they were squeezed through a wringer. He puffed out his cheeks and sat back in his seat. 'Look, I'm sure it's nothing...'

'Of course it's fucking nothing!' said Raff. 'What the hell are you talking about? Riley would never do anything like this.'

'Yes, I know...' He put his head in the palms of his hands for a moment, slowly slid them away and looked at Taylor, then Jack.

Taylor spoke first, calmly. 'What motive could Riley Kane have had?'

'They go back a long way. They played in the same team in the AHL for quite a while, the Kingsport Thunderwolves, from Ontario.'

'What's your point?' said Raff. 'That's common knowledge.'

'Then why aren't they, I dunno, closer?'

'It was nearly 15 damn years ago! You yourself played with Jonas…'

'Only half a season!'

Raff said to no one and everyone at the same time. 'Who *was* Jonas close to?'

'No one, I guess.'

'Exactly.'

'Look,' Quinn pressed on. 'I know Jonas didn't socialise with his teammates off the rink, but he did say hello to people in passing. He wasn't an asshole, just an introvert. Except for when it came to Riley. Since I've been at the Mavs, I don't recall them ever exchanging words off the ice. Not even in the changerooms. Perhaps they had some running feud from back in the day?'

'Bullshit,' said Raff dismissively. 'Riley's no murderer.'

'You're probably right. If it is bullshit, then the detectives…' he looked back at Jack and Taylor, who had been observing the interaction between player and coach with interest '…will find out, won't they?'

'Where can I find Riley Kane now?' said Jack. The fellow may or may not be pleased to see the detectives so soon again, considering it was Jack and Taylor who quizzed him yesterday.

'He's a gym junkie,' said Quinn. 'Try there.'

Chapter Eighteen

THE RIGHT WINGER was an even bigger specimen than Quinn. As they entered the hotel gymnasium, Riley Kane was working the heavy bag with unbridled enthusiasm. Jack estimated his height to be at least 6'4", maybe more. Weight around 110 kilos.

'He'd give you a run for your money,' said Taylor, puckering her lips appreciatively.

'Simple combination routine,' said Jack. He sucked air through his teeth and added, 'Jab, body rip, hook, alternating right and left hand. Plenty of energy. The man is a formidable unit, that's for sure. And bloody huge into the bargain. King bleedin' Kong.'

'Could you take him?'

'He'd be about 10 years younger than me. Although it's hard to tell with these ugly hockey players. So he's got the age advantage, as well as the obvious reach and extra weight. But I reckon I'd take him down in minutes.'

'Is that arrogance, DS Lisbon?'

'Nope. Observation. Watch him closely. Sure, he's

thumping the bag with a lot of newtons, maybe close to 4,000, but his technique is flawed.'

'Looks pretty good to me.' She placed her hands on her hips as she watched almost in awe as the Canadian's upper arm muscles flexed and bulged. 'You're sadly lacking in the tattoo department compared to him, too.'

'Compared to everyone. Even you, sunshine. Actually, I meant to ask about that one of the black cat on your–'

'I'll tell you later,' she said with a wink. 'Now tell me why Kane's a poor boxer compared to the great Jack Lisbon.'

'Because…wait, he's shifted up a gear. Can you see? A real tricky combination. Jab, cross, uppercut, cross, hook. Good lad, terrific speed.'

'It's all a blur to me.'

'Right, but at the end of each combo, you're meant to draw your hands back to protect your face. He's not doing that. Careless. I'd take him in round one, as long as I kept out of the way of his punches.'

Taylor laughed. 'But he's not fighting anyone, is he? Why would he keep pulling his gloves back to his face? Pointless.'

Instead of explaining that it was all about developing good habits and not being a lazy sod, he determined to show her the value of a proper defence in a private boxing lesson. Get Skye involved: another way of bringing Taylor closer to his little family. He was confident Taylor could take care of herself in a scrap where the odds were close to even, but with street criminals getting more and more brazen, the odds were too often stacked against the police. No, he'd be a lot happier if she set about improving her combat skills as a matter of priority.

Kane slowed the tempo, cradled the swinging bag in his arms, shifted to the other side to begin another attack.

'Sorry to interrupt,' said Jack, mashing on a fresh stick of spearmint gum. 'Take a breather, pal. Me and my colleague here would like a word in your shell-like. Won't take up too much of your time.'

'Hey, you two again!' The man, for a split second, smiled jovially, then reined it in to a nod. 'To what do I owe the pleasure?'

'You seem in a pretty good mood for someone whose teammate was murdered less than 48 hours ago.'

He wiped his face with a towel, rather slowly, Jack thought. Getting his words together, making up some bollocks. He dragged the towel languorously down his cheek. 'Some people cope with grief in different ways.' He sniffed hard with one lip curled. 'If you believe everyone should be crying their eyes out, then that's pretty naïve in my opinion.'

'And you like to get violent with the heavy bag to cope when tragedy strikes, is that right?' Jack thrust out his jaw challengingly.

Kane shrugged then wiped his armpits with another towel. He dropped his 16-ounce Everlast gloves to the floor, ripped off the strapping underneath. Then he bent down slowly, extracted a water bottle from a sports bag and drank deeply. He looked at Jack and said, 'I'd prefer to use the word physical. Violent? That's emotional language.'

'You're right; physical's the right word in this context,' said Taylor. She smiled at Kane. 'You've got a lot of power behind those punches. I wouldn't want to get in the way of them.'

He laughed awkwardly and said, 'Never hit a woman in

my life and I never would. It's the way I've been brought up.'

'But you have no trouble hitting men?' said Jack.

'Are you fucking serious, bro?' Ridge lines appeared on Kane's forehead. 'There's a famous line by the comedian Rodney Dangerfield. *I went to a fight the other night and a hockey game broke out.* Kinda sums up our culture. Fighting's a fundamental part of hockey, so yeah, I've got no trouble hitting dudes. But then again, the same goes for every single hockey player who ever laced up a pair of skates. Male ones at least.'

'You hit hard. Jonas Eriksson was hit very hard. Repeatedly.'

Kane held out his hands for the detectives to inspect. 'Does that look like I've been hitting someone with my fists?'

'Who said anything about fists?' said Taylor, who nevertheless stared carefully at the man's barnacle-like knuckles.

Jack went further, grabbed Kane by the wrists and tugged him closer, scanned the back of the hands, turned them over and looked closely at the palms.

'What the hell are you doing, man?' Kane's voice contained an edge, hinting at the type of anger Jack knew could boil over into rage.

'Reading your future, sunshine. Possibly not a rosy one if you're withholding information from us.'

'I'm not fucking withholding anything!' Kane yanked his hands free of Jack's grip. 'Look, I already spoke to you yesterday, yeah? And you were as polite as pie. Now you're just being an asshole.'

'Please forgive my colleague,' said Taylor. 'He's had a rough couple of days trying to find a sadistic killer. It's nothing personal against you. Perhaps we can continue the conversation seated?' She gestured towards a scrum of plastic chairs beside a vending machine.

'Sure,' said Kane. 'But no more touchy feely shit. Try that again and I'll be making an official complaint against you, Detective Lisbon.'

'I apologise,' said Jack contritely. 'For some reason I was under the impression ice hockey players could take it as well as dish it out.'

Kane only grunted as Jack draped his jacket over a plastic chair. Taylor bought a couple of colas from the machine. Kane refused the offer of a free soft drink as a peace offering, citing a strict diet.

'Yeah,' Jack patted his stomach, rock hard from his daily exercise regime. 'I find working out with a lot of aerobic activity allows me to occasionally stray from the path of deprivation. Enjoy myself a little, know what I mean? But, each to their own, I guess.'

Kane bunched his cheeks, looked back and forth between the two detectives, giving little shakes of the head. 'If you've got new questions you forgot to ask me yesterday, fire away. I've still got 30 minutes of my workout to go and I'm not happy about being interrupted.'

Taylor glanced at scribbled notes to refresh her memory. 'According to the statement you gave us,' said Taylor, 'you left the party at 11:30pm, came back to the hotel at 7:30am. One of the last to return to base.'

Kane grinned like a split watermelon. 'I got lucky. Met a local chick who thought it would be an adventure to hook up with a hockey player. She'd been to the match and the afterparty, where I got talking to her. We partied on at the nightclub then went back to her apartment. The rest you can figure out for yourselves.'

'Regine's nightclub?' prompted Taylor.

Kane made a pistol gesture with his thumb and forefinger and pulled the imaginary trigger. 'That's the one. I can give you her phone number if you want to check that I'm not lying.'

'Good idea,' said Jack. 'Give me the details.'

Kane dug around in his bag, found the mobile and, in moments, the contact number for a woman called Jade. He showed it to Taylor and she jotted it down.

'Did she give you a last name?' said Jack.

'Nope.'

'Got the address?'

'You'll have to ask her when you call. It was dark and we were kinda occupied in the back seat of the cab, if you get my meaning.'

'You didn't mention this romantic pick-up yesterday,' said Taylor. 'Why not?'

He shrugged. 'Didn't think it was necessary. Didn't want to involve the lady for no good reason. But now you've come back for a second round with me, I figure I'd better put all my cards on the table so you'll leave me the hell alone.'

Jack said, 'Tell us about your time with Jonas Eriksson at the...what was the name of the club in the AHL?'

Kane grinned and said, 'I see you've done some research. The Kingsport Thunderwolves. We played one season together, then Jonas got drafted into the NHL by the Boston Bruins. Man, we were all so happy for him.' Kane delivered one of those far-away, wistful expressions. In a TV show, Jack mused, it would be accompanied by a wobbly mirage and a flashback scene to those years gone by.

'Were you friends at the time?'

'Not really. I'm sure everyone's told you what an introvert he was. Well, he's been like that all his life. Transformed into a machine when you put a hockey stick in his hand. But put a beer in his hand, and he didn't have a clue. He reckoned he had some kind of mild autism. Me, I think he just said that to avoid having to deal with people.' Kane bent down to retie a loose shoelace, bobbed up again and said, 'Sometimes I used to think that was a good tactic of his. Dealing with people can be a real pain in the ass.'

'Your coach thinks the self-diagnosed autism call was wrong, too,' said Taylor. 'That Eriksson used it as an excuse to be the lone wolf.'

Kaned nodded enthusiastically. 'Yep. By staying away from people, you wonder how he could've trodden on someone's toes bad enough to want to kill him, huh?' He shook his head and added, 'I just don't get it.'

'Neither do we,' said Jack. 'There's gotta be an enemy. A person who really despised Jonas. You can't think of anyone like that?'

'The only person I can think of is Jari Aalto. He's a real son-of-a—'

Jack held up a hand. 'Apart from him.'

'Why'd you cut me off?'

'He's been mentioned by others. Doesn't check out. He's in Melbourne as we speak, so that excludes him.'

'He could have paid someone to do it,' suggested Kane. 'A hit man.'

'People tell us he's barely got two pennies to rub together,' said Jack. 'Sure, he may have had motive, but we're missing the other two key ingredients. Means and opportunity. He had neither of those.'

Kane hoisted off his soaking wet t-shirt, revealing a tattoo of his own surname in a gothic font etched into his stomach, just above the navel. 'Is there anything else? If not, can I please get back to my workout? I'm hitting the bars with a couple of my buddies later.' He eyeballed Taylor. 'Care to join us? I'm sure you'd be a lot more fun than your sourpuss partner here.'

Jack stood so fast the plastic chair tipped over backwards. He snapped out a lightning shadow punch that missed Kane's nose by a millimetre. 'Next time, pal, I follow through.'

Back in the car, Jack took a couple of deep breaths before clicking his seatbelt. Although Riley Kane was an A-grade tosser, Jack couldn't find a reason to push him any further at this stage. Unless Jade failed to back up his alibi. He turned to Taylor and grinned. 'See how unprepared Kane was? I could have sent him sprawling on the floor if I'd wanted to. Knocked him out cold. Don't matter if you're a hulking effin' gorilla. If you've got no defence, you've got no chance.'

She nodded and said, 'Right, got it.' A hand wandered onto his thigh as he started up the engine. 'Have you got a defence against this, Detective Lisbon?'

He turned to her and said, 'Against you, I'm defenceless.' Doing his best to concentrate as Taylor massaged his leg, he shifted into second and turned into Strudwick Avenue.

'Will the mysterious Jade be able to cope with the Lisbon charm?' Taylor wondered out loud. 'Please don't throw a fake punch at her, Jack. Do you promise?'

'Not unless she strikes first.'

Chapter Nineteen

THE STRANGULATED SOUNDS of Jimmy Barnes belting out the chorus of "Working Class Man" poured through a set of powerful surround-sound speakers. The weatherboard home smelled of sandalwood incense and dust. A ceiling fan cranked slowly but failed to make a dent in the muggy heat. Constable Aden Trevarthen made a wind-it-up gesture with a finger. The resident of the premises got the message, moved to the sound system and turned it down.

'Still too loud,' said Constable Noah Semmens. 'How about you turn it off, Mr Clayton?'

The bearded man, bleary-eyed and loose of limb, complied with a shrug of indifference. 'If you blokes can't appreciate the great man's voice, then there's no hope for you.'

'You'd be lucky to be 30 years old,' said Trevarthen. 'What's somebody your age doing listening to that daggy 80s stuff?'

'Because there's been very little written or produced since those days that I've been able to connect with. With the exception of 90s grunge. I don't mind some of that. Kurt Cobain, that Daniel Johns from Silverchair. Geniuses.' He lit a scraggly roll-up cigarette and collapsed into a worn paisley-patterned sofa the same vintage as the music. With a languid wave of the hand he invited the constables to make themselves comfortable in tatty armchairs. Both declined the offer and remained standing at parade-ground attention.

'Much as I'd like to get into a discussion about rock music,' said Trevarthen, 'and why a man such as Jimmy Barnes, who purports to be an Aussie, thought it was relevant to sing about working class struggles in the United States and not this country, is nothing short of odd,' said Trevarthen, 'we're not here about that.'

Semmens side-eyed his partner, face muscles stretching in incredulity, and looked back to the man. 'Yeah. We're here about the gig you and your band played at the Yorkville Arena on Friday night.'

'Hmmm.' James Clayton, lead singer of the band "Cover Up", lying on his side, adjusted a black silk dressing gown embroidered with dragons. Thank God, thought Trevarthen, as parts of the rock singer he'd prefer not to see began to appear through the gap in the robe.

'Is that all you've got to say?' said Semmens. 'Hmmm?'

'No,' he said, flicking ash into a tin ashtray on a glass-topped coffee table but only getting half of it in. 'But you hadn't asked me an actual question.'

'Sorry for not being crystal clear.' Semmens took a step closer to the couch. 'Would you mind sitting up? I feel like we're visiting someone in a hospital bed.'

Clayton swung up into a sitting position. 'I've been expecting a visit from the boys and girls in blue. It's obviously about the murder, correct?'

'Indeed it is,' said Trevarthen. 'We're simply checking in with everyone who attended the afterparty with the two teams. Although you and your band aren't in any way suspects, is there a chance you may have seen or heard something that raised your suspicions?'

A shake of the head. 'Me and the other two band members stuck to ourselves pretty much. When we play, we're absorbed in our music, not really paying much attention to what's going on in the crowd. You know, we heard the news and saw the press conference. If we'd had anything useful to offer, we would have called the police already. We're all very shocked by what happened, so close to where we were playing. It's mind-boggling.'

Trevarthen handed Clayton a couple of A4 photo prints. They were from various angles, in various settings. One was an enlarged passport photo taken recently. 'Did you see this man at the party?'

'That the victim?'

'Yes.'

He nodded understandingly. 'I thought so. I partly take back what I said before. I actually do remember this guy. People were crowding him for attention for a while, but soon drifted away, which I thought was strange.'

'He was known for his social awkwardness.'

'That would explain it. He had a kind of wet-blanket vibe about him.'

'Did you notice if anyone came back to him later for a chat?'

'Honestly, I can't say with certainty.'

'Describe your set.'

'We played for one hour solid, no breaks, had a quick complementary drink at the end of it, then we left.'

'No interaction with the partygoers?'

'Nope. We talked more with the bar staff. The lowly hired help finding their community.' He gave a short laugh. 'As for the crowd, there were a lot of guests from overseas not familiar with our Australian pub-rock style of music. When it's locals watching us play, there's usually lots of banter, people yelling out requests. But on Saturday, I dunno, it just didn't have that feeling.'

'Funny,' observed Semmens. 'According to Ned Campbell, the crowd was really getting into it.'

Clayton shrugged. 'People perceive things differently. Some were dancing and singing along to the old favourites, but it was definitely a minority.'

'What time did you and the band leave the arena?'

'It was some time between 11:15 and 11:30pm. We were told to get a move on because the venue was about to close. We packed our gear, put it in the van, then I drove Vicky and Sly – my bandmembers – home. There were still plenty of people filing out of the joint as I drove off.'

'Who told you to get a move on?'

'The manager, Ned Campbell. He wasn't rude about it, though. He said the cleaners were coming in soon and they'd appreciate not having to work around people.'

Trevarthen's ears pricked up. He remembered something DS Lisbon had said about Campbell's statement. How he'd fallen asleep. 'How did Mr Campbell seem to you when you spoke with him?'

Clayton crushed out his cigarette and rubbed his hairy chin thoughtfully. 'A little zonked, to be honest. Not drunk, though. Exhausted. I've seen the same look in the eyes of my band members when we play long gigs, night after night.' He chuckled. 'They probably see the same in me. But we soldier on.'

'Did he look like he might have crashed into a deep sleep soon after you saw him last?'

'I'm no expert, but if that happened, I wouldn't be surprised in the slightest.'

'Do you think he may have been drugged?' said Semmens.

Clayton stood, wandered into the kitchen of his small two-bedroom weatherboard home. 'You guys think because I'm in the music business I know all about drugs?'

Trevarthen said flatly, 'Yes. That's what we think.'

'Speak for yourself,' chuckled Semmens. 'I've got a younger brother in the music industry. You'd never meet a more well-behaved lad.'

'Isn't he in the church choir?' said Trevarthen.

Semmens nodded. 'You saying that doesn't qualify as the music industry?'

Trevarthen ignored his partner's remark, turned his attention back to Clayton. 'Well? Care to comment?'

Clayton said in a serious tone, 'Well done, officer, because you are absolutely right. I do know shitloads about drugs. Namely, to stay away from them. I've seen people die around me from overdoses. There's some evil gear floating around this town. But,' he added, flicking on a kettle, 'in this case I don't know. I've seen people get all drowsy from cold and flu pills, antihistamines, so maybe Campbell had taken something like that.'

'Possible,' said Trevarthen. 'Or he could have been drugged in order for the killer to enter the building undisturbed.'

'Not for me to speculate about that,' said Clayton. 'But yeah, if I was on a jury, that might sound plausible. You blokes like a cup of tea or coffee? I've only got instant.'

The two constables declined, thanked Clayton for his time and left.

An hour later they were interviewing the aforementioned Vicky and Sly, who lived as a de facto couple in a more modern house on the other side of town. About the same age as Clayton, more conservative in their appearance and lifestyle, but like him, mega fans of 80s and 90s music. Office workers who lived out their fantasy muso life on a part-time basis. The hosts' offers of glasses of cold water were accepted with gratitude.

The same photos of Jonas Eriksson made an appearance. Without prompting, Vicky and Sly offered roughly the same assessment of the victim's last night alive as had Clayton. Eriksson seemed to have enjoyed early interest from some fans, then there was a general backing off until all they remembered was a sea of faces passing before the band as they played. People at the bar, at scattered tables, a few patrons dancing.

'Did either of you see Jonas Eriksson leave the party?' said Trevarthen.

Neither had.

'Did you notice anyone having a proper conversation with him?'

'No,' said Vicky.

'Actually,' said Sly. 'Now that you mention it, I think maybe I did.'

Trevarthen's ears pricked up.

'Maybe?'

'Yeah. It could have been something, and it could have been nothing.'

Trevarthen gritted his teeth, battled to stop his frustration from showing. 'Who was with him?'

A shake of the head. 'I couldn't say exactly. I did notice

a guy talking to Eriksson, but I only saw it for about a minute. Less than that probably. I remember because we were about to play a Rose Tattoo classic, "Bad Boy for Love", and I had a feeling the cable connecting my guitar to the amp was loose. There's some awesome riffs in that song, and not having the gear working perfectly is a crime. I told James and Vicky to chill while I checked the cable. Sure enough, it was loose and needed pushing in properly. That's when I spotted this guy, in the far corner of the room, leaning into this Eriksson guy's ear. Body language was intense. Doing a bit of finger pointing.'

'Angry?'

'Couldn't say. Maybe. Or maybe just super enthusiastic about whatever he was talking about. Some people are like that, aren't they?'

'How did Eriksson seem?'

'I'd describe his body language as impassive.'

'Facial expressions?'

'Again. I couldn't say; they were in a pretty dark spot.'

'You're absolutely sure you wouldn't be able to ID the guy who was with Eriksson?'

Sly shook his head. 'I'm sorry.'

Semmens produced a copy of the match program, opened it to the pages with the Mavs players' profiles. Sly waved it away. 'Seriously, mate, I couldn't identify the bloke; it was less than a minute.'

'Never mind,' said Trevarthen. 'If it comes to you in a dream, give us a yell.'

'Will do.'

As Sly walked the officers down a hedged pathway to their patrol car, rippling heat mirages rising from the asphalt, he said, 'The bloke who was talking to Eriksson was tall.'

'Most of them are tall,' said Semmens.

'No, this one was real tall. Like a basketball player.'

Trevarthen stopped, scanned the program again. The tallest player in the tournament stood at 6'4". He pointed at the profile. 'Could it be him?'

'I...yes...I think it could be.'

Trevarthen made a phone call, passed on the gist of information given by Sly to Detective Lisbon, then plotted a course for the police station. He wanted to write up a summary of the two interviews while it was fresh in his mind. He cursed under his breath as the radio crackled. Comms dispatching them to attend the third home invasion over the course of the last week.

'It's better than paperwork, isn't it?' said Semmens, buckling up.

Trevarthen could only nod in agreement, then grimaced as it dawned on him it was merely a delay in having to write up a report. And this new job would also require a report. Too many damned reports. He spoke into the radio. 'On our way.'

Chapter Twenty

'I MANAGED to speak to three out of the four bar staff who worked Saturday night,' said Constable Kylie Smith. 'None of them had much to say.'

'What about the fourth one?' said Jack as he pulled the car into the driveway of a low-set rendered brick house in the middle-class suburb of Mortimer.

'Still working on it, sir. But, based on what the others had to say, I doubt that the guy will give us the key to solving the case.'

Jack pondered for a moment. 'Any of them holding anything back, do you think?'

'No, sir. They were very enthusiastic about wanting to help the police, apologetic at not being able to. Two females burst into tears; the male didn't but was close.'

'Did you show all the photos to them?'

'Of course.'

Jack rubbed his face. 'Sorry, Kylie. I know you're about the most thorough uniform we've got.'

'No need to apologise. I actually made them take a long

look at every single person in the match program. One of them remembered serving the victim a couple of drinks. Straight double whiskies.'

'How many? Was Eriksson drunk?' Toxicology would show how much alcohol was in his system, but it wouldn't say anything about how he behaved.

'She reckons only three or four. He was polite, although he didn't say much, didn't smile, but he appeared to be sober.'

'Doesn't mean he was.' A functioning alcoholic for many years himself, Jack knew it was possible to have a skinful but still fool people into thinking you were sober. 'Make sure to follow up on the last of the service staff. 'Probably a waste of time, Kylie, but you never know. Good work.'

Jack ended the call, turned to Taylor. 'Let's see what this Jade Gunston has to say for herself.' Ben Wilson had managed to find the woman's full name and address in seconds on the driver licence database.

The walk to the front door took them past a lush front garden that was largely well-maintained lawn edged with hibiscus, oleander and frangipani. A child's trike and other colourful toys lay scattered about the yard. The house itself was a newish build, shiny as a pin.

Jack made a "be my guest" gesture and Taylor pressed the buzzer. It took three more goes before the door was eventually opened by a smiling woman in her mid-twenties dressed in ragged, high-cut denim shorts and a loose, unbuttoned blouse. Like Riley Kane, her midriff was adorned with tattoos, with the addition of a piece of dangly belly button jewellery. The detectives barely had time to introduce themselves before they were ushered in. Gunston, all big teeth and a mane of thick black hair that ran the length of her back, was as happy to see the police as she would have been to see a representative of the lottery who'd come to tell her she's won the jackpot.

'Jayden!' she called into the small bedroom as she led her guests down a narrow hallway. 'Hurry up and tidy your room and then you can come and meet a couple of detectives. I'll come and get you when they've finished talking to me.'

The sound of a small boy delirious with excitement came from the room. 'Yay!'

Jack drew in a deep breath. The last thing he wanted was an unruly child getting under his feet. Taylor whispered in his ear. 'Don't worry. I'll distract the kid if he's too much of a handful.'

Jack whispered back, 'I think I'll have my hands full with the mother.'

'Sorry?' beamed Gunston.

'Just saying to Detective Lisbon what a lovely home you have,' said Taylor.

'Oh,' said Gunston, blushing. 'It's nothing to get too excited about, but I'm rather proud of it.'

Jack's curiosity needed satisfying before he asked any questions about Riley Kane. 'I'm not seeing much evidence of a male presence about the place. Just you and your son, is it?'

'That's right.'

'You renting or...?'

She insisted they sit while she fetched them a jug of lemonade from an adjoining kitchen. 'Oh, no. I own the house. Outright, no mortgage. I make my living online.'

The penny was dropping for Jack. No doubt part of the Onlyfans phenomenon, raking in a fortune making "adult content". He wasn't one to judge, each to their own and all that. And in reality, how different was it from how Misty Roach made a buck? A lot safer, for starters. Gunston interrupted his thoughts as she delivered the drink and glasses on a tray. 'I guess you want to ask me about Riley Kane?'

'Yes, we would,' said Taylor.

Gunston's phone vibrated on the glass coffee table. She picked it up. 'I'll just set it to silent. Just got a question from a subscriber, wanting to know whether we're entering a bull or a bear market. I'll answer them later.'

Jack clunked glass against his teeth. 'Come again?'

She smiled so broadly that crow's feet formed for a moment before melting away. 'I run a YouTube channel with an investment and money-saving theme.' She waved a hand around. 'Just about everything you see in this home was bought second hand.'

'How many subscribers do you have?' said Taylor.

'As of this morning, just clicked over half a million.'

Jack edged forward. 'Are you bleedin' serious?'

She nodded demurely.

'And you make enough money from that to live on?'

'It's basic common sense, really. I think my success is down to my personality as much as it is the actual advice. I don't really know that much about the stock market. Just regurgitate what I read. Most of my viewers are interested in the money-saving side of things. How to make your measly budget stretch further, feed your family for $20, that kind of thing. Plus I do sponsored spots for various apps, stuff like that.' Gunston paused for a moment, then screwed up her nose playfully. 'I have to admit.' She held her hands in the air in surrender. 'I did score a small inheritance that helped get the mortgage down. But it's been mainly me. I quit my secretarial role a year ago when I started making way more money online than the job paid me.'

'You've done all this as a single woman?' said Taylor, unable to hide the admiration in her voice.

'Yep. Jayden's the product of a failed relationship. He couldn't handle me making more money than him. We argued about it all the time. In the end he just packed his shit and walked away. I was sad for a while, but now I don't care. I do fine as a single mum working from home. He's still jealous of my success, but he's a good dad to Jayden when he gets custody every second weekend.'

'Which leads me to the next question,' said Jack, reaching his glass of lemonade. 'How did a single mum get invited to a glamorous after-party at the ice hockey?'

She shrugged. 'Like I said, I never pay full-price for anything. A woman on a Facebook group had a ticket for the game but an emergency came up and she couldn't go. She put out the call for someone to take it. It cost $25 instead of $150, so I jumped all over it. I don't get out much and it sounded like fun.'

'That doesn't explain the invite to the party.'

'That was an accident. After the first half...'

'Period,' corrected Jack.

'Oh yes. At the end of the first period a man came up to me out of the blue, asked if I'd like to attend the event in the corporate suite after the game. He said they needed some single ladies for the event, so I said yes and he handed me the invitation. Jayden was staying over at my mother's place, so I snapped at the rare chance to party on. Again,' she tapped her temple, 'free entertainment. I had no idea what to expect, but it turned out to be a classic one-night stand with a hunky guy.'

'Is that a rare occurrence for you?' said Taylor.

'Totally,' she laughed. 'I'm not on any dating apps or

anything like that, rarely go out, but I'm only human, aren't I?'

'He's a lot older than you,' ventured Jack.

'Really?' she said, still smiling. Jack wondered if anything was capable of throwing her off kilter. 'I'm 27. How old is he?'

'Thirty-eight,' said Taylor.

'I wouldn't call that a lot older,' said Gunston. 'Anyway, the younger generation these days are airheads and I've got nothing in common with them.'

Taylor pulled out her notebook. 'Can you please tell us how you came to meet Riley Kane and what time you left the party with him?'

'The band was about to play its second song. I was standing at the bar, kinda wondering whether to stay or go home. It felt a little uncomfortable.' She locked eyes with Taylor. 'You know how it is when you don't know anyone at a party?'

Taylor nodded. 'It can be awkward, that's for sure. So, did he approach you?'

'Yep. He appeared at my shoulder, asked me what my favourite drink in the world was. I thought that was a much better line than the old "what are you drinking". I had to look up to talk to him,' she giggled. 'That man is like the Eiffel Tower.'

'What next?' said Jack.

'He got me a Black Russian, he had a beer, then we danced.'

'Was he with you the whole time?'

'Yes.'

'We have a witness who claims Riley Kane was talking rather animatedly to Jonas Eriksson for a while. Are you sure you don't want to rethink that?'

For the first time Gunston's carefree and joyous demeanour shifted. 'Well, he may have gone to the toilet once or twice, but not for long. I mean, I had a toilet break myself, so yes, there were a couple of brief moments we weren't together.'

'And did you leave the venue together?'

'Ah...yep. We did.'

Jack's ears pricked up. 'What time was that?

'He grabbed my hand and led me out of the room as soon as the band played the last song. I can't tell you exactly what time that was, but I'd say it was about 11:30pm.'

'You hesitated just now. Why?'

'I'm sure it's nothing, but when we got downstairs, he told me he'd forgotten something in the changing room and that he had to go and get it because he was afraid someone might steal it. He said it could take a while, so he called me an Uber, put $100 cash in the driver's hand and told her to take me to Regine's. Riley said he'd meet me there soon.'

'You were OK with that?'

'Sure. You hear a lot about weirdo taxi drivers, but this one was an older woman, so I had no issues with it.'

'What was it Riley had forgotten at the arena?'

She blinked hard. 'You know what? I never thought to ask. And by the time he turned up at the nightclub, I was already excited about...well...being with him. So I never found out.' She tucked her chin to her chest, like she was ashamed of her having a sexual desire for the man.

'Were there still people leaving the arena when Kane went back in?'

'Yes, in dribs and drabs.'

'Can you tell me what time Riley Kane arrived at the nightclub?'

She took a sip of lemonade. Jack wondered if she was

preparing an alibi for the man. 'I saw him inside at around 1:00am.'

'That's a long time, isn't it? An hour and a half from when you left in the Uber. It's only a 15-minute drive from the arena to Regine's.'

She shook her head. 'No. He apologised profusely. He said he'd been in the club for a while already and got caught up talking to some of his buddies.'

It sounded plausible. He turned to Taylor. 'Message Wilson. Ask him to have another look at the CCTV from the nightclub for Saturday night. I want to see if Kane was lying about when he arrived.' Back to Gunston: 'So, confirm it for me again, so we're clear. The subject of what he'd had to go back for wasn't discussed.'

She looked at him with no expression on her face, almost like a mannequin. 'That's correct.'

Taylor said, 'Much as we're trying to establish the movements of Riley Kane, we'd also like to know if you had any interaction with the victim.'

'No. I saw him at the beginning of the party, but then I never noticed him again. I was too preoccupied with Riley.'

'Did Mr Kane have any interaction with him?'

'Not that I noticed.'

'Interesting,' said Jack. 'Because another witness is fairly confident they saw Kane having an intense conversation with Eriksson during the evening.'

'It's possible, I guess, but if it happened, Riley said nothing about it.'

'We're just about done, Ms Gunston,' said Jack. 'One last question. Have you had any contact with Riley Kane since Saturday night slash Sunday morning?'

'No, sir.'

As they stood to leave, Jack said, 'Your son. Didn't he want to say hi to the cops?'

Tears welled in the corners of Gunston's hazel eyes. 'Oh wow...I'm just realising the seriousness of this horrible crime. Perhaps we can leave it for another time?' She smiled with trembling lips.

Taylor touched her on the shoulder. 'I think that's a good idea.'

———

WHAT DID YOU MAKE OF HER?' said Jack, picking a scenic route back to the station.

'She's holding something back.'

He nodded. 'And those tears at the end. Real?'

Taylor nodded. 'In the sense they were wet and had salt content? Yes. Were they genuine? I don't know...'

Chapter Twenty-One

JACK AND TAYLOR sat in swivel chairs at Jack's corner workstation; standing behind them – Constable Wilson and Inspector Batista. All stared intently at Jack's monitor. The cheery woman on the 15-minute YouTube clip wore an even broader smile than the real-life version. A background of fake books packed tightly on a tall but equally fake bookshelf, the lighting coming from the left to cast a faint shadow on Gunston's face. A simple setting, yet it came across as highly professional. Sound and image quality as good as a TV network.

The latest offering, ten ways to make the most of supermarket specials, had been posted last Wednesday night and had already racked up more views than she had subscribers. Comments in the tens of thousands.

When Jack clicked out of the platform, Wilson said, 'The stats back up her claims. A catalogue of material stretching back two years, half a million plus subscribers, all her videos getting tons of views. People with channels doing that can earn up to $10,000 a month. Even more if they have sponsored ads.'

Taylor whistled softly. 'I'm in the wrong business. I could be as engaging as her.' She looked up at the Inspector. 'Surely QPS rules don't preclude me from moonlighting and–'

'Don't even think about it. We need you here.'

Jack was about to query Wilson on the nightclub security camera footage when his mobile rang. Emily Eriksson. He answered, told her he'd be putting her on loudspeaker, if she didn't object.

'No, not at all,' she said.

'Can I record it?'

'Of course.'

'Fire away, then.' Jack pressed a button to record the conversation.

'I've been wrestling with my conscience over this. But I think it's time to tell you. Jonas was being threatened with blackmail.'

The officers exchanged wide-eyed looks of anticipation.

'Please go on,' said Jack.

She sighed deeply; the sound of a cigarette lighter sparking up came down the line. 'He wouldn't be specific about it, but I've got my suspicions. I could be way off the mark, of course.'

'Detective Claudia Taylor here, Emily. Please tell us who you think might be behind this and why?'

'I can't tell you who, but years ago Jonas was involved in something shady. It happened in Prague, years ago. He's hinted at it now and again, but would never go into details. Too ashamed of what he did, I think.'

'How many years ago?'

'Perhaps ten? I can't be sure. If you look on his mobile phone, I'm sure there'll be evidence of it.'

Jack gritted his teeth. 'Unfortunately, his phone's missing. We believe the murderer took it. We'll be seeking a production order from the magistrate to access Jonas's records, but that doesn't guarantee anything. We can see where a text or image has originated from, but if something's been deleted, we have no idea of the content.'

'Oh...'

'You know which provider he was with?'

She named one of the big telcos and gave a sad laugh. 'He was always complaining about the poor coverage where he lives.'

'Thank you, at least that's something.' It was bugger all, but it didn't hurt to be polite to grieving widows. 'Why didn't you tell us about this before?'

She sniffled. 'Stupid, really, since he's dead. But if he was involved in something dodgy, maybe illegal, I didn't want a story to come out that might tarnish his memory. Is that silly of me?'

'Not at all,' said Taylor. 'You obviously loved him very much.'

'I still do!' she wailed.

Jack gave her a minute to settle. 'Was he playing hockey in Prague in those days?'

'Yes. He played a couple of seasons for a team there. Can't remember the name off hand.'

Jack scratched his head. 'Is there anything more about this you'd care to share with us? Names of former teammates who he argued with or...'

Racking sobs rang out in the police station. 'I'm sorry, no.'

'That's fine, Emily. We'll contact the police in the Czech Republic, Interpol, too. I'm sure they'll be keen to help.'

Jack wasn't so sure his words would be backed up by fact. He thanked Emily Eriksson for her courage in calling and terminated the call.

Inspector Batista said, 'I'll make the necessary calls to our international colleagues.'

With Batista back in his aquarium, Jack asked Wilson about the nightclub's CCTV.

'The pictures are good, but a lot of the time people entered in groups; sometimes they had their heads facing down or away from the camera.'

'Did you identify any individuals from the Mavs and Hawks?'

'Yes. Plenty. Among them, Quinn and Pascoe, two of the men you asked me to look for especially. Also, the coaches of both teams and plenty of others.'

'You haven't mentioned Riley Kane.'

'Well, that's interesting. We've got him inside at 2:07am, getting up close and personal with a young woman. We've also got him leaving at 4:30am in the company of the same woman. But there's no footage of him arriving at the nightclub. I guess he was one of the ones the camera simply failed to catch for one reason or another.'

'Either that or he deliberately muddied the waters by concealing his face when he arrived at the nightclub because the timing would mean he could have murdered Jonas Eriksson and got to Regine's undetected.'

'But the CCTV at the arena?' said Wilson. 'The Inspector and I went through it and didn't see anything unusual.'

'Have another look,' said Jack. 'Jade Gunston said Kane

went back into the stadium to retrieve something and then got a taxi to the nightclub.'

'That's right,' said Taylor. 'Gunston was sure there were people filing out of the gates when he went back in. He could have blended in with the exiting crowd and snuck back in undetected by the cameras.'

'Dammit, you're right.' The Inspector was already moving towards his office. 'Come on, Ben. Let's have another look.'

'Make a copy of the file, please, sir.' Jack was on his feet. 'Make it several copies. Whoever's in the office can help on this. I'm liking Riley Kane for this one.'

'Detective Lisbon?' said Trevarthen, whom Jack noticed for the first time.

'Yes? And weren't you attending a home invasion?'

'We were. Jumpy neighbour dobbed in the kid next door who was climbing into his own bedroom window.'

Jack nodded. 'I don't blame that neighbour with the way things are going in this town. So, what did you want to say?'

'You mentioned Ned Campbell said the CCTV turned off at midnight? If it's Kane, he could say he picked up whatever it was he went back for and exited just after midnight. According to Dr Proctor, the likely time of death was 12:30am. That would put Kane in the clear.'

'There's always a margin of error in these things. Especially in the cold environment, so pinning down the TOD exactly will be close to impossible.'

'Then how do we nail him for it?' said Taylor.

Jack winked. 'There are ways and means.'

Ten minutes later, a Eureka moment. 'Got him!' said Taylor. The other officers crowded around her desk.

'Bullshit,' said Jack. 'I've been back and forth a hundred times and didn't spot him. He's six-foot bleedin' four!'

'That's because he's crouching a little to blend in. All the players are wearing their team polo shirts and jeans. He's got a regulation short-back-and-sides haircut, like many of them.' She stopped the video and advanced it one frame at a time until one player's tight shirt rode up a fraction. She pointed, 'Look. Part of a tattoo on the stomach. You can just make it out if you squint.'

'That means…what does that mean?' said Noah Semmens.

'It means a man's vanity with a lady cop around might have been enough to bring him unstuck.'

THE MAN STOOD on the hotel room balcony wearing only a pair of shorts. Tattoos and muscles on display as they were in the gymnasium. Without looking at either of the detectives he said, 'Feel free to arrest me if that's the best you've got.'

'Do you seriously expect us to believe your bullshit?' said Jack, standing in the gap between the sliding bi-fold doors and the wall. 'That it took you around one and a half hours to locate your wallet in the arena and then get back to your new lady friend at Regine's disco?'

A stream of frothy cola sailed over the railing as Riley Kane burst into laughter. 'Disco, granddad? No one says that any more.' He turned around, leaned back against the railing, extended arms resting on the top like a bird's wings.

'That tattoo on your stomach gave you away, mate. Despite the extreme effort you put in to be unnoticed. A waste of time, since your lady friend dropped you in the shit anyway. Told us you went back inside. In my mind, with the purpose of murdering Jonas Eriksson.'

'You're mental, you are. Jade told you what she did because she's a good person who tells the truth. As for me killing Jonas, that's a fantasy. You told me Jari Aalto had no means or opportunity. But he had motive. Well, I've got *no* motive. Zero. No reason to harm poor Jonas.'

'Still,' said Taylor. 'Why *were* you striving so hard to get back into the stadium unseen? You looked ridiculous ducking down among your teammates, almost waddling so the camera wouldn't pick you up properly. Reminded me of Basil Fawlty.'

Jack laughed; Kane stared in bewilderment.

'I've no idea who that is, and I don't fucking care,' said Kane, who now made no effort to rein in his temper. 'I'm about sick of you stupid cops harassing me. The reason I was "crouching", as you put it, is because I dropped my phone just before I went inside and I bent down to pick it up.'

'So it's just a coincidence that you exited the arena when the CCTV had stopped working?' said Jack.

Kane's eyes widened as he held out his massive hands. 'You think I would know something like that? I'd never been to that arena prior to the match. As I said before, you are off your head. Clutching at straws. Instead of bothering me, get out there and find the real killer. Now, if you've got no intention of arresting me, I'd kindly ask the pair of you to piss off.'

Chapter Twenty-Two

WITH SKYE TUCKED up in bed, exhausted after a weekend at her schoolmate's house, Jack paced the wooden deck of his wide veranda. A slight breeze penetrated the scrub around his property; the night creatures croaked, chirped and squawked. His mood was down after that last meeting with Riley Kane. Hopefully the working week starting tomorrow would bring some better news from forensics, or a dark-horse witness would show up with conclusive proof of the killer's identity.

He'd been hoping to have a cosy three-way chat with Taylor and Skye about the new…what should he call it… special friendship with the lady detective. Unfortunately, there was no Taylor for company tonight; she'd made the three-hour drive to Cairns Hospital to comfort a loved one. Her sister Annie had taken a turn for the worse, a reaction to chemotherapy. The woman had a nasty melanoma with a nasty name – acral lentiginous melanoma – on the sole of her foot. It was removed a couple of years ago and all looked rosy. Recently, a new one was detected on her hand.

The surgeon had cut it out, but something malignant had been left behind. Not his fault, just one of those things.

The arrogance of Kane made Jack's blood boil. The way he flirted so openly with Taylor only made it worse. The urge to rearrange the bloke's smug face was almost too hard to quell.

There was nothing solid to pin the murder on him, yet Jack's gut screamed Kane was the culprit. Physically, he was strong enough to have killed Eriksson with relative ease. And the timing was perfect for him to have done it, yet his excuses were all plausible. Most curious in Jack's mind: he hadn't seemed at all fazed to learn one-night-stand Jade had dropped him in it. Not even a flinch. Like he expected it and had prepared for the police to bring it up.

Doubt crept into Jack's mind: if Kane had casually gone back into the stadium with her knowledge, then he must have considered the possibility the police would question her and that she would answer truthfully. And if that was the case, why the charade of ducking his head when going back inside the stadium? Unless….unless he really did drop his phone. *Dammit.* Another look at the footage was inconclusive. If it was shown to a jury, a half-decent lawyer could make the case that is exactly what transpired.

Bugger it, he thought. And dialled a contact in the UK who, he was convinced, could find certain information and do things all the police forces in the world were incapable of.

'Alright, Micky?'

'It's bleedin' early over here, Jack. Must be one of those urgent cases and not a social call. Correct?'

'You got it, mate.'

'What's up? I'm kind of busy myself today. I'm being interviewed on the telly.' Even though the sun had barely risen in the UK, Jack's long-time friend and ally Micky Knox was his usual cheery self. 'So I can't give whatever you want my full and undivided attention right away.'

'You're not on my payroll, sunshine. Every favour you do for me is appreciated more than I can express.'

'Leave off. You'll have me bawling in a minute.'

'I doubt that,' said Jack, cracking the top of a can of diet lemonade. 'I've never seen you cry. Not even when I whipped your arse in the boxing ring. But tell me, why on earth would anyone want to put your ugly mug on the telly?'

'Generous with the compliments, as usual, I see. As it happens, I've sponsored a local football club that was on the verge of folding and everyone wants to know about this geezer who's stepped in to pull them back from the brink.'

'Is that what it's really about, Micky? Sure you're not currying favour with the town council for some dodgy property development?'

'I can't believe you said that,' Micky chuckled. 'I've got enough money now; why not dabble in a bit of philanthropy, hey? We had to do it tough at our crappy gym in South London, so I figured it'd be nice to give the kids in this area a bit of a leg up.'

For a couple of minutes they waxed nostalgic about the old days at McNair's gym, neither of them mentioning the murder of Alex Gallagher and the subsequent robbery that helped fund Micky's future. Jack's too, but in a different direction. It was a secret both of them wanted buried deep and safe and forever. The subject was rarely mentioned and never over the phone. Jack touched briefly on his new romantic entanglement, which brought howls of enthusiastic approval from Micky. Finally, Jack got to the nitty gritty of the case. Outlined the circumstances and the key figures he'd like Micky to find some dirt on.

'Jack, my son, that's gonna take time. I mean, stuff from Prague that happened ten years ago? Lots of the press material is gonna be in bleedin' Czech, innit? Not to mention any dark-web stuff. Honestly, pal, I can't really make a start until tonight. I've got too much preparing to do for this interview. After that I'm gonna need to catch my breath for a spell. Believe it or not, I'm nervous about fronting a camera.'

'I can believe it. Took me several press conferences before I had the confidence to deal with the media vultures. Now, it's second nature. It'll be the same for you.'

'I don't want it to become second nature. This is a one-off.'

The men made their farewells with some last-minute reminiscing and a promise from Micky that he'd visit Australia soon.

Humidity levels had climbed over the hour Jack had bent his friend's ear, making it too uncomfortable to remain on the veranda. Or maybe it was the hungry mosquitoes. Either way, the comfort of modern air-conditioning in his bedroom won the argument.

THE BONE-JARRING sound of his alarm, set to the Clash's raucous "White Riot", jolted Jack out of a deep slumber. A pity, since his dream was a replay of his passionate night with Taylor.

'Micky!' He tossed the top sheet away, swivelled to a sitting position, turning on his phone's loudspeaker function and setting the device on his bedside table. 'Do you know how early it is here?'

'I sure do. Five in the morning.'

'I didn't ring you until 6:00am your time. You're taking a bleedin' liberty.'

'Just returning the favour,' said Micky with a mock evil laugh. 'Want to know what I found out or not? Happy to let you go back to sleep, pal.'

'Of course I want to know.' Jack hunted through drawers, found his last clean item of underwear, then a lone t-shirt. Shorts he'd been wearing for nearly a week. He'd been so busy there had been little time for boring domestic chores like washing clothes. Luckily, Skye did her own if dad wasn't on the ball. There'd be no time to run a load and hang it out before work; he'd have to buy a new collared shirt on the drive in.

'Buckle up.' Micky started with the main suspect, Riley Kane. 'As a lad he got into a spot of bother with the law. Aged 19, he went on a drunken rampage in the small town he lived in in Ontario, Canada. Smashed up some cars, broke a picket fence. Blamed it all on a "friend" who plied him with liquor and then egged him on. No jail time, fifty hours of community service.'

Jack inhaled sharply, now in the kitchen and priming his coffee machine. Aden Trevarthen, his sparring buddy, had put him onto the idea of drinking a strong coffee before his morning run. Turned out to be a great idea, boosting his performance and even burning more fat than he would without it. Once addicted to alcohol, Jack was now addicted to coffee, so Trevarthen didn't have to try hard to argue his point. 'I knew that pratt had a violent streak. What else?'

'Ah...nothing. That's it. His record's been clean as a whistle since then.'

'Have you looked everywhere?'

A sigh. 'Jack, I've looked in more places than everywhere.'

'What about the other names I gave you? Surely you've had some hits.'

'Better news. Let's start with Jari Aalto. The bloke got in trouble for smoking marijuana as a teenager in Finland. And when I say trouble, it was a warning. The laws were strict in those days, even for liberal Scandinavia, but his father is a lawyer. I guess that helped him avoid having a tainted record.'

'Didn't do him a lot of good in the long term. The man's an alcoholic.'

'In itself, not a death sentence. You yourself, Jack, were—'

'Yes, we're all aware of that. No need to rake over old coals. So, nobody had any run-ins or grudges against Jonas Eriksson?'

As he listened to Micky's reply, he fixed himself a double espresso.

'Not that I can find. Not every human interaction ends up online, on a police database or in a court report. Our little chat right now, for example. Unless someone is listening in, there'll be no record of it. Like it never happened.'

Jack swallowed his coffee in one gulp. Knox was as astute as they come. 'You're right, mate. Any of the others arouse your suspicions?'

'One did, yeah. In your backyard. The arena manager.'

This one took Jack by surprise. 'Ned Campbell? He seemed pretty innocuous to me. Small of stature, small of character.'

'Sometimes they're the ones to watch out for, innit?'

Jack carried the phone back to his bedroom. Daisy sat

up in her dog bed, panting excitedly, tongue lolling. Jack got dressed for a run, stretched quadriceps and hamstrings, neck and shoulders. Daisy leapt out of her bed, sat beside Jack and gazed up. She knew when her master laced up his training shoes that a run wasn't far away. 'Our people have had a good look at him. He's had no significant interaction with Jonas Eriksson that we can tell. No motive to kill him.'

'He may not have a motive to kill him, that's true. But would he be morally bankrupt enough to assist someone else to kill him? I chose the word bankrupt on purpose, because that's what he was. Now discharged, of course.'

'How long ago?'

'Fifteen years. Which has given him plenty of time to recover, with more or less a clean slate. But, he hasn't really. He appears to have racked up a massive debt again. The repayments must be crippling.'

Jack didn't know how Micky did it. For the police to look deeply into Campbell's financial affairs would require a court order. He had to ask: 'How the hell do you know that?'

'Of course, I could hack into the banking system, but I'd have to know which bank he was with. This would take too long, and it's too risky for me. Penalties if you get caught don't bear thinking about. But I found a searchable Australian electoral roll, sitting on a server in Serbia of all places. They've got 'em for a number of countries. Dodgy as hell, and it cost me a couple of quid. Which you can pay me back in the form of a pint next time we meet.'

'Electoral rolls don't contain financial information; even I know that.' Jack found the dog lead and connected it to Daisy's studded collar. 'I know you're playing me like a fish on a line, Micky. Consider me reeled in.'

'Right. So I found where the guy lives.'

'Micky, stop. He lives right here in Yorkville. He rents a rather nice apartment on the Esplanade.'

'According to the electoral roll, your guy Edward "Ned" Campbell is registered as living in a multi-million dollar home in the well-heeled Melbourne suburb of Toorak.'

'You're kidding.'

'Nope. Using this electoral roll, I rang a couple of the neighbours either side and across the street. Said I was a cousin in the UK, that I hadn't heard from Ned in a while and I was worried about him.'

'You can spin a good yarn, Micky.'

'I learned from the best. Anyway, one old woman had no hesitation in telling me she's seen repossession guys around on a couple of occasions. They've pulled up in a van and carted off furniture, electrical goods, effin' framed oil paintings, you name it.'

'He never even hinted at this.'

'Why would he? People like him are in complete denial of reality.' A slight pause before he added with gravitas, 'He owes money, lots of it. And probably not to the bank, either.'

Jack muttered under his breath.

'Sorry, Jack?'

'Who's letting the repo guys into the house?'

'The woman's not sure; thinks it's most likely a house sitter. She reckons the residents in the street aren't very sociable.'

'It all makes sense,' Jack pulled the door behind him. 'He told me he'd tipped everything but the kitchen sink into this dream of establishing a proper professional ice hockey league in Australia. Teamed up with this Herbert Jubb character. By the way, did you find anything on him?'

'You didn't ask about him.'

'Put him on the to-research list.'

'Jack, you'd think I didn't have my own business to run, my own life to live?'

'Sorry, mate. But back to Ned Campbell for a second. I'd be very nervous if I were him, staking everything on this project. I went to the game the night Eriksson was killed. The game's electric, right up my street. But it's way too foreign for the Aussies to make it a major sport. That's just my opinion. I could be way off the mark. But even if he's right, it's going to take him years to get the money back.'

'And that's why…'

'That's why he's taken money to look the other way while somebody kills Jonas Eriksson. Self-ingested a sleeping drug to make it look like he was a victim, too.' He wrapped the lead around his wrist a couple of times, patted the dog on the head. 'Only question is, who paid him? It's gotta be Kane.'

'That's for you to figure out, Jack.'

'Right. Daisy's champing at the bit. Gotta go.'

'Aren't you gonna ask how my TV interview went?'

'Of course!' He involuntarily disconnected the call as the mutt took off and nearly pulled Jack's shoulder out of its socket.

Run. Shower. Call Micky back.

'How did the interview go?'

'I've emailed you a link to the video. You can make up your own mind, but I think it went pretty good.'

'Well.'

'Well what?'

'You think it went pretty well, not good.'

'Fuck off, Jack. I'll not be taking grammar lessons from an ill-educated git like you.'

'I'll be sure to check it out,' Jack laughed.

'Anything else while I'm here?'

'No, mate. But keep your eye on the case online. Over here, it's getting plenty of column inches or pixels or whatever you call it these days. As usual, the pressure's on for a quick result.'

'You haven't been ignored completely over here. The story made page four of yesterday's *Daily Mail*. Not bad when there's uncontrolled knife crime on our streets and wars are raging on our doorstep.'

As Jack hung up, Micky's words hit home. Despite his own whining about crime in Yorkville, there were many worse places to be.

Apart from in Ned Campbell's shoes.

Keys. Jacket. Hilux. Highway.

Chapter Twenty-Three

'I WOKE up this morning with a headache driven by pessimism,' announced Inspector Batista, standing on one side of the blank whiteboard. 'However, Detective Sergeant Lisbon has assured me he's now got a new lead, which means I might not need a third aspirin to get through the day.'

The officers gathered in the clinically sparse incident room laughed politely.

'On the negative side, we have no murder weapon, and forensics is yet to provide us with anything conclusive,' Batista continued, rubbing his hands together in his trademark praying mantis fashion. 'I spoke briefly with Margaret Proctor this morning. She's usually optimistic, but this time she believes the scene of the crime, the rink and the cold conditions inside the arena are going to work in the perpetrator's favour.'

'Don't chuck in the towel, sir,' said Jack, bookending the Inspector on the other side of the whiteboard. 'What I learned last night could help point us in the right direction.'

He proceeded to outline Ned Campbell's apparent financial worries and his hunch that the man was desperate enough to do anything to get his hands on money.

Micky Knox had long ago agreed that Jack could take the credit for any breakthroughs or discoveries that originated in St Albans, UK, rather than as a result of Jack's own hard work in Yorkville, Australia. In fact, Micky, rather sensibly in Jack's view, insisted on being left out of the equation altogether.

'Good idea with the reverse search of the electoral roll,' said Constable Wilson, whose mouth immediately flipped to a disappointed frown. 'Although I'd actually taken the initiative of doing that very thing with every person on the Mavs' list. Plus Herbert Jubb, Emily Eriksson, Jari Aalto and Ned Campbell. The file I created is in everyone's email inbox.'

'Great work, Ben,' said Jack, giving the junior officer a wink of encouragement. 'But I've got to give credit to an old pal of mine.' He felt the heat under the collar as he busted out the white lie. 'He told me about an old telephone debt collector's tactic. Ring the neighbours up and down the street and spin them a line. Amazing what people will tell you voluntarily when they think they're helping someone in a pinch.'

'A bit sneaky, DS Lisbon,' said Taylor, twirling a pen between her fingers. 'I like it.'

'Probably, and forgive my word choice,' said Batista, 'skating close to the edge of ethical behaviour.' He coughed into his fist. 'Still, when there's a killer lurking in our midst…'

'The killer might have fled town,' said Kylie Smith. 'There's nothing to prove that person is still here.'

'All the more reason to employ every possible means.'

Batista nodded towards Jack. 'What do you intend to do with this information?'

'Confront Ned Campbell. In fact, with your permission, sir, I'd like to turn up the heat on him by bringing him to the station for a proper grilling.'

'If he refuses, hint as strongly as you can that he might be arrested for being an accessory. I'll take the opportunity to remind you all that a person can be charged with this offence even if the principal offender is unknown. The new magistrate, Brent Overton, has vowed to co-operate with Yorkville CIB more than the last one did. Just last week he joined the local Rotary Club, of which I am Sergeant at Arms.'

Jack nearly swallowed his gum. 'I thought that was an office in motorcycle gangs?'

'It's shared terminology. My point is, we have an ally in the courthouse.' Batista grabbed a pen and wrote the name NED CAMPBELL at the top of the whiteboard. Under that: DEBT? LOOKED THE OTHER WAY FOR MONEY. PAID BY KILLER?

'I'm liking Riley Kane for this murder,' said Jack, adding the man's name to the board. 'Only problem is, I can't figure out why he did it.' He stepped back and looked at the assembled officers. 'But that will be irrelevant if we can gather enough evidence to prove his guilt. I've got a feeling he'll tell us the *why* when he's in cuffs and admits his guilt.' He scanned the small assembly. 'When you've got the time between normal policing duties, I'd like all of you to get on the phones and ring the neighbours of everyone on Ben's list. No need to be sneaky like I was. Tell them you're the police and ask them to spill their guts. Stress that anonymity is guaranteed.'

Murmurs of assent bounced off the walls.

'Now I'll need to make an expanded list including the neighbours' phone numbers,' said Wilson, chirpy now that he had another key job to do.

'Then do it!' said Batista.

NED CAMPBELL OPENED the door until the security chain reached its limit.

'Let us in, and hurry up about it,' barked Jack.

A rapidly blinking red eye appeared in the crack for a second, disappeared, and the door opened fully. The resident was dressed in baggy white Y-fronts and a singlet so filthy it looked like it had been dragged out of a skip bin. The signs of several days' binge-drinking were on full display: dirty salt-and-pepper stubble, matted hair with a couple of greasy clumps pointing in different directions, manky body odour.

'Yes?' he squeaked, scratching at his underarms.

'Good morning, Mr Campbell,' said Taylor in her friendliest manner. 'We'd like you to accompany us to the Yorkville police station. We believe you have information that could move our enquiries forward.'

'Wha…?' He squinted, held his hand up against the sun belting down. 'I've already told you everything.'

'Garbage,' said Jack. 'Before we go anywhere, go and take a shower. You effin' smell like death.' He barrelled his way past the man, Taylor close in his wake. 'And clean your teeth. The fumes coming out of your gob are enough to set the building on fire.'

A kettle on the bench and a tea caddy next to it drew Jack's attention. He flicked the on-switch, told Campbell to get a move on and he'd have a cuppa waiting for him before they took the drive to the station. In a croaky voice Campbell requested a milky, sweet tea before shuffle-staggering down a hallway.

Fifteen minutes later, Campbell was back. Transformed. Dressed in chinos and a checked, short-sleeved shirt, hair slicked down, beard shaved smooth as an egg, and now a hint of peppermint mingling with the alcohol that had seeped deeply into the man's core. Eyes still bloodshot, expression – confused.

He accepted the tea with shaking hands. He'd only taken three swallows when Jack gripped him by the elbow. 'I deem you sufficiently refreshed. Let's move it.'

———

THE STARK, white ambience of interview room 2 had an immediate sobering effect on Campbell. Eyes more alert, perky body language. Jack put it down to the aircon being set to a temperature colder than the freezing Yorkville cinema. With his ice hockey lifestyle, it should suit Campbell perfectly.

'I told you, I don't know how I fell asleep. I readily agreed to a blood test in case someone doped me. The results will come back and show you that's exactly what happened. I've got nothing to hide.'

Jack smirked. 'People who say they've got nothing to hide always have something to hide.' He moved to stand with his back to the one-way glass. Batista was ensconced behind it, making sure Jack didn't step over the line with his interrogation techniques. Not that the chief's presence there always had the desired effect.

'Well, I don't,' said Campbell flatly.

Taylor said, 'We know about the repossession of goods from your Melbourne home. What's that all about?'

Campbell crossed his arms. 'I can't see how that has anything to do with poor Jonas.' He sucked in a breath. 'You're concentrating your efforts in the wrong places.'

Jack resumed his seat. '*Poor Jonas.* I've heard a couple of people say that. Riley Kane said it too. The exact words.' He drilled into Campbell with his eyes. The man in the hot seat gulped. 'And you know what's interesting about that?'

A shrug.

'No sincerity behind it. Like the way you just shrugged your shoulders. You don't give a monkey's. You're an egotist. Only worried about how things will work out for you.'

'Not true.' Campbell chugged half a glass of cold water. 'I want to see ice hockey take off in this country. Not for my own sake, but for the sake of the players, the coaches, the fans. And it will happen.'

Jack shook his head. 'You've put everything on the line for this. I'd wager you've borrowed heavily to make sure your share in the venture was big enough to be attractive to Herbert Jubb. A man like him would be choosy about who he lets get close to the action.' He waited a couple of beats then said, 'You previously told me you'd taken out a second mortgage on your home. With your bankruptcy record, I doubt a normal bank would touch you. The lender would be imposing a bleedin' high interest rate. Who loaned you the money?'

'I'd rather not say.' He uncrossed his arms and let his hands rest on the table.

'How much exactly have you invested?' said Taylor. 'We can easily ask Herbert Jubb. Tell him you refused to co-operate fully in a murder enquiry. How would that look for you? A man with a cloud over him, questioned by police and not answering fairly standard questions about money, might not be a good fit for his enterprise. He might boot you off the team.'

A shake of the head. 'No, he won't. I've contributed a lot, and he'll do the right thing by me.' He narrowed his eyes. 'I'm not telling you because what you're asking about has nothing to do with the murder.'

'Oh really?' said Jack, extracting a stick of gum and tossing the packet in front of Campbell. 'Like some?'

Campbell shook his head. 'No, thanks.'

'Well, you can chew over my theory instead. Sound good?' Before Campbell could respond, Jack stood and began to pace back and forth behind Campbell's back. 'This is what I think. You, sir, are in a world of money trouble.'

'I've had enough and I'm leaving.' Campbell attempted to stand; Jack pressed on his shoulders with both hands, sending Campbell back into his seat.

Jack glanced at the door, half expecting Batista to come in and give him a bollocking. The door remained closed; Jack pressed on. 'You leave when I say you can.'

'You're recording this interview, aren't you?'

'Of course,' said Jack. 'You can see the light's on. Smile for the camera.' He resumed his seat opposite Campbell. 'The sooner you start telling the truth, the sooner you can go back to your apartment and start drinking again. Something tells me if we had a look in your cupboard, we'd find only the cheapest booze, am I right?'

Campbell sniffed. 'Go ahead, get on with it then.'

'You borrowed more money than you can afford to pay back because you believe in this dream. I can appreciate that. A man of conviction. Now your creditor, whoever that is, is getting heavy, repossessing stuff from your home. Do you have any immediate family? Wife, children?' Jack already knew the answer to that one.

'No. I'm a lifelong bachelor.'

'Something to be grateful for. At least no one else suffers from your selfish behaviour.'

Campbell glared at Jack and grunted something under his breath.

'What's worse,' Jack continued, 'the money you make as a consultant and whatever you're getting as the arena manager doesn't cover the repayments. Correct so far? All of this is easily verifiable.'

A reluctant nod.

'Excellent. Progress. We like that, don't we, Detective Taylor?'

'Very much. Progress is good.'

'Now,' Jack resumed. 'Someone, let's name him...ah... Riley...offers you a chunk of cash to look the other way, maybe take a sleeping pill, so he can sneak back into the arena with no one here...'

'No one awake, at least,' said Taylor.

'Yes.' Jack held a finger aloft. 'Good point. Had you been awake, you might have witnessed something you weren't supposed to, reported it. Lots of possibilities. But with you out like a light, there was only one possibility. The killer being able to roam free about the stadium and do as he pleased.'

'Nonsense,' said Campbell. 'You can't prove any of this.'

'Not yet,' said Jack. 'But I will. Now, we have to add that...what's the murderer's name again, Detective Taylor?'

'Riley.'

'Yes, Riley. He knew the cameras would cut off at midnight, because you told him.'

'And, this is where your theory falls down,' said Campbell, suddenly a lot more talkative. 'Why was Jonas Eriksson here so late? An introvert like him would have wanted to get out of there as quickly as he could.'

'Because Riley asked him to stay behind.'

'What?' Campbell scoffed. 'To be killed?'

'No. For some other reason. A witness saw them talking animatedly at the party. I think Riley convinced Eriksson to remain in the stadium. Perhaps to patch up an old argument.'

'Listen, I came here of my own free will. Unless you plan to charge me with something, can I please go?'

'For now, yes. But I'll be seeking a warrant from the magistrate to trawl through your bank accounts. If there's been any large unexplained deposits, we'll trace them to their origin.'

He beamed. 'Be my guest. You'll find nothing.'

'Then you'll be in the clear.' Jack flicked his wrist, glanced at his watch. 'Interview terminated at 10:46am. Thanks for your time, Mr Campbell. You're free to leave.' He switched off the camera, fixed Campbell with a steely glare and whispered, 'Next time you come into this room, there's a good chance you'll need legal representation. Do not leave Yorkville until I say you can. Have a nice day.'

Chapter Twenty-Four

TAYLOR NODDED APPRECIATIVELY when the deferential young waiter handed her the wine list. Herbert Jubb, a trim man of medium height and build sporting a mane of silver hair and a neat, white moustache, thanked the man and told him to come back in five minutes to take their order. He smiled at Taylor and said, 'I know absolutely nothing about wine. Never bothered to learn. The simple reason is, I can't abide the stuff; red or white, it doesn't matter.' He put two fingers in his mouth and made a fake puking sound.

'I'm no expert either,' said Taylor, folding the enormous list and placing it back on the table. 'But I do like it. That's why I always choose the house red.' She looked about the room. 'And here at Luigi's, there are no bad wines, just expensive and very expensive. But it's a moot point, since I'm on duty and the QPS has strict policies that could see me in a load of trouble if I had even one glass.'

'Not even one! I find that rather…tyrannical,' said Jubb. 'A pilot or bus driver, I can understand, but for a copper? Ridiculous.'

'It is what it is.' She frowned, waited a moment then grinned. 'When the waiter comes back, you can order me a non-alcoholic beer. Perfect on a hot day like this.'

'It's a shame Detective Lisbon couldn't make it.' Jubb donned a pair of rimless reading glasses and scanned the menu. 'He's a bit of a legend in this state. Even abroad.'

Jack had been called away to the courthouse, together with Semmens. Overton was making a decision about what to do with the offenders they had arrested at the service station on the night of the murder.

'It is a shame. But he trusts me to have the wherewithal to squeeze every last bit of information out of you.' She smiled with a dose of chutzpah.

Jubb squirmed in his seat, Taylor's flirtatious attitude hitting right in his millionaire's ego. Then his face suddenly turned serious. 'Despite the affable façade, you know I'm totally gutted about what happened to Jonas Eriksson. An utter tragedy.' He dropped his voice to a whisper. 'You know his ex-wife is here in town?'

'Yes, we've had discussions with her.'

He tossed his head back and tut-tutted himself. 'What an idiot I am. Of course you would have. And lots of other people, too.'

The conversation was interrupted as the waiter came and took their drinks and meal order at the same time. As he retreated to the kitchen, Jubb said, 'You *must* find who did this. I don't care about the tournament being cancelled, you know.' He paused, took a breath. 'Well, I do, of course. The concept of an ice hockey super league in Australia has been set back massively, perhaps by years. You couldn't get PR worse than this. And I'm bleeding money. I have to arrange refunds to everyone who bought tickets for the next two games and honour the bookings with the hotels for the teams.'

'You're paying for that, too? Must be a fortune.'

'Detective Taylor, I'm a billionaire. I can take a hit like this.' He put his glasses back into a case. 'But my losses pale into insignificance compared to the loss of life.'

Some might think Jubb was laying it on a bit thick; Taylor thought otherwise. The way his face moved matched the tone of his words.

'I'd like your opinion of Ned Campbell, if you don't mind.'

Jubb looked at an oil painting of a crocodile lurking in the mangroves that hung on the wall to his right. He rubbed his moustache, took a small sip of mineral water and switched his gaze back to Taylor. 'I've always been a risk-taker. No risk, no reward. Often it's a case of take the risk, and get no reward.'

'I guess that's why it's called a risk,' said Taylor, pulling out her notepad. 'OK if I jot down some notes while we chat?'

'I'd be surprised if you didn't,' he said with a deep-throated laugh. 'One of the biggest risks you can take is when you hire staff. Ned Campbell has exceeded my expectations as an employee, and I'm happy with his performance.'

'Despite the fact he's a binge-drinker with massive financial problems? I assume you do your due diligence when it comes to employing people?'

They stopped talking for a moment as the waiter brought their meals. Chargrilled octopus tentacles with salsa verde for Jubb, fettuccine carbonara for Taylor.

'Yes,' said Jubb, stabbing a piece of octopus. 'And I am fully aware of his issues. However, he brings an unparalleled desire to see this dream of mine succeed. In many ways, he's even more enthusiastic about it than I am.'

'Did you realise that licenced commercial agents have been repossessing Mr Campbell's property?'

'Debt collectors?' Cutlery clanked onto a plate. 'Are you kidding me?'

'No. We have a witness. And this morning we questioned Campbell about it and he didn't deny what was happening.'

Jubb rubbed his face. 'He told me he was a discharged bankrupt. He made some bad investment decisions in the past, borrowed too much. He said things were on the improve, dammit.'

'With that in mind, do you think Mr Campbell would do something…irrational…to get money to cover his debts?'

A slow shake of the head. 'I don't know what to think. I'm still digesting what you've just told me.' He chewed another piece of octopus, twisted his mouth in thought. 'Maybe I can bail him out.'

Taylor's eyebrows jumped a little. 'Are you sure that's wise?'

He pointed a knife at Taylor as he made his point. 'As an administrator, he's the perfect fit for me. I'm paying him over the odds as far as the award wage goes for a similar position.'

'He told Detective Lisbon he was only running the arena until you could hire someone local.'

Jubb wiped his mouth with a napkin, took a sip of foamy lager. 'That was the deal, true. But Ned was doing such a good job, I was planning on offering him the gig full time.'

'And now?'

'Now I'm definitely going to. And help him with his drinking issues. I'll put conditions on his contract, of course. Three strikes, that kind of thing.'

'Will people still want to use the arena after someone was slain in the middle of it?'

He nodded. 'I've got a couple of popular music acts booked for concerts throughout the coming year. None of them have cancelled after what happened, tickets are still selling. So I think people will understand it's not the arena's fault Eriksson was killed there.' A pause. 'There'll be plenty for Ned to do even without ice hockey being played. Then again, maybe with time we can play more exhibition games, even championship games for the current league. I'm an eternal optimist, even in the face of tragedy.' He forced a weak smile.

Taylor twirled fettucine around her fork and said, 'Do you think it's possible that Mr Campbell took a large sum of money from the murderer to, as it were, look the other way?'

'In my experience, anything is possible.' He leaned to one side as the waiter brought a fresh jug of water. 'But you don't get to be where I am by being a poor judge of character. Yes, Ned's got problems, but would he willingly be an accessory to murder to get himself out of strife?' He left the question hanging in the air.

'That's what I'm asking you.'

'No,' he replied flatly. 'I'm sure he wouldn't.'

The waiter delivered coffees with biscotti on the side.

'I wonder if you have any theories yourself on who the murderer might be?' said Taylor, spooning two sugars into her cup. 'You've got an overview of everything that others don't.'

Jubb took another peek at the crocodile painting,

perhaps seeking answers from the ancient creature. 'I've hardly been thinking about anything else since it happened. And, to be honest, I haven't got a clue. I don't know the players personally beyond small talk, although I've had substantial contact with the coaches and the teams' managing staff to get things set up. I can't imagine any of them being involved. Why would anyone from the Mavs want to jeopardise the future of their franchise in a new league by killing one of their own?' He shook his head. 'Makes no sense.'

'The Hawks have no stake in a future super league in Australia. Maybe one of them did it?'

He sipped coffee then said, 'If so, who? I can't even begin to think of anyone. There was a dust-up between Eriksson and their goalie, what's his name…?'

'Kirin Pascoe.'

Jubb pointed a finger. 'That's him. But that's part and parcel of the game.'

'That's what I've discovered.' Taylor's gut told her Jubb was sincere on every level. She had one more avenue to pursue. 'What about on the night of the party? You were there, weren't you?'

'Indeed I was. The atmosphere was amazing. Great music, friendly banter.' He placed a palm on his forehead. 'How did it go so wrong!'

'Did you see anyone interacting with Jonas Eriksson?'

He smiled. 'Of course. He was player of the match, remember? People were crowding around him. He signed a couple of autographs, shook hands, and was basically nice to everyone who spoke to him.'

'Not easy for an introvert, don't you think?'

A shake of the head. 'No. Like I said, he was nice to people, but you could tell he wasn't enjoying it a great deal.

Probably wanted to go back to his hotel room and put his feet up in front of the TV. Only he never got the chance...'

Jubb dabbed the corner of his eyes with a cloth napkin. 'Oh my...sorry.'

'Please think hard, Mr Jubb...

'Call me Herbie.'

'OK, Herbie. Can you confirm a certain young woman was present at your home after the party?'

'You mean Lena?' he said, as if clearing up a puzzling item on an invoice.

The question hadn't thrown him in the slightest.

'Lena Holstrom, yes.'

'Is that her last name?'

'You didn't know?'

A shake of the head. 'No idea. She kind of invited herself along to my place as the event was winding down.'

'That didn't strike you as odd?'

He wiped his mouth with a napkin. 'When I was a young man and broke, women had absolutely no interest in me. Once I made my first million, I quickly learned that money and influence are powerfully attractive forces.' He pointed at himself with both index fingers. 'I mean, look at me. Average looking, and that's being kind.'

'You're married.'

A nod. 'My wife knows I occasionally meet other women. She's been in hospital for several months and I'm not sure she'll be coming out again. Motor neurone disease. It's reached the stage of dysphagia, in other words, she's having trouble swallowing.' His eyes misted over. 'It's a cruel, cruel thing, Detective Taylor. But,' he said with a shrug, 'my infidelity has her blessing. I don't go out of my way to pick up women.'

'I understand.' Not her place to pass judgement. 'I won't

ask anything personal about your interaction with Ms Holstrom. However, I would like you to confirm when you arrived there, when she left, and if there were prolonged periods in that time when you don't know where she was or what she was doing?'

'Sure. We arrived at my house just after midnight, we had a nightcap and went to bed. I called her a taxi at 7:30am after coffee and scrambled eggs. The only time I didn't see her was when she went to the bathroom a couple of times. I'm a sound sleeper, so if she got up and prowled about the house in the middle of the night, I couldn't tell you.'

'Thank you for being so honest with me.'

He smiled. 'Lot's of businessmen are baldfaced liars. I'm not one of them.'

'One more question. Did you see anyone having an intense conversation with Jonas Eriksson at any point during the night? Perhaps off in a corner somewhere?'

'I'm afraid once Lena had my attention, she held it.' He sighed deeply. 'I do wish I had seen something that could help your investigation. When people like Jonas Eriksson give off signs they'd prefer their own company, I totally respect that.'

As Jubb dropped his credit card on the small tray with the bill, Taylor said, 'Somebody didn't respect Eriksson.'

'Find that somebody,' said Jubb. 'Just fucking find them!'

Chapter Twenty-Five

BRENT OVERTON APPEARED in the doorway, ready for business. As he strode into the courtroom, clutching papers and head bowed, the magistrate's animated face put Jack in mind of an excited rodent. He took his place and announced, 'Please be seated, everyone.'

Jack and Semmens occupied seats at the very rear of the courthouse. In all likelihood, they wouldn't be giving evidence, just representing Yorkville CIB. Today, Overton would listen to the prosecutor and the defence lawyer from Legal Aid and make a decision on when a trial would take place, if at all. Jack glanced at his phone in case he'd missed a text from Taylor about her meeting with Jubb. Nada.

'The accused are charged with two crimes, both occurring on the same date,' intoned Overton.

'Does the fact they went on a spree make it worse?' Semmens whispered to Jack.

'For me, of course it does. I can't speak for Overton.'

'A shame the victims can't be here to make the little shits squirm with guilt for what they did.'

'No point,' said Jack. The system didn't accommodate for victims at a first hearing. There were many reasons for the convention; Jack didn't agree with them, especially when there was violence and intimidation involved. He said to Semmens in hushed tones, 'Look at the faces of those lads. No remorse. They think it's an effin' picnic.'

The magistrate tapped the microphone. 'May I ask for silence in the court? Thank you.' He looked at the three youths sitting in the dock, then at the prosecutor, Mandy Mellors, who sat behind a desk a couple of metres from the dock. Overton asked her to outline the Crown's case. Jack hoped the woman would speak with authority, demand the lads be treated as adults and thrown in youth detention for a long period. There was a good chance she would; Mellors was known among the legal fraternity as a hard nut.

'Your Honour, the three young men before us today are charged with two extremely serious crimes, and I ask that you make a recommendation to proceed to trial as soon as possible. On Friday, 29 January, they broke into the house of a home-based sex worker. A client was present at the time. The accused, wearing balaclavas to hide their faces and heighten fear, terrorised the resident and her client, threatened to tie them up. The client was, in fact, punched in the face to subdue him and then robbed of his cash. He sustained a serious injury which required hospital treatment.' She flipped over a piece of paper. 'And if that wasn't enough for one evening's entertainment, these thugs...'

'Please, I won't tolerate inflammatory or derogatory language in this court,' interjected Overton. 'Our focus is on rehabilitation, and terms such as the one you used do not align with that policy. Please, just stick to the facts of the matter.'

'Forgive me, your Honour. I withdraw the term.'

Jack smiled to himself. She had described the lads to a tee. He looked at them; each one was grinning like he was at a stand up comedy show. *Let's see what else she's got.*

'The offenders soon thereafter stormed into a service station and threatened the manager with physical violence if he didn't hand over the takings from the till. Luckily, he was able to lock himself in a back room and then trap the accused inside the service station until the police arrived. While trapped, the accused set about vandalising the store, breaking items and stealing food.' She shuffled papers, looked at the magistrate. 'If not for the quick thinking of the manager, these three...youths...might still be at large, still committing crimes, still frightening the life out of law-abiding citizens.'

Jack stood and applauded – in his mind. In the courtroom, he remained seated and impassive. For the next couple of minutes, the jaded lawyer from Legal Aid, Todd Simpkins, waffled in a monotone about the need for rehabilitation, cited the lack of a prior record and stressed that the lads still had their whole lives before them: why ruin everything by being tough? The boys in the dock nodded at each of the man's well-rehearsed platitudes.

Finally, Magistrate Brent Overton cleared his throat. 'Would the accused please rise.'

They stood together, shoulders back and chins jutting out. Their mothers stood. They had been compelled to attend the hearing by a court order and had watched on with a seeming lack of interest. None of the young men had a father or male authority figure in the home.

'In light of the fact that the accused are all under the age of eighteen and due to the backlog of cases in the system, I am unable to proceed to trial at this time. I have no other option but to release the accused on bail. You will reside at your mothers' addresses, and not contact each other. You are banned from social media. You will comply with a curfew of 7:00pm. I'm adjourning this matter for three months, at which time we will proceed to trial. If you breach bail conditions, you will be remanded in custody.' He adjusted his glasses, glanced down, then back at the accused. 'I note you all appear to be relieved that you are not going to a junior correctional facility.' He took off his glasses, gave them a wipe, and concluded. 'In my opinion, a custodial sentence for each of you is a distinct possibility. Keep your noses clean between now and trial, and the length of any sentence that may be imposed will be shorter than if you breach bail conditions. Do not think you can do as you please.'

Outside in the scorching heat, Jack and Semmens watched the three boys high-fiving each other before their mothers dragged them in different directions.

'Overton said no contact,' said Semmens. 'A high-five is direct physical contact. Breach of bail conditions, straight up.'

'Technically, yes.' He pressed the car fob-key and the Territory's doors unlocked. 'Get in, sunshine. This juvenile system does my head in. If we find Eriksson's killer and he turns out to be under 18, I think I'll scream.'

Semmens burst out laughing. 'Good one, Sarge.'

'I'm not kidding.' As he started the engine, the recollection of Overton's summary gave him encouragement. Those boys better enjoy the next three months at liberty; after that, they'd be taking a holiday at His Majesty's pleasure.

Chapter Twenty-Six

JACK READ Taylor's three paragraph summary of yesterday's lunch meeting with Herbert Jubb. He shook his head when he got to the part where the billionaire intended to extend a lifeline to Campbell. Jack wouldn't have been so generous. The perfect alibi for Lena Holstrom, too.

Next up, Proctor's analysis of Ned Campbell's blood sample. Alongside the expected alcohol, she found traces of the drug flunitrazepam, aka Rohypnol, in his system. Unusually, it showed the dosage ingested was between 1 and 1.5 mg, well under that generally administered by predators who wanted to make sure their victims were out cold. 'My hunch is, he's taken it himself,' Jack said, sensing the boss's presence behind him.

'Based on what?'

'Nothing.' He spun around in his swivel chair to face the Inspector. 'That's why it's called a hunch.'

'I'm not sure,' said Taylor, fiddling with a scrunchie. Back to her favourite yellow. 'If he's colluded with someone, they're both going to want the dosage to be mild. Enough to make Campbell really drowsy, but not dangerous to his health.'

Jack stood and walked to the window, prised open the blinds and watched the morning traffic trickling into town. He turned around and said, 'If I were the murderer and we'd struck a deal to use this shit, I would have given him enough to put his lights out forever. With Campbell still alive, there's a chance he'll spill his guts.'

'I'm not sure I agree, DS Lisbon. If he admitted to taking the roofie, whether he self-administered or swallowed it in the full knowledge that someone else gave it to him, he'd be virtually admitting he was an accessory to homicide.'

Jack shook his head. 'We're going to nail him for being an accessory, I have no doubt. And he'll admit it, because he'll believe that by doing so he'll get a lesser sentence.'

Batista gave a short barking laugh. 'I've never met a detective as confident as you, Lisbon. Even when we've got no evidence. Remarkable.'

'No evidence *yet*.' He tossed his jacket over the back of his chair. 'Now, if you'll allow me to read the rest of Proctor's gibberish, maybe I'll find some.'

Twenty minutes later, his eyes were aching from reading the detailed results. As far as evidence pointing to a suspect, there was none. The ice samples scraped off the rink contained no DNA, hairs, skin flakes, soil or other contaminants from shoes. Apart from those of the victim, of course. And because it was apparent the killer blows had come as a complete surprise to Eriksson, he was unable to grab at the attacker, perhaps get hold of hair or fibres or... dammit...something! Random items of trash sampled around the two gates leading onto the rink *did* contain a ton of DNA, but without getting a court order to demand

Kane or any other suspects submit to swabs, it was completely useless.

He looked over to Taylor, eyes glued to her computer screen. 'Are you reading the forensic report?'

'Yes, a second time. It's disappointing.'

'Not Proctor's fault.' Jack snatched at his takeaway coffee, sucked the last droplets out of it. 'Perhaps we need to run another sweep of the stadium and surrounds. Also the executive box, the players' effin' hotel rooms.'

'I half agree.'

'What bit don't you agree with?'

'The bit we've already done; the stadium precinct. If the killer's one of the Mavs, the hotel rooms are where evidence might be secreted. The weapon, for instance.'

Jack shook his head. 'Something smaller, perhaps, not the weapon. But,' he paused, 'you never know.' He chewed his pen for a minute. 'Wanna do something sneaky?'

'What?'

He beckoned her with an index finger. 'Come here and I'll tell you.'

'WHERE'D YOU GET MY NUMBER?' said Kane, who had rung back after Taylor left a message on his mobile. 'I don't recall giving it to you.'

'I'm the police,' said Taylor. 'We can find anyone's phone number. Big brother is watching and all that,' she laughed. Ben Wilson had easily tracked his number via the Law Enforcement Assistance Program used by Victoria Police and shared with the QPS.

'Did you call to harass me some more?' he challenged.

'There's a rumour we're all packing up and leaving town soon.'

'Oh?' she cooed. 'Then it's a good thing I acted on my instincts. I've actually changed my mind about having a drink with you.'

The thought of a date with a detective must have set off a trigger in Kane's ego; he readily agreed to meet anywhere, anytime.

'How about midday at the Pelican Bar?' She gave him the address, although there was no need. Every cab driver in town knew where it was.

HE LEANED against the reception counter, held out his ID, and smiled at the woman behind the desk. 'I'd like a swipe card to access the room Riley Kane is staying in. And I'd like it now.'

She frowned, her eyes squinting behind a giant pair of glasses. 'I'm not sure I can do that, sir. I'm pretty sure you need a warrant.'

Jack drew a deep breath. 'You seem like a nice person. I really don't want to have to break it to your boss that you think it's OK to obstruct a murder investigation. You don't want me to do that, do you?'

Uncertainty froze her face for a moment. 'Mind if I clear it with my supervisor first?'

He shook his head. 'There's a good chance key evidence in the case is about to be destroyed.' He dropped his voice as another front-desk employee passed behind the woman. 'Now, your supervisor is probably one of those goody-goody sticklers for the Privacy Act, am I right?'

She nodded. 'She reminds us about it constantly.'

A roadblock he had to smash through. 'In other, less urgent circumstances, I would of course obtain a warrant first. However, if I believe that the destruction of this evidence could see a murderer walk free, I am by law entitled to take action now. But I need your co-operation.' He busted out his affable smile. 'See my problem here?'

'One second.' The woman opened a drawer, pulled out a white plastic rectangle, encoded the magnetic strip, handed it to Jack. 'Room 403. Right by the lift.' She lowered her voice a touch. 'Housekeeping has been, so you won't be disturbed.'

'Thank you.'

'Please promise me I won't get into trouble for this.'

'You won't get into trouble.' His fingers were crossed that he, too, wouldn't get into trouble. As long as he was careful. Very bloody careful.

Walking to the lifts, he felt his phone vibrate in his jacket pocket. An SMS from Taylor. *In Pelican Pub bathroom. Kane already on 2nd beer. Think he'll want more. Will text if anything changes.*

Conflicting emotions gripped him: relief that the coast would be clear for a while, perhaps hours. Jealousy like he'd never felt before. Her words – *Think he'll want more* – could be interpreted a couple of ways. More beer, or more Taylor. It would be worth it when he found the evidence to nail Kane's arse to the wall.

The lift dinged at the fourth floor and the doors slid open. Outside the room, he gave a couple of sharp knocks in case someone was inside. He pressed his ear to the door and listened hard. Nothing. Another knock and another listen. Satisfied the room was empty, he snapped on a pair of rubber gloves, held the card to the sensor, the green light flashed, and he was in.

The first thing that struck Jack was the neatness. The room looked like housekeeping had prepped it for a new guest about to arrive at any minute. The second thing he noticed was the size of the room. Small. Which would make things a lot easier for him.

Bathroom first. Nothing in there but a tiled shower, toilet, a mirrored vanity cabinet over the sink. He opened the cabinet to find on the top of two shelves the usual assortment of shampoo, hair "product", deodorant, all arranged like soldiers, labels facing out. On the bottom shelf, a zip-up toiletry bag. Would the Rohypnol be in it?

Jack slowly unzipped the bag. Inside, a host of items but no pill bottles. As far as medications, just a small packet of a popular brand of aspirin in foil strips.

On the bedroom floor at the foot of the bed, a green suitcase with a combination lock covered in stickers from around the world. The zip was undone halfway around. Jack's heart sank. He'd been hoping to have to bust it open: a killer wouldn't leave a weapon in an unlocked bag. Still, worth a look. Nothing but clothes, neatly folded, a bottle of sunscreen, size 13 shoes and a pair of rubber sandals. The inside pocket contained some printouts with itineraries, some handwritten notes about match tactics, a used boarding pass. As he feared, nothing even resembling a weapon.

He dropped to a push-up position, looked under the bed. Nothing but dust.

Last place to look, the small closets. Another fruitless search: a suit in a drycleaning bag, some ironed shirts on hangers, along with two pairs of slacks.

About to head out the door, he remembered how they'd first interviewed Kane on the balcony. There were a couple of potted plants out there. From the case in Portugal last year, he remembered how a killer had abandoned a handgun in a planter box.

He slid open the balcony door, looked at the two adjoining balconies to make sure no one was there. A quick look at his phone. No warnings from Taylor that Kane was on his way. There was a small waste bin in the bathroom. He could empty the soil into it from the pots, transfer it back. The temperature outside was scorching; he'd lose a litre of sweat mucking about in the dirt. Do it inside? And create a potential mess? And if there was nothing in them? As a compromise, he found a butter knife in the kitchenette, in which there were also no items that could have been used to club Eriksson to death. Jack gripped the knife close to the end of the handle so he could poke to maximum depth around the sides of the pale pink geranium plants. Each prod went straight to the bottom of the pots.

He stood back, hands on hips, small beads of sweat lining his upper lip, bigger ones dripping under his shirt. *Bugger this for a joke.* Then it dawned on him – before he started probing, the soil had looked like it had been undisturbed for weeks, if not months.

As he let the door click closed behind him, he pulled off the rubber gloves and headed for the lifts. If there was one positive he could draw from the futile exercise, it was that the lovely woman on the desk would likely keep her job. When the case was solved, he'd send her a gift. A pot plant.

Chapter Twenty-Seven

BRENT OVERTON, imperious behind his polished Tasmanian oak desk, looked over the top of his glasses as Jack entered the spacious office.

'Is this about the three lads I granted bail?' Overton said with a degree of empathy. 'Believe me, I would have preferred to proceed straight to trial, but what I said about the backlog is real. My hands are tied by the system.'

'It's not about those toe-rags, no.' Jack shook his head. 'I need a search warrant.'

'I hope you don't use descriptions like that in court?'

'No, never. Perish the thought.' He decided to indulge the beak a little. 'And you were right to pull up Mandy Mellors for calling those lads thugs in the courtroom. Bad form.'

'No matter how horrendous the crime or evil the criminal, we must maintain decorum in the legal process.'

'Totally agree.'

The magistrate set his glasses on the table, steepled his

fingers. 'Yorkville CIB normally lodges these requests via email or over the phone. Why the personal visit?'

Jack wanted to say, *because Batista made the claim you were an ally and I wanted to suss you out properly*. Instead, he said, 'I've just picked up Detective Taylor from another assignment, we were passing by, so I thought I'd drop in. Two birds, one stone and all that.' He flashed his best disarming smile. 'Where I grew up, it was all about the personal touch.'

'You're an old-school copper, is that what you're saying?'

'In a nutshell.' He raised his eyebrows as he gestured towards a guest chair. 'May I?'

Overton jerked his head back and said, 'Where are my manners!' He chuckled and added, 'Perhaps I need to get back to being old-school myself?'

'Never mind.' Jack stretched his legs out in front of himself, crossed them over. 'In another nutshell, I want to search all the skip bins outside the Yorkville Grand Hotel.'

'Up for a bit of recreational dumpster diving on a sunny day?'

Jack burst out laughing. 'I'll pay that one…what do I call you?'

'Outside the courtroom, simply Brent.'

'And you can call me Jack.' A grandfather clock chimed two, reminding him that time was ticking. 'We're already four days into this case and we're going nowhere fast. The press are on the Inspector's back for results; all we can provide is templated responses.'

'I see.'

'You know, Brent, we've cracked a number of high-profile murders in Yorkville over the last couple of years, and none have taken this long. To be honest, it's frustrating the crap out of me.'

'So the warrant you want me to sign is based on frustration, not reasonable grounds that you'll find something in these skip bins?'

He had to be careful with this new guy. Overton might be an ally, but he also might be inclined to follow the rules as much as possible. Jack bent forward and placed his hands on the table.

'Been doing a spot of gardening?' said Overton, nodding at a smudge of dirt on the cuff of the detective's shirtsleeve.

Jack retracted his hands instinctively. 'What? Oh...no... Dropped my keys in a flowerbed.'

'So, what are the actual grounds on which you seek this warrant? Got a witness statement, for example?'

He coughed into his fist. 'We have a suspect, Riley Kane. Security footage showed him re-entering the arena on the night of the murder when everyone else had gone. We believe he drugged the manager, who had traces of Rohypnol in his blood, murdered Jonas Eriksson, and left the area after midnight when the CCTV automatically cut off. Since he's staying in a hotel, it makes sense the murder weapon could be in one of their bins. He's unfamiliar with the town, so he's not likely to have another hiding place in mind. He has no garden to bury it in...'

'What is *it*?'

'No idea. Something big and heavy. Something perfect to toss into a large garbage bin, dust your hands off and forget about it.'

Overton rubbed his jaw. 'I've got to take into consideration the privacy of the other guests. It's not just garbage from your suspect that could be in the bins.'

'He's probably aware of that!' Jack thumped his fist on the table; the magistrate's in-tray levitated a fraction before falling with a rattle. 'Imagine, you can kill someone, drop the murder weapon in a communal skip, knowing full well that effin' privacy considerations will spare you a life sentence!'

'I see how that could be a clever tactic.' Overton spoke calmly, as if Jack's outburst hadn't even happened. 'Have you searched everywhere else for the weapon?'

'High and low. Everywhere we don't need a bleedin' warrant.' Jack half closed one eye. 'We've been over the stadium twice, with help from Cairns CIB. It's the crime scene, you see. An environment where it was possible for the perpetrator to kill the victim and get away without leaving any physical clues. None that we can find, at least. Our pathologist, Margaret Proctor, is as frustrated as I am. She's never encountered anything like this.'

'Give me one more reason.'

'How about the fact that the council contracting company is scheduled to pick up the rubbish from the hotel in the next two hours? Is that a good reason? Because I can't think of any more.'

Overton nodded slowly. 'To be honest, I'm convinced more by your passion than by your arguments. Another magistrate would have shown you the door.' He signed the warrant, handed it to Jack. 'Don't tell anyone I said that.'

Jack tapped the side of his nose. 'Mum's the word.' As he turned the door handle to step out into the waiting area, Jack said, 'I'm grateful, Brent. I was prepared for a rejection on this one.'

'I almost denied it when you smashed your fist on my table.' He rubbed his hand lovingly over its polished surface. 'This baby wasn't cheap.' He looked back at Jack with a serious glare. 'This was a one-off. I won't issue another warrant on such spurious claims. Count yourself lucky this time.'

Taylor stopped scrolling through her phone when Jack clambered into the driver seat, frowning like he'd lost his dog. 'No luck?' she said.

'Yes luck.' He held the document in an outstretched hand. 'Bingo.'

THE SAME RECEPTIONIST gave Jack a warm smile. 'Back so soon?'

'Yep.' He placed the warrant on the counter. 'Please let the manager know me and my team are about to go through the skip bins at the back of the hotel.' The uniforms were due to arrive in about half an hour, once an accident on a major arterial road had been cleared.

'Pardon?'

'We're looking for evidence.'

'You'd better hurry then.'

'Why?'

'The truck's turned up early.'

A group of guests trundling suitcases along behind them stared in disbelief as the man with the scarred face and bent nose sprinted across the lobby, phone to his ear, barking instructions. Out again in the belting heat, he made a sharp left, leapt over more suitcases as a couple exited a cab, followed the concrete path. In less than thirty seconds he'd reached the loading area. He pulled up in dismay as a behemoth of a front loader truck held aloft in its forks a blue skip bin overflowing with garbage. Jack took off again, yelling at the operator, but the roaring din of the machinery drowned out Jack's words. The trajectory of the bin couldn't be stopped; the bin reached its tipping point, the contents spilling out into the belly of the truck. Then, the unwelcome sound of the hydraulic blade pushing the garbage towards the back of the hopper, compacting everything inside.

Jack dropped his head after realising a line of four bins had already undergone the same treatment. He turned to walk away when he heard the beeping sound of the truck reversing. He turned back. A ray of hope. The driver was lining up the forks to fit them into the sleeves of one last bin. If he could stop the driver, there was a chance at least one bin could be searched before its contents were crushed into a dense mass. Jack picked up a stone from a small gravelled garden that lay between the path and the wall of the hotel, took aim and threw it at the driver's window.

The truck stopped dead, the window wound down. An angry bald man with Māori tattoos on his face glared at Jack before unleashing a tirade of unintelligible abuse. Jack struggled with the Kiwi accent at the best of times.

'Police,' said Jack, brandishing his ID and advancing on the truck like he was the terminator. 'Step down from the vehicle immediately. I need to inspect that last bin.'

The driver killed the engine, jumped to the ground. Trembling with anger, he held his hands by his sides, fists bunching. 'Why'd you throw a rock at me, bro? You coulda smashed the glass, cut my eye.' Without waiting for a reply he added, 'I'm on a tight schedule, so turn around and piss off or I'll break your legs and throw you in with the rubbish.'

Jack stopped walking towards the man, realised he mustn't have heard him above the noise. He bellowed, 'I'm a police officer. Sorry to hold you up, but I order you to stand aside while I inspect the bin.'

The man shook his head. 'I think you're full of shit.' He marched towards Jack, clearly intent on inflicting physical harm. Jack reached into his jacket, levelled his Glock at the middle of the man's body. 'Stop!'

At that moment, the station's Kia Stinger pulled up behind the garbage truck. Trevarthen and rookie Stan Billington alighted, saw their colleague in a pickle, and within seconds the truck driver was facing down the barrels of three pistols. His hands shot in the air. 'Alright, guys. Peace out!'

'Holster your weapons,' said Jack. He walked over to the driver, still trembling, but no longer due to anger. 'Take a seat over there and relax.' Jack pointed at a shaded, jasmine-covered pergola by a cyclone fence. 'I'll call your boss later, square everything away, OK?'

'Sure thing. What's going on, anyway?'

'Nothing for you to concern yourself about. What's your name?'

'Jethro.'

'I'll put in a good word for you at the contracting company, Jethro. Say you were a great help to the police.'

His face lit up among the intricate ink lines and swirls. 'For real, bro?'

Jack patted him on the arm. 'Sure.'

After the three men had spent a couple of minutes rifling through the top layer of the full bin, Jack went back to Jethro. 'Tip it out for us, will you?'

A minute later, Jethro had expertly used the forks like a rhino attacking a jeep, manoeuvred the bin onto its side until the contents spilled onto the asphalt; he backed it up until the bin clanked back into its normal position. Jethro beamed like a child when Jack gave him the thumbs up.

'Want me to help you look for whatever it is you're looking for?'

Tempted, Jack declined the offer.

With the baking sun sapping every ounce of energy out of the officers, Jack was about to call it a day when Trevarthen called out, 'Eureka! I've found a mobile phone.'

Jack stood up from the stinking trash he was sorting through and thought to himself, *Hallelujah.*

Chapter Twenty-Eight

THE LAST PERSON Jack wanted or expected to see representing Riley Kane was the woman sitting across the table. Denise Hutchinson, from the firm Chapman, Kinberg and Associates, was a woman he'd slept with a few years ago. Once. He'd been strongly attracted to her, but now couldn't figure out where that attraction stemmed from. Their one-off fling was no secret, Taylor knew about it, and it didn't seem to bother the detective constable at all. But it bothered Jack. Especially in this cosy setting. Unfortunately, he was in no position to dictate whom a suspect chose to run interference. Sweat dampened his collar despite the low temperature in interview room 2.

He pointed at a mobile phone inside a plastic evidence bag that sat exactly in the middle of the table. 'Seen that before, Mr Kane?'

Kane looked at Hutchinson, all business in her pale blue silk blouse and tailored navy blazer. She wasn't the best choice for a criminal defence lawyer; her area of expertise was corporate law. Must be filling in for the usual guy, Jack reasoned. That bloke was sharp as a razor and knew every law backwards. Him missing was a bonus. After a while Hutchinson nodded, giving Kane the go-ahead to answer.

'I don't know. Looks like a regular smart phone. Could be anybody's.' He patted his pockets, gave a fake smile of relief, then smirked at Jack. 'It's not mine, I can tell you that. Although I wouldn't put it past you assholes to pickpocket someone's cell.' Kane then glared at Taylor. 'And what a turncoat you are, Claudia. Ask a man on a date, then treat him like a common criminal. You should be fired for manipulating people like that. Highly unethical.' He pouted, folded his huge arms and rocked back in his seat.

'Excuse me,' Jack interjected, tapping his finger on the table. 'She went to meet you in order to obtain further information. Which she did. On my instruction.'

'What information?' said Hutchinson. She darted a look at her client. 'You not giving me the full picture?'

'Upon questioning the suspect,' said Jack, 'DC Taylor learned that the Riley Kane is a lech, a creep, whatever you want to call it.'

Hutchinson opened her mouth to object but Jack cut her off. 'Anyway, that's a side issue. What's relevant is this mobile phone, which one of our officers found in a hotel skip bin. This phone belongs to the murder victim, Jonas Eriksson.'

Hutchinson frowned. 'So what? Where's the connection to my client?'

'Yeah,' said Kane, emboldened beyond his usual arrogance by having a lawyer sitting next to him. 'So fucking what?'

'Language,' said Taylor. 'You're not in the pub now.' She side-eyed Jack; he was barely able to suppress a grin. 'We believe you took the phone from Mr Eriksson after you killed him because there's incriminating evidence on it. Texts, messages. You later disposed of it in the hotel skip bin, where, you hoped, it would be crushed, never to be found again. Unfortunately for you, Detective Lisbon was too quick.'

'I'll say this for you, Claudia,' said Kane. 'You're not only a very sexy lady, but you also have an incredible imagination. I've never seen that phone in my life.'

'Never seen your deceased teammate use his phone?' said Jack. 'I find that hard to believe.'

Kane sighed deeply. 'You know what I mean. Of course I've seen him use a phone. Is it that one? How the hell would I know? That one could be anyone's.'

'I assure you, it's his. We've shown it to Emily Eriksson. She recognised this bit.' Taylor picked up the plastic bag, pointed to a hole in the unit's casing where part of the metal had chipped off. 'There's also blood on the back, which forensics will most likely establish belongs to the victim.'

'OK, so it's Jonas's cell phone. I've never sent him anything, and vice versa. What are these photos and texts you mentioned before?'

Jack took a slow sip of water, made everyone wait for a moment. 'Our digital forensic team in Brisbane will open up this bad boy and expose all its dark secrets tomorrow morning. We'll get a production order to serve on the telco, and then we'll receive a log of all the calls he's made and received on this number. Ever since he's had the number, if necessary.'

'So you've got nothing!' Kane scoffed.

'Don't worry, we will,' assured Jack. 'And when I decide it's time to arrest you, you'll give us your fingerprints and DNA, like it or not.'

'Would you care to submit to a fingerprint check now?' said Taylor like she was asking someone to board a plane. 'There are dabs all over this one. Eriksson's and someone else's. You can help us rule you out of our inquiries by cooperating. It's a quick and easy process.'

'Don't agree,' said Hutchinson out of the side of her mouth. 'Nothing to be gained from it.'

He nodded. 'The lady's right. No chance.' He pointed an index finger. 'Something else. Someone was snooping around my hotel room. Stuff's been messed with, and not just by housekeeping. I've seen the TV shows where the cops use sticky tape to lift prints, then plant 'em somewhere else. You're trying to frame me because you have no idea who did it.'

'And you reckon DC Taylor's the one with the imagination!' laughed Jack. 'We'd need all kinds of warrants for that. Plus you'd have to know about it before hand.' He locked eyes with Kane. 'When bent cops plant evidence, they always get caught.'

'Did you have a warrant to go looking in the bins?' Hutchinson spoke like she was about to score a point. Her shoulders slumped when Jack dropped the document on the table.

'Do you think we operate outside the law, Denise?'

'No. Of course not.' She scribbled a few lines on a large-format notepad. 'Just making sure.'

'Look,' said Kane. 'Can you show me some respect? I'm here voluntarily, to help you catch whoever killed poor Jonas.'

Jack tut-tutted, looked at Taylor. 'There he goes again with the poor Jonas routine, without a skerrick of sadness.'

'What the hell is a skerrick?'

'Forgive me,' said Jack. 'I've picked up some of the local

Aussie slang over the last five years. It means a very small amount. Even less than the trust I have that you're telling us the truth...about anything.'

Kane leaned to his left, whispered something to Hutchinson, whose artificially enhanced lips twitched as she listened.

'Care to share something with us?' said Jack when she nodded and folded her hands on the table.

'My client would like to wrap things up now. He would also like me to convey as a parting comment, and these are his exact words, that this is a circus and you two are a pair of stupid clowns.'

Jack sneered. 'How childish. Too much of a coward to say it to my face, I get it.'

The sound of Kane's chair skittering backwards and crashing onto the concrete floor rang out like a gunshot. Hutchinson screamed in horror, her hands flew to her face. Kane reached across the table, grabbed Jack by the collar and snarled. 'Fuck you!'

In less than a second, Jack leaned across to get closer to Kane, worked a hand up towards his own chin. A flex of his upper body and shoulder muscles, a thrust of his forearm against Kane's wrist, and he easily broke the man's grip.

'Get back,' Jack growled deep in his throat.

Kane swung a left hook that whooshed past Jack's ear as he ducked under the punch. Jack pushed up from his knees, unleashed an uppercut that found its mark, sent Kane sprawling backwards. Kane sprang to his feet, rubbing his jaw, a line of blood trickling from the corner of his mouth, his fingers clenching and unclenching. The fellow was tough, Jack had to give him credit. You don't play ice hockey if you're afraid of a stoush.

'I said get back!' Jack repeated.

'Do as he says,' said Taylor. 'You don't want to end up in hospital, do you?'

Kane was still weighing up his options for another forward thrust when the door burst open. A voice barked, 'Everyone freeze!'

Jack cast a glance towards the source of the words, did a double take. In the doorway stood Inspector Batista, holding a taser with a finger on the trigger, feet shoulder width apart, a wild look in his eye.

'I cannot believe what I just witnessed from behind the glass.' Batista quickly calmed when he realised the fight was over, let the hand holding the taser drop to his side.

'Find yourself another lawyer,' said Hutchinson, voice quavering. She snatched at her notes and shoved them into her handbag. 'Good luck with that.'

Jack said, 'Interview terminated at 19:35.' He pressed a button to switch off the wide-lens camera in the corner of the room. He locked eyes with Kane. 'You're lucky, sunshine. I should press charges against you for assaulting a police officer, but I don't think I will.'

'You're not?' said the Inspector. 'You have to. It's all on camera.'

Jack moved his neck from side to side until he heard a crick; it felt like he'd sustained a slight sprain from when Kane tugged hard on his shirt. 'I've had worse sparring with Trevarthen. This dickhead never laid a finger on me.' He drew in a deep breath. 'I'll say I provoked him if you want to take it further, sir.'

'Calling someone a coward isn't provocation. He's assaulted you, Jack.'

'A good lawyer could get him off based on the camera footage.'

Batista muttered something incoherent under his breath

then said, 'It's your mess, Lisbon. You sort it out. I've already missed half of my Rotary meeting.'

With the boss gone, Jack said, 'You've gone and painted yourself into a corner, Riley.'

'I want the camera back on again,' he demanded. 'You're still interviewing me.'

'I'm afraid you've forgone the luxury of even making requests, let alone giving orders,' said Taylor. 'Throwing a punch at a police officer...' she whistled through her teeth '...doesn't get much more serious than that.'

'She's way too smart for you, pal,' said Jack. 'I can't believe you thought for a second that she'd be interested in a bozo like you.' Jack placed both hands on the edge of the table, drilled a death stare into Kane's blazing eyes. 'Listen to me good. You make one false step between now and next time we speak, and I will press charges. That was all baloney about provocation, sunshine. For the Inspector's ears. I didn't provoke you. You've got serious anger issues that need to be controlled. Perhaps a stint in Copperhead Prison will fix you. For now, I'm letting you go back to your buddies, but there's conditions attached. Breach them and you're screwed.'

Twenty minutes later, Taylor and Jack had taken and logged Kane's finger and palm prints, as well as a DNA swab of the inside of his cheek.

And, for good measure, he got Trevarthen to drive him back to the hotel wearing a pair of handcuffs, which Jack promised would be removed before Kane stepped out of the vehicle. As a favour.

Chapter Twenty-Nine

BATISTA HAD MADE the executive decision at 9:00am that sufficient time had now elapsed and the Yorkville Entertainment Arena was no longer to be considered a crime scene. Still closed to the public until further notice, however owner Herbert Jubb decided to allow the Mavericks to enter the stadium. They would have the opportunity to lay flowers on the ice, say prayers or bid their final farewell to Jonas Eriksson in their own way. Emily Eriksson was the only other person outside the players, coaches and administrators invited to the ceremony.

And the media.

A scrum of reporters and camera crew were on hand to catch the drama of the occasion. Jubb might have been devastated by what had transpired over the last few days, but he clearly wanted to show them that the dream was still alive, even if Eriksson was dead; that those behind the movement might be bowed, but they were not beaten.

The two detectives watched discretely from a distance. It would have been poor form to have a visible police presence at the private memorial. Or so said the Inspector. Jack knew the real reason – the media would give them hell, shouting questions about why there had been no arrests.

From the passenger seat of Jack's Hilux, parked under shady trees about 20 metres away to the south on the opposite side of the street, Taylor pointed a camera at the players as they alighted from the bus, tried to take as many photos as possible. To get a pictorial record of who spoke with whom, who kept away from whom, body language, facial expressions. A freelance photographer assisting the police sat in another unmarked car, 20 metres away to the north, also snapping away at frequent intervals.

'Remind me why we're doing this again?' said Jack, rubbing throbbing temples with firm, circular movements of his fingers.

'Because we're waiting for digital forensics to get back to us about the mobile phone. Until then, we watch and try to learn something. Your words, Jack.'

He chewed a fingernail, found it tasteless and went for a packet of gum. Cinnamon for a radical change. 'I was hoping I'd said something more useful than that load of bollocks.' He stopped the head massage, counted off on his fingers. 'Autopsy – done. Analyses of physical evidence – done. Interviews of major persons of interest – done. Not much else we can do except wait for something to happen.'

'Am I detecting a note of defeatism, Detective Lisbon?' She put the camera down as the last of the mourners entered the arena, took a takeaway container from the console. 'That's not like you.'

He reluctantly turned down the music that had just started to play over the radio. JS Bach's Toccata and Fugue in D minor. Normally he'd turn that one up until his ears ached. 'Has Kane committed the perfect crime? Why is he so defiant, huh?'

'Because we didn't find his prints on the phone?'

'He would have worn gloves, innit? That's covered in the course you must have studied at the academy, How to Murder Someone and Not Get Caught 101.' He began to tear up a piece of gum wrapper. 'I was never expecting to find his dabs, to be honest.' His chest rose and fell as he sighed. 'Am I completely wrong about Kane?'

She tilted her head to the side. 'He had the means, the opportunity. The bandmember ID'd him as having an intense conversation with Eriksson. On the face of it, he looks like our guy.'

'I feel like this one might slip away from us, sunshine.'

She touched his forearm lightly. 'There's always the chance someone who knows something vital will get an attack of the guilts and come forward. You know how these things can happen. It might take a little longer to solve this one, that's all.'

He turned to her and smiled. 'You know how to say all the right things. As long as it doesn't become a cold case that a bored detective pulls out of the archive 20 years from now.'

'Was that a pun?'

'What?'

'Cold case.'

'No.'

They sat in the car in silence for the next half hour. Jack nudged her with his elbow when people started emerging from the entrance. When the media had departed and the last player had filed out, Jack opened his door. 'I'm going to talk to Jubb.'

'What for?'

But he was already out of earshot.

Taylor watched as Jack trotted towards the businessman, about to get into a late-model Mercedes. A friendly chat, smiles and nods. The two men shook hands, Jack returned, his slow gait matching the downbeat attitude she'd detected.

He clunked the car door closed. 'They're leaving tonight. Players took a vote inside not to take up Jubb's offer of another couple of days' holiday.'

'They don't like our town?'

'They don't like what happened here. You must have a place that has bad associations attached?'

She nodded. 'I do. But I'm not ready to talk to you about it yet. You?'

'Sure. McNair's gym, South London.' He wasn't ready to talk about what he did there. He'd never be ready for that chat with anyone except Micky Knox.

A muffled version of "London Calling" started playing in Jack's pocket, then loud as hell in his hand until he pressed the green button. Wilson. He put the call on loudspeaker. The Brisbane digital forensic team had accessed Eriksson's mobile. 'They've found some interesting stuff, sir.'

'Don't tease me. What is it?'

'Nudes from a woman called Lena.'

Jack shook his head, said to Taylor, 'Emily was on the money there!'

'What?' said Wilson.

'Nothing. Thanks for that.'

'Hang on. Like the guy on the TV ads says, *wait, there's more*. We've also got some blackmail demands. Old photographs going back ten years showing Eriksson and another person surrounded by bags of narcotics.'

'Are they from Kane?'

'I doubt it.'

'What do you mean, you doubt it, dammit!'

'Perhaps it would be easier if you came back to the station and had a look for yourself? Brisbane's uploaded everything.'

Jack threw the 4x4 into reverse, overtook the Mavs' team bus, which was sitting exactly on the speed limit. The twelve-minute drive to the station took exactly 10 minutes.

Chapter Thirty

SHE DIDN'T BOTHER HIDING her face as she posed coquettishly in front of a mirror. On the contrary, she hammed it up by employing lip-licking, pouting and tongue-poking expressions as accompaniments to the bare-flesh main course. The selfie photos of a topless Lena Holstrom found on Eriksson's mobile sent a creeping, sweaty heat up the sides of Jack's neck, into his scalp, as if he were outside under the blazing sun. The flush wasn't caused by any form of arousal; it was the embarrassment of having Taylor look at the same photographs over his left shoulder. And of Batista looking at them over his right shoulder.

'OK,' said Jack. 'I think we've seen enough of these.'

'What about the texts she sent?' said Taylor. 'We haven't analysed them. They were scorching hot. Like something out of "Fifty Shades of Gray". Have you read that one, Detective Lisbon?'

'No, I haven't. I prefer hard-boiled crime fiction for my reading material. Sleuths like Mike Hammer.' He clicked out of the file, the screen now showing an array of folders prepared by Brisbane's digital forensic experts. It contained all the images and texts from the discarded phone, listed by month and stretching back a number of years. There was no itemised call log. That would be coming later today from the telco, who had been served with a production order to produce all data linked to Eriksson's mobile phone. His Internet provider was also served with a similar notice.

'Does this bring Holstrom back into focus as a suspect?' said Taylor. 'I think it might.'

'Her alibi is watertight,' said Jack. 'Plus there's only three of these photos. The last one was taken ages ago. He never responded to her come-ons and she gave up. As for hiring a hitman, she couldn't afford one.'

'That's how I read it, too,' said Batista. 'The girl's an attention seeker and a liar – remember she claimed she didn't send any spicy pictures to Eriksson – but I don't think she's a murderer.'

'The Inspector's right,' said Jack. 'I say we focus more on the ten-year old photo and the texts associated with it. Often people are killed when a long-term grudge can't be borne anymore.' He recounted a couple of cases from his days in the London Met where gangsters would plot and plan the demise of rivals over years, waiting patiently for the perfect opportunity to strike. Also to make sure they had every contingency covered. 'But,' he concluded, 'they nearly always got caught out by something insignificant; an eyewitness they didn't account for, a once-loyal foot soldier wooed by an enemy outfit who sends the police an anonymous tip.'

Taylor, hands on hips, smiled. 'That's more like the Jack Lisbon we know. There is no perfect crime, and the murder of Eriksson is no exception.'

Jack buzzed Wilson, asked him to come to his desk. He was there in under two minutes, eager as a border collie eyeballing a flock of sheep. Batista and Taylor parted slightly so he could get closer to Jack.

'I take it you've had a good look through these files, Ben?' said Jack. 'I'd like your take on it.'

'There's not a whole lot to see. The guy's an introvert, so there was never going to be a lot of communication with other people. It only took me two hours to review the whole lot.'

'What stands out to you, Ben?' said Batista.

'Texts between him and his ex-wife dominate in terms of volume, but there are others. From his coach and other staff. Reminders for doctors' appointments, spam he hadn't deleted, the kind of stuff we all get these days. As for images, most of the photos stored on the phone are ones he took himself.'

'And not many of those, either,' said Jack, who had also trawled through the files. 'Looks like records of cities he visited. A selfie or two near prominent landmarks. And once he'd been to a place, looks like he didn't take photos on any subsequent trips.'

Taylor said, 'I get it. Some people spend so much time taking pictures and posting them on Facebook and Instagram, they forget to live their lives. Eriksson wasn't like that. In fact, his social media presence is virtually non-existent.'

'Let's get back to what was sent to him,' said Batista, a note of frustration in his voice. Not surprising, since the media were hounding him: about the lack of police presence at the memorial, but more importantly about the lack of an arrested suspect. 'Forget about the X-rated stuff from Lena Holstrom. Let's start with the texts between Quinn and Eriksson.'

'From what I could tell, it backs up what Quinn

claimed,' said Taylor. 'The amount demanded is the same as what he showed us on his banking app.'

'A thought about that, if I may?' said Wilson.

'Yes,' said Jack. 'Thoughts are most welcome, considering I don't have too many at this stage.'

'You mentioned a banking app. Can you be sure Quinn showed you a live version of the interface?'

'What do you mean?'

'I mean, maybe it was a fake. Perhaps he'd created what looked like a page with his account, but it was actually just a jpeg or similar.'

'We saw him logging onto it,' said Taylor.

'Did we?' Jack stood, suddenly excited, and added, 'We just saw him tapping on the screen. He could have been doing anything, like…'

'Like opening an image he'd made that showed the money had been paid,' said Wilson. 'Maybe it hadn't? You can do anything with programs like Photoshop and Canva these days.'

'I'll get a production notice to get access to Quinn's accounts,' said the Inspector. 'The existence of these texts is evidence enough to convince the magistrate that demands had been made by Quinn.'

'Not threats, though,' said Taylor.

'Quinn's language in the texts is strong enough, I think,' said the Inspector. 'Overton will play ball.'

'That's going to take some time,' said Jack. 'They're all leaving town tonight.'

'We can extradite him from Melbourne,' said Batista. 'If he's our man, we'll get him.'

Jack nodded. His gut told him Quinn really had logged onto the app and that Wilson's theory was a stab in the dark. Kane was still his number one suspect. Maybe there was a connection between Kane and the 10-year-old gangster-style photo of the two shirtless men and the drugs, and also with the blackmail demands? He asked Wilson if he'd done an image search for the second person in the photo.

A nod. 'I've had a couple of hits. Because the image isn't clear, taken in poor lighting, the AI has suggested several people, but I've narrowed it down to one. A guy called Mikel Bubla.'

'Isn't he a shite Canadian singer?' said Jack.

Nobody laughed.

'Who is this guy, Ben?' said Taylor.

'A Czech hockey player. He was a big star back in the day. A celebrity in the Czech Republic. He leads a reclusive life in Switzerland now. Importantly, he and Eriksson played a season together in the same team in the Czech Extraliga in 2015.'

Jack stood, cleared his throat and, pacing back and forth, read aloud the text with the blackmail demand. *'Deposit $60,000 USD by the end of the week or this photo will be released all over the Internet. You will be arrested and spend the rest of your life in prison. We will send you the details of how to make the payment exactly 24 hours from now.'*

'Emily Eriksson told me he'd been getting threats, but he was vague,' said Taylor. 'She had an inkling it was something to do with his past, that it happened in Prague. Dammit, she was right.' She paused, then added. 'On the other hand, he was murdered only hours after receiving that demand. So it makes no sense that the blackmailer, whoever it is, has anything to do with the murder.'

'Unless it's a massive red herring,' said Wilson. 'Made to distract us from the real culprit.'

Batista scratched his prominent chin. 'The text originated from the United States. And there's a follow-up text received on Eriksson's phone 24-hours later with the number of an account in...where is it?'

'The Bahamas. Purportedly. We don't know if the account number is real.'

'Rather an elaborate set-up to throw us off the scent, don't you think? Are you suggesting the photo of Eriksson, Bubla, and the pile of drugs is also a deep fake, Ben?'

'I'm saying it's a possibility, sir. It's also possible that it's entirely real. If it is, then Detective Taylor is right and this had nothing to do with the murder. A blackmailer wouldn't murder the person they're trying to get money out of before that person had even received payment instructions. It's coincidental to the murder, but not the reason.'

Taylor said, 'I've just run an internet search on my phone and found an old news story. Apparently, there was a huge drug heist near the Czech city of Ostrava in 2015. A truck delivering the goods, worth millions, was hijacked near the border with Poland and the load stolen. It was never recovered. This picture with Eriksson and Bubla...it makes sense. Whoever took the photo might have been cut out of the proceeds.'

Jack shook his head. 'Eriksson was a journeyman living a modest lifestyle. Either he didn't get a cut either, or he blew his share somehow.'

Batista tugged his cuff. 'I'm referring this matter to the FBI. As well as the Czech Police, the Polish Police and Interpol. Logic tells me these are separate crimes. Everyone agree?'

The three other officers nodded. Jack said, 'I'm amazed Eriksson was able to play so well after having that threat land on him right before a match.' He also figured Micky Knox had missed this one since Jack had asked his mate to look for clues in Prague, nowhere near where the drugs heist happened.

'Unless it was fake and he knew it,' said Wilson.

'Like I said, I'm handing this one on to higher authorities,' said Batista. 'They can determine if it's real or not. Either way, Eriksson's not going to be arrested for drug trafficking.'

'Emily will totally lose her shit when this one breaks,' said Taylor. 'I feel so sorry for her. His reputation will be ruined if it turns out he was part of that drug robbery.'

'Look on the bright side,' said Jack.

'What bright side?'

'It won't be you who has to tell her. It'll be some anonymous FBI officer calling over the phone.'

Batista sent Wilson back to reception to relieve Constable Billington, clapped his hands and flashed Jack an optimistic smile. 'We've made progress, thanks to your gut instinct about the skip bins.'

Jack frowned. He didn't feel like they'd made much headway despite the discovery of the phone. To make an arrest, they needed something more.

'Claudia, send out another brief to the media,' said Batista. 'Say we've got two solid suspects in our sights, with more developments to come tomorrow. I'm hopeful this Quinn thing will bear fruit.'

'Sir.'

'With respect,' said Jack. 'Wilson's theory could turn out to be a bag of bollocks. I reckon the two grand was paid, fair and square.'

The Inspector grabbed his shoulder firmly. 'Let's just wait and see, huh?'

'Sure.' Alone at his desk, utter pessimism gripped Jack's

gut. He'd never felt it to this degree. There was something eluding him, but what was it?

He picked up his mobile and called someone who could always make him feel better. 'Hi, sweetheart.'

'Dad. You watching the TV?'

'I don't know what you think I do all day, but watching TV isn't it.'

'Pity. That horrible woman Holly Maguire from Channel 11 is on. She said the police showed no respect because you didn't attend the memorial. I think *they* showed no respect by filming it. Then she said the cops aren't doing enough to find whoever murdered the ice hockey player. I know how hard you work, the long hours. She's a total bitch.'

'Skye!'

'Sorry, Dad, but she is. I hate her. It's still on if you want to catch the end of it.'

'I don't have to now that you've told me all about it, hey?' Curiosity had already got the better of him; after the call he'd look for the story online.

'I guess I have. Anyway, when you do catch the killer, she's going to have to apologise to you, isn't she?'

His heart ached with love for the kid. Unconditional support. 'That's not how the media operates. They rarely apologise unless they're forced to.'

She sighed. 'Are you coming home at a normal hour today?'

He looked at the time in the corner of his monitor. 4:30pm. 'No.'

'Why?'

'Because I'm coming home early. We'll take a run around the back paddock with Daisy.'

'It's been raining all day, in case you hadn't noticed.'

'All the more reason.'

'Can I ride the trail bike while you run? I can't keep up with you.'

'Deal.'

He pocketed the keys, headed for the door. Taylor looked up and said, 'What's up? Your shift doesn't end for another hour.'

'True. But some things are more important than the job.'

Taylor trailed him out the door and into the car park. With concern in her voice she leaned in the driver's side window and said, 'You sure you're OK? You never leave early.'

'Never better, sunshine. I just need to be with the kid. I'll make up for it by coming in early tomorrow.'

'Want me to pop around later?'

'I'd like that. And so would Skye.'

At the first set of lights he opened the glovebox, fished around for a CD. Classical wouldn't cut it for this drive. He shoved the Sex Pistols' *Never Mind the Bollocks* album in the slot, cranked up the volume and banged his head in time to the thrashing beat.

Through the noise he could still think.

Taylor was right. This one might take a little longer.

But that was OK. Holly Maguire be damned.

Chapter Thirty-One

THREE MONTHS LATER

ONCE AGAIN, Jack and Semmens found themselves in the rear of the courtroom. The trial was over and done with in a matter of hours. The prosecutor demanded nothing less than a custodial sentence; the defence lawyer entreated the magistrate to show compassion and leniency towards the three young men.

A hush descended as Brent Overton fiddled with his glasses and leaned into the microphone. 'Would the defendants please rise,' he intoned. The magistrate's face was impassive as he stared at the three men in the dock. Their hair had been trimmed since the first hearing; they were neat and clean, dressed in sober dark suits. One wore a green-and-red tie; the others' shirts were open at the neck. There was no cockiness or arrogance in their expressions this afternoon; instead, fear and uncertainty clouded their eyes.

'What do you reckon?' whispered Semmens. 'The prosecutor was on fire.'

'A very stern caution,' said Jack. 'After a long, fatuous speech.'

'Having listened to the evidence brought before me, I have come to a decision,' said Overton. 'But before I give it, I want you to know that the crimes you committed are serious ones. Had adults carried them out, they would be facing many years in prison.

'The effects of your actions will be felt for a long time. The home invasion, in particular, where you, Billy Ryan, stole money and hit one of the victims so hard he required arduous and expensive dental surgery, was particularly grave.

'And then, not satisfied with having terrorised two innocent people, you had the temerity to steal a car and attempt to hold up a service station.

'Billy, Austin, Zach. In making my decision, I have taken into account your past records, as well as reports and recommendations made by social workers, and of course the evidence presented by the prosecutor and the spirited defence put up by your own representative.' Overton glanced at a piece of paper, then looked up again. 'However, I have also been influenced by the rising levels of youth crime in this town, which shows no signs of slowing down despite the sterling efforts of the Yorkville police.

'Above all, I have to do my bit to protect the community. Therefore, I sentence each of you to one year in the Northern Springs Youth Correctional Centre.'

Jack thumped Semmens on the thigh and said, 'Finally. A bloody win for our side.'

One of the lads seemed to be on the verge of saying something, his lips twitching. 'Watch that Austin, the one in the middle,' Jack said to Semmens. 'Any minute now.'

'Don't look at this as the end for you,' continued Overton, 'but a chance to reflect on the life choices you have made so far and what you can do to make sure you don't end up in court again.'

'Fuck you!' called out Austin. 'No one cares about us!'

'Bingo,' said Jack.

'You want me to make it two years?' said Overton calmly, holding up a pen. 'I just have to write the words.'

Austin's lips formed a tight knot.

Overton droned on for several minutes about second chances, redemption, rehabilitation, hope. When he finally cleared the court and the lads were led away, Jack said to Semmens, 'If I were still a drinking man, this would call for a pint.'

'What does it call for instead?'

He wanted to say a naughty weekend away with Detective Claudia Taylor. Instead he said, 'I'll settle for coffee and cake, sunshine.'

ALL THE STAFF at the office stood and applauded as Jack and Semmens made their way inside. 'Well done,' said Batista, clapping each officer on the back as he passed by. 'It's not often we get a result like this. Hopefully, it will send a message to potential young offenders to think twice about committing serious crimes.'

Jack tossed his jacket over the back of his chair. 'One swallow doesn't make a summer.'

'I'm not sure about that,' said Batista. 'I told you Overton was an ally. He plays it fair, according to the law.'

Jack narrowed one eye. 'I thought you'd gone soft, sir. When I suggested that you make representations to the magistrate to have them detained until trial, you said no.'

The Inspector gave an understanding nod. 'Because I knew he'd come good at the actual trial. Us appearing too heavy-handed from start to finish is a bad look. We're here to mop up the mess out there, the judicial system metes out the justice.'

With no other serious crimes on the books, Jack cleared a backlog of boring emails, responded to an enquiry from a local state school requesting DS Lisbon give a talk to the kids. Something he would genuinely enjoy doing. A pile of paperwork relating to a successful drug raid the previous month beckoned, but he wasn't feeling it. That job could wait another day or two. He stood, moved over to Taylor's desk. 'Wanna take a break for 30 minutes?'

She spun in a 90-degree arc in her chair and looked up at him. 'Sure.' As she went to grab her things, an alert went off on her phone. A crowing rooster sound. 'Oh, my. I don't believe it.'

'What?'

'Coffee can wait.' He stood in bewilderment as she logged back onto her computer, clicked the mouse feverishly, cursed softly, closed the open window, re-opened it. She pointed at the screen. 'Look!'

Jack bent at the knees and pressed forward to see better. 'What am I looking at?'

'An Instagram post of a woman holding a trophy,' her voice quavered. 'Read the text.'

He read it aloud: *Given the passage of time I feel it's OK to post this now. Got given this trophy by one of the Mavs ice hockey players visiting my hometown of Yorkville. Forgot to post three months ago cos too sad after that Swedish guy got killed. RIP #jonaseriksson.*

'How the hell did you find this?'

'Wilson's not the only smart person around here. When the bank confirmed Eriksson had paid the money to Quinn exactly as he claimed, I decided to do something on the quiet. I was doubtful it would work, so I didn't say anything about it. But it has.'

'What effin' worked?'

'My own boolean search.' She scrolled down to the end of the post. 'Ah-ha! Here they are. The woman who made this post has done what everyone else does, added hashtags. They also happen to be the terms the program's been looking for over the last six weeks. Finally, they've appeared together in the same post.'

Jack saw the line of five hashtags at the bottom of the post: #yorkville #icehockey #mavericks #mavs #jonaseriksson. 'What program?'

'It's a social listening tool. Searches across all the major platforms in real time. We've got our own proprietary one running in the background, the one Wilson's got an eye on, but I wanted to try my own combination of terms.'

'So you input all of those words as terms that had to show up together in the one post?'

She shook her head. 'I said a long shot, not an impossible shot. I didn't specify Mavs or Mavericks. There's an American pro basketball team of the same name and nickname, which would have had so many online mentions it may have screwed things up.' She scrolled back to the top of the post, turned her head up to Jack and grinned. 'Look at the profile. Seems she's used her real name.'

'Let's pay this woman a visit, shall we?'

'One second.' Taylor saved the image to her desktop, edited it by cropping everything out except the shiny silver trophy and the two hands holding onto it. Zooming in to read the inscription produced a blur of words. The camera must have decided to focus on the woman's face at the expense of everything else in the frame.

'I've got another idea.' She opened an internet browser and ran an image search. Lots of results. The fifth one took their breath away.

———

MIMI FOXGLOVE'S bedroom was painted lurid pink. Shelves lining three walls were adorned with blue-eyed china dolls, fluffy toys, and, in the top right corner by her white-and-gold Queen Anne dresser, the trophy. Jack nodded at it and said, 'May I?'

'Of course.' The large-framed woman was in her early thirties. She sported pigtails adorned with blue ribbons and wore a checked blue-and-white pinafore over a puffy-sleeved white blouse, white ankle-length socks and a pair of red slippers. As he took the three strides to get to the trophy he whispered in Taylor's ear, 'I've got a feeling we're not in Yorkville anymore.'

He snapped on blue rubber gloves and pulled down the trophy, immediately adjusting his grip as its immense weight caught him by surprise. Shaped like a ten-pin with a stylised hockey player on top wielding a hockey stick, it sat on a round wooden pedestal. 'Can you tell me who gave you this?'

'A friend of mine.'

'Can you tell us his name?' said Taylor.

'Her name.'

'A woman gave you this?' said Jack. 'Your post said one of the Mavs' players did. So it wasn't the man whose name's on the inscription?'

She gave a guilty tilt of the head. 'I'm sorry. I don't go out anywhere. I've got agoraphobia. Sometimes I…exaggerate things on my Instagram page.' She gave an awkward laugh. 'It was my friend who comes and sits with me sometimes when I'm feeling down. He gave it to her and she gave it to me.'

Jack said through gritted teeth. 'The name, please!'

'I don't want to get her into trouble.' A tear ran down Mimi's chubby cheek.

A voice came from the doorway. Both detectives turned around. Mimi's mother, who'd let them into the house just minutes ago, stood with slumped shoulders, desperate sadness etched in her eyes. 'Please go easy on her. Mimi's a little–'

'Dorothy, mum! I'm Dorothy today.'

'Come with me.' Mrs Foxglove escorted the detectives into the loungeroom. 'You'll want to be speaking with a woman called Gemma Ransome.'

Taylor whipped out her notebook. 'Got an address?'

Mrs Foxglove gestured with her head. 'Right next door.'

Before they left the house, Jack held out the trophy so Taylor could take a snapshot and send it to the Inspector. In particular, she made sure the inscription was in sharp focus. ECHL Championship 2007. David Quinn. River City Blizzards. A valued player in our mighty team.

JACK WRAPPED hard on the aluminium flyscreen with his gnarled knuckles. A timid voice came from behind the door. 'Yes?'

'Police. Open up!'

Within ten minutes the woman had caved. 'Holy shit. Mimi's got a fucking Instagram account? I can't believe it.'

'I think Mimi's smarter than you give her credit for,' said Taylor.

'Am I in trouble?'

'Massive trouble,' said Jack. 'You'll be charged with being an accessory after the fact to murder. The charge carries a maximum sentence of life imprisonment. Same as if it was you wielding the weapon instead of David Quinn.'

'No!' She began to sob hysterically. 'All I did was...say I'd...look after it...'

Jack was having none of it. 'Bullshit. You knew what was going on; that's why you handed it over to Mimi, thinking she'd stick it on one of her fantasy shelves and no one would ever be the wiser.'

'Please!' she wailed, hugging herself with thin, heavily tattooed arms. 'I've never done anything bad in my life.'

'How did it come to be in your possession? Remember, telling lies won't help you.'

'I met David at Regine's nightclub. He had the trophy tucked under a jacket, asked me to put it in my handbag. For safekeeping. It barely fit, but I squeezed it in somehow. Later, we came back here and...you can guess the rest.' She sobbed. 'When he was leaving in the morning, he said I could keep it.'

'Then why'd you give it to Mimi?'

'She needs things to brighten her life. It's why she collects all that crap.'

Jack shook his head. 'I don't believe you for a second. It didn't seem odd to you that he brought a hefty trophy to a nightclub?'

A hesitant head shake. 'Not really. I didn't think about it.'

'Pull the other one. Quinn confided in you about what he did.' He said to Taylor, 'This town's going to become famous for ice hockey groupies. Who'd have thought it?'

'Not me.' Taylor said to Gemma, 'Grab whatever you need for a night in the cells before I formally arrest you.'

A small child, a girl of about three, waddled up the corridor. Jack pinched his nose hard. *Why do they always have little kids?* 'Listen, you got someone to look after the wee tyke?'

'My…m-m-mother,' she blubbered. 'But she can't know about this!'

'Sorry, Gemma,' said Taylor. 'Everyone will know about this by the end of the day. You won't be coming back home unless the magistrate grants you bail. With a crime this serious, I wouldn't count on that happening.'

On Gemma's behalf, Taylor made a hasty phone call to the mother, prepared her for the worst. Mum readily agreed to take the child, promised to arrive within the next twenty minutes. Taylor then formally read out the charge, advised the woman of her rights, including the right to legal representation, and snapped on a pair of handcuffs.

'No need for the cuffs, sunshine,' said Jack. 'She ain't going anywhere, are you, love?'

'Fair call,' said Taylor, taking the cuffs off again.

Head bowed, all Gemma could do was choke back the sobs.

In the squad car, Jack called the Inspector on his private number. No preamble. 'We've made one arrest in the Eriksson case, sir.'

'You're kidding! It was some local hitman after all, hey?'

'No, sir. We've arrested the accessory. The killer is David Quinn.'

'I'll call Victoria Police to pick him up and arrest him. Then we'll extradite him to Queensland.'

Jack grinded a chunk of chewing gum overtime. 'Can you hold off on that for a bit?'

'Why? We need to act now.'

'I want to tie up some loose ends in my mind. Make sure he can't wriggle out of it.'

'I don't know, Jack...'

'Trust me. I've got a couple of theories, but they need confirmation. I want to talk it all over with you and Taylor.'

Batista took in a deep breath. 'Alright. But if he gets away while we muck about...'

'Sir. Relax. He's blissfully unaware of anything right now.' He terminated the call, indicated a left turn and pulled into the station. He looked over his shoulder at Gemma Ransome, ninety percent of the life gone from her eyes.

Too bad.

Chapter Thirty-Two

'THE UNDERSIDE of the trophy proves it was fake, sir.' Jack leaned the heavy item on its side. 'Check out the name of the manufacturer. Eccleston and Sons, Caulfield, Victoria. You imagine the ECHL's gonna commission this little Aussie business to make their trophies?'

'But why? It makes no sense?'

'And look here.' Jack pointed with the tip of a pen. 'What does that look like to you?'

'Could be a tiny speck of blood.'

Jack nodded. 'Yep. Could be. He would've wiped it down with something, washed it, who knows. But his adrenaline would've been through the roof, so he's missed a spot.'

'Might not be blood either,' said Taylor.

Jack recoiled. 'Don't be a killjoy, DC Taylor. Of course it's effin' blood.' He placed the trophy in a large plastic bag, ready for delivery to Proctor.

'The Inspector asked the most important question just now. Why?'

'You have an answer, Claudia?' said Batista.

She nodded. 'I believe I might have an idea. The 2007 championship match mentioned on the trophy? I trawled back through the team lists from that final game. Quinn wasn't on it. I believe the fact he didn't play might have something to do with Eriksson. What, exactly, we'll find out after we arrest him. I think killing him with this fake trophy on centre ice was symbolic.'

Jack nodded and looked at the Inspector. 'We talked about this in the car on the way back to the station, sir. I propose we contact other players and staff from that match. One of them might be able to clue us in on the circumstances.'

'Do it,' said Batista. He waited a moment, then switched it up. 'Now, let's talk about the "how". What about the CCTV of the team leaving the arena? We clearly saw Quinn outside the entrance well before the estimated time of death.'

Jack held up a finger. 'If you remember, some of them were leaving in groups of three and four. I wouldn't mind having one more look at the footage. Let's get Wilson in, too. The lad's got an eye like a hawk.'

Ten minutes later, with Gemma Ransome in the interview room conferring with a lawyer from Legal Aid, the video played out on the large monitor in the incident room. 'Stop it…there,' said Jack. Wilson clicked the mouse. 'What do you see?'

'I see David Quinn, three of his buddies,' said Taylor.

'Go again…and…stop.'

'What the?' said the Inspector. The men on the screen had stopped and formed a little scrum as Riley Kane passed them on the right, bent down, and, a fraction of a second later, was gone. 'He was telling the truth. He did drop his phone.'

'Yes,' said Jack. 'I was so sure it was Kane; I was blinded to the obvious suspect right in front of us. Go again, Ben.'

The video resumed, only this time it was just Quinn's three teammates walking down the path, away from the stadium. Quinn had disappeared, too, as if by magic. 'I thought something like this might have happened when I remembered an episode of a TV series back in the day,' said Jack. '*Banacek*, it was called. Bleedin' brilliant, it was. Anyway, in this particular episode, an American footballer got tackled, a whole bunch of guys piled on, and when they peeled away, the bloke was gone. The whole thing was captured by TV cameras, and no one was able to figure out what the hell had happened. A bit like our situation.'

'This is too much of a coincidence,' said Batista, rubbing his jaw. 'It's like a choreographed dance. Kane and Quinn must have been in cahoots.'

Jack shook his head. 'No, sir. A coincidence is all it is. So what if Quinn returned to the stadium? It's all about when he left the second time. After the CCTV was switched off.'

Batista waved a hand. 'Then why does this even matter?'

'Because he lied about it. He swore he never re-entered the stadium.'

'Correct,' said Taylor.

'And it was Quinn who drugged Campbell?' said Batista.

'Yes,' said Jack. 'But that one will be hard to prove without a confession.' He grinned. 'Which I plan to get. From both of those toe-rags.'

Taylor said, 'If Quinn got wind of Campbell's money worries, he may have paid him generously to voluntarily take the roofie. And out of the goodness of his heart,

Campbell obligingly told Quinn about the cameras going off at midnight.'

'No such payment showed up in Quinn's bank statement,' observed Batista.

'Course not,' said Jack. 'Would've been cash, innit?'

'Alright,' said Batista. 'I think we've got the makings of a very good case. The bogus trophy's enough on its own, I believe, but it doesn't hurt to tick everything off.' He paused for a moment, then added. 'Last item on my list. What about the musician who reckons he saw Kane speaking intently with Eriksson at the party?'

'The two men are almost as big as each other,' said Jack. 'One inch difference in height. Trevarthen only showed Sly a photo of Kane. I'd wager if we now showed him one of Quinn, he'd probably concede it could've been him, too.'

'OK,' said Batista, looking in turn at Jack and Taylor. 'The lawyer's had enough time with that stupid woman. Go get 'em.'

Chapter Thirty-Three

THE RED-EYE special from Cairns touched down with a thump, then trundled smoothly along the runway of Melbourne's Tullamarine Airport. Neither a delay in the final stages of taxiing due to congestion on the runways nor a mechanical issue with the aircraft's doors that slowed disembarkation was able to spoil Jack's mood.

Vicpol had requested Jack come down to be on hand while they made the arrest. He had an inkling it may have been Batista behind the so-called request; Jack's image all over the media as a senior figure in bringing the case to a close would be fantastic PR for the Yorkville CIB, the QPS in general. Jack grinned to himself as he strode through the airport terminal. After the mauling the police had received in the press over the last three months, the arrest would also be a spectacular middle finger to Holly Maguire and co.

Inside the bustling reception hall, a burly male Detective Chief Inspector, a slimmer female Detective Senior Constable, and four uniformed officers in bulky kit greeted Jack with firm handshakes. 'Good flight, I hope?' said DCI Archie Brownstone.

'I slept most of the way. Food was dreadful, the coffee was worse.'

The uniforms laughed, Brownstone and his partner merely nodded. 'You've landed in the coffee capital of the world,' said DSC Imogen Turner. 'You might like to sample some of it later?'

'Nothing beats my machine at home,' said Jack. He wondered for a second if Turner had just hinted at a personal invitation, then dismissed the notion.

'The Mavericks' flight arrives in exactly one hour,' said Brownstone. 'You up for it?'

'I'm always ready,' said Jack.

Jack had checked the result online. The Mavericks had played a match in Adelaide last night. David Quinn scored four goals in a comfortable win for his side. It would be the last victory he'd ever enjoy.

An hour later, the flight from the city of churches landed bang on time. The police officers stood shoulder to shoulder on the carpeted area of the small waiting lounge: detectives in front, uniforms either side.

Passengers began to file out, none suspecting one of their number was about to be arrested and hauled away. Business class done and dusted, the athletic figures of track-suited athletes began to amble through the gate.

'I see him,' said Jack. David Quinn, flanked by two teammates, breached the passenger tunnel. The son-of-a-bitch wore a broad grin, obviously pleased with his efforts in last night's battle.

'Focus now, people,' said Brownstone, as he stepped forward, Turner and Jack half a pace behind him. The DCI manoeuvred his way between a couple of Mavs players until he was face to face with Quinn. The American's smile began to slowly fade. 'David Quinn?'

'Yes?' His eyes were darting all over the place, expanded as he clocked the phalanx of officers. His broad chest was rising and falling quickly; Jack sensed the fight or flight mechanism was about to kick in.

'Step this way, please.' Brownstone held out his ID, opened his mouth to inform Quinn of his fate, when all hell broke loose.

Quinn roared, grabbed two female passengers in each of his huge hands, pulled them towards himself as a temporary shield, then shoved the screaming women towards the detectives. The collision gave him the split second he needed to take off. He dashed to the left, easily hurdled a row of empty seats, sprinted in the same direction the exiting passengers were streaming.

The uniforms were first to head off in pursuit, yelling at Quinn to stop and the public to get out of the way. Their heavy vests and other equipment slowed them down, and Jack overtook them in a heartbeat. Tracking Quinn, his head sticking up above the crowd, was the easy part. Catching him – that was the hard part. DSC Turner's pounding footsteps sounded over Jack's left shoulder, her beefy boss unable to keep up the chase.

Adrenaline surging through his system, Jack found another gear. 'David Quinn!' He managed to shout. 'Stop immediately!'

But Quinn wouldn't listen. He dropped his carry-on duffel bag, bolted for an escalator, shoving and barrelling people out of his way as he went. Then, a skidding right towards an emergency exit sign.

Cold Shot

'I'm with you,' panted Turner. She put on the afterburners and overtook Jack. Quinn was a fast runner, but they were gaining on him. *You're not on skates now, sunshine.*

Ten metres, five...

Quinn's hand was now on the push handle. Turner launched herself like a cannonball, drove her shoulder into the fugitive's legs, just behind the knees. He crumpled to the floor, screaming. He spun his body around to confront whoever it was that tackled him, saw Turner winded on the ground. He lashed out hard with his right foot and collected her in the side of the head, sent her tumbling.

By now, Jack was upon Quinn. He dropped to one knee, with blinding speed unleashed a power jab flush on Quinn's nose. As blood spouted, Jack repeated the dose with a right cross, one more left, a whooshing uppercut, to finish him off.

'Get back, DS Lisbon!' yelled a deep male voice behind him.

Before Jack could comply, two pairs of strong hands grabbed his shoulders and lifted him to his feet. He looked on as two more young constables hauled Quinn to an unsteady upright position, spun him around and slapped on a pair of handcuffs.

Jack glared at Quinn, covered in blood and mumbling incoherently.

'That's the trouble with you show ponies,' he spat. 'No effin' defence.'

DCI Brownstone, clearly in need of a stint at bootcamp, stepped forward and huffed, 'Thanks, Detective Lisbon. We'll take it from here.'

A crowd of rubberneckers was watching from a safe distance, many holding aloft their mobile phones. Jack smiled: the plan had been to alert the media immediately after Quinn's arrest. He knew the world would know about what just happened in a matter of minutes. It prompted him to pull out his mobile and text two words to Taylor. *Got him!*

Chapter Thirty-Four

ONE WEEK LATER

THE WARM AFTERNOON sun kissed the surface of the water as Skye prepared to cast her line into the sea. The location was a "secret" spot, according to Trevarthen. A secret the other two parties set up a hundred metres either side of them must have known about.

The long, crescent-shaped foreshore, with hundreds of boulders littering the beach, was partly sheltered to the west by a line of tall trees. A rocky outcrop 25 metres from shore was the perfect spot for the barramundi to hang about. From his fold-out camp chair, to Jack this view looked like heaven on Earth.

Even with other anglers competing for fish, the water was teaming with barramundi, and there was more than enough to go around. The fish were practically throwing themselves at the shiny hardbody lures today. At the rate they were hauling them in, and with the minimum legal size being nearly two feet, the big Eski would soon be full, even after scaling, gutting and filleting the catch.

'She's got the hang of this pretty quick,' said Taylor, leaning back in a banana lounge and watching Skye through reflector sunglasses.

Jack laughed as he cracked open a can of soft drink. 'She's already caught four to my two. And she's strong enough to land the smaller ones herself.'

'Daaad! Help!'

This wasn't a small one. Jack grabbed the landing net, handed it to Skye while he wrestled the monster and reeled it in. He strained with every fibre to lift the barra up and into the net. He cut it loose, resumed his seat, and Skye tossed the line in once more. 'No more help, sunshine,' Jack called out. 'You're on your own from now on.'

'From what I read in the paper, you busted a gut catching Quinn.' Taylor laughed. 'No wonder you've got no energy left to help your daughter again.'

'Don't believe everything you read in the paper. You should know that by now.'

She sat up, spun around, lifted her sunnies and looked into Jack's eyes. 'You know, I just remembered something Quinn said to us when we first interviewed him. We were talking about that Finnish guy. Jari Aalto. Remember?'

'Uh-huh.'

'He said Aalto was an empath.'

'Yeah. I know exactly what you're going to say next.'

'What, smarty pants?'

'That it's ironic, because Quinn himself turned out to be a bleedin' psychopath.'

She frowned. 'Such a sad story, for so many involved.'

'Don't worry. We'll get to relive it all over again when Quinn's tried for murder in six months' time.' Jack pulled his straw fishing hat down tighter as a breeze sprang up out of nowhere. 'Shouldn't take too long since he fessed up to everything. I was expecting a bit more resistance from the tough guy.'

'Hoping for it, more likely.' Taylor smiled as she watched an eagle soaring in the distance. In a more serious tone she said, 'He really thought Eriksson took him out at a training session on purpose so he wouldn't get to play in that final match.'

Jack shrugged. 'He might have had a point. His medical records showed the pelvic injury Eriksson caused him was on the extreme end of serious. The surgeon's report said it was like Quinn had been hit by a speeding truck, not a man on skates slamming him into the boards. But then to set up the elaborate murder, with that fake trophy? That does take the mind of a psychopath.'

Jack's phone rang. 'Where is it, dammit?' He patted a pile of towels, plucked out the device. 'Inspector. I hope it's important, it's my day off 'n all.'

Out of the corner of his eye he saw Taylor grinning with her head tilted back.

'I'll put you on loudspeaker. Taylor's with me. She'll be interested, too.'

'I've had a call from Interpol. Mikel Bubla's been arrested for the drug heist in 2015. All thanks to you locating that phone, Jack. They want to give you some kind of reward.'

'Come on, sir. That's a bit over the top.'

'That's not the best bit. They've also managed to track down the blackmailer. A guy called Finlay Farnsworth. He was in on the heist, was promised a cut of the loot, but, like Eriksson, got nothing. Apparently, he thought he was the only one to miss out. He targeted Eriksson only because Bubla was too hard to find.'

'But not for Interpol?' said Jack.

'They've got resources you and I can only dream about.'
'I guess so.'
'Daaad!'
'Sorry, sir. Emergency. Gotta go and help a young girl land a fish.'

More from Blair Denholm

vinci-books.com/revolution-day

In a nation built on lies, one detective risks everything to uncover the truth and prevent catastrophe.

In Soviet-era Moscow, Detective Captain Viktor Voloshin defies the regime to investigate a brutal murder. With anonymous bomb threats, deadly black market operations, and his own demons haunting him, the detective must confront corruption at every turn.

Keep turning the pages for a free preview…

A free prequel novella...

vinci-books.com/takedown-free

Get the explosive prequel to The Fighting Detective series, absolutely free.

Revolution Day: Chapter One

'ARE YOU THERE YET?' Burov barked, his words difficult to make out over the crackle of the two-way radio.

'Nearly, Comrade Colonel.'

'You'd better be, Voloshin. Recover the body, get it to the morgue as fast as possible.'

'ETA five minutes.' I quirked an eyebrow at my driver, Lieutenant Yegor Adamovsky. He nodded and returned his attention to the road.

'I want this case solved and put to bed. Understand? It's a potential PR disaster for Gorbachev, the Party, the entire country.'

'Yes, Comrade Colonel.'

'The Central Intelligence Directorate's asked us to conduct a quick preliminary investigation until they take over.'

'When will that be?'

'When they tell us,' said Burov. 'Over and out.'

Yegor chuckled.

'Shut the hell up and drive.'

Masses of red flags lined both sides of the highway. Our clunky Militsiya Lada sedan skipped across Leninsky Prospekt, slick with ice. Snow flecked with dirty grey gravel lay in thick drifts at the sides of the four-lane highway. Trolleybuses and trams stopped at regular intervals to pick up shivering commuters. We hurtled along a five-kilometre section of road that bisected a vast wooded parkland. Yegor wrenched the wheel left and right as the car fish-tailed down the highway.

'Oi!' The burr of the engine and static radio chatter compelled me to shout. 'I'd like to arrive in one piece if you don't mind.'

'We have to hurry, Comrade Captain. You heard what the Colonel said.' He gave me a wide-eyed stare. 'Only a handful of officers are at the scene. If word spreads about what's happened and we aren't there to lend our authority, well...'

'I know that.' I took a deep breath. 'But getting there five minutes earlier won't make much difference. Especially for the victim.'

'What do you mean?'

'He's already dead.'

Yegor nodded. 'Yes, of course. But there could be a panic if we don't...'

The car tilted, just missed a truck passing in the opposite lane. 'Watch out, you moron,' I spat. Yegor, teeth clenched, regained control of the swaying vehicle. 'Slow down immediately.'

'Sorry.'

My warning all but ignored, we drove the next 500 metres at 95 clicks an hour, an insane speed for the icy conditions. A concrete barricade blocked the road ahead. I stared at Yegor, his boot still firmly planted on the accelerator.

'Slow down, for God's sake.'

He slammed his foot on the brake, the vehicle slid sideways. The rear right wheel struck the gutter and the car bounced twice before landing with a clunk. I gripped Yegor by the forearm. 'You'll kill both of us. What's wrong with you?'

'Sorry, Comrade Captain. You know the old saying. *What Russian doesn't enjoy a fast ride?* Anyway, you can relax. We're here.'

Sergeant Anatoly "Tolya" Pronin waited for us on the side of the road near two Militsiya vans. In the highway's outer lane a squat, round cop from the Traffic Directorate Branch waved a striped baton like an orchestra conductor at drivers who slowed down to rubberneck. Probably anticipating a car accident in the icy conditions. Thank God they'd be spared the horrific crime scene a hundred metres from the highway.

'So glad you've arrived, comrades.' Pronin saluted, waited for my acknowledgement.

'Put your hand down, Sergeant,' I said. 'No ceremony needed with me. You should know that by now.'

'Yes, Viktor Pavlovich.' He dropped his hand, the tight lines at the corners of his mouth softened. After eighteen months at Yugo-Zapadnaya Militsiya station the men still treated me like a newcomer. Gavril Peskov, the man I replaced, a fixture at the station for thirty years, suddenly dropped dead at his desk. Massive stress-induced heart attack. He had a reputation for being a hard-arse, a stickler for procedure. By comparison, I was a free spirit and the crew were still trying to figure me out. 'Would you like some details?'

'I'm listening.' I raised a flap of my ushanka fur hat and pointed at my ear. Pronin smiled but I heard Yegor groan. 'Talk and walk. Time's ticking.'

As we set off into the forest, we passed a hulking, ruddy-cheeked officer who snapped out a salute, then thrust his hands behind his back. I smiled at Pronin. 'See, that's how you do it. Short and sweet. So, what else have you got for me?'

'Okay,' Pronin inhaled deeply. A furrowed brow told me he was anxious not to forget anything. 'I placed Sasha Kozlov on guard at the start of the forest path.' He glanced at his watch. 'About an hour ago. Kirill Gregoriev's manning the track where it exits to the Chekhov Institute, one of those colleges for foreign students, on Bolshevistskaya Street.'

'Anyone approach our men with information?'

'Kozlov's turned away a few brave joggers who don't give a damn about the cold. Otherwise, not too many eager to enter the forest with Militsiya about. The Traffic Division cop's been very diligent, too. One glare from him would scare off anybody.'

'And the guy at the far end of the path?' I sidestepped a puddle with little chunks of ice floating on the surface.

'Don't know, sir. I haven't spoken to Gregoriev for a while. Too busy keeping the dead man company.'

'Witnesses?' My hopes weren't high. A lonely track on a bitter winter's morning isn't the most pleasant place to spend time. Just after dawn, an anonymous male called in from a payphone. Reported the crime and promptly hung up. A potential A-grade witness scratched from the start.

'But there was one person near the scene when we arrived.'

'Who?'

'An old woman in a blind panic. She stumbled upon the victim just after first light. She buried a dog here.'

'She did what?' I stopped, spun around to face Pronin. 'When? This morning?'

'Uh, no sir. I should have been clearer.' He consulted a notebook. 'Let's see. Her name's Nina Petrova. Lives in an apartment block less than 300 metres away. Apparently, her terrier died last summer. Couldn't afford to dispose of the little fella properly, so she and her son, Vasily, dug a hole and buried him here. The dog that is, not Vasily.' He laughed uneasily, checked his notes again. 'She visits every week. Probably goes without saying, but she's a bit loopy.'

'People can't go burying animals in public parks.' I gestured for Pronin to lead on through the forest. 'Has to be a public health violation. She could've buried the bloody thing in the cemetery down the road.'

'I'm pretty sure that's just for humans, Comrade Captain,' said Yegor. He leaned in closer to my shoulder as the path narrowed. 'Should we see the victim before we interrogate her?'

I ignored Yegor's question. "Where is she then?' We need to interview her in depth.'

Pronin coughed into his fist, steam from his breath poured between his fingers. 'Gone home, sir.'

'You have her address, I take it?'

'Of course.' Pronin pointed over my shoulder to the northern edge of the park. 'Her apartment's over there. Did you really expect a 90-year-old babushka to wait in the freezing cold until the chief investigator showed up?'

'Yes,' I replied. 'Obviously.'

'Viktor Pavlovich, with respect, she'll be more inclined to answer questions in the comfort of her own apartment.'

As if confirming his argument, a gust of wind shrieked through the power lines.

'Witnesses have better recall when the time between the incident and the interview is minimized,' I said flatly. 'That's basic police work. Something you should know.'

'We couldn't keep her here. She was raving, struggling not to lose it. Deep shock. Rita Vasilyeva took her home before she passed out in the snow.' Pronin nodded towards a uniformed woman standing about 30 metres ahead, hands behind her back, her gaze fixed on something hidden in a dense thicket of birch trunks. 'The old woman's son was home. He's with her now, waiting for us to return.'

'Any other civilians see the body?' We continued to shuffle along the path, skirting ice-encrusted puddles and slippery mud.

'Yes, Comrade Captain. Some schoolkids were hanging around when we arrived, but they scarpered. Vasilyeva and Gregoriev gave chase but the little bastards pissed off.'

'How many?'

'Three.'

'You saw them?'

'No, not me. Rita and Kirill spotted them standing around the corpse. When the officers called out, the children took off like startled deer.'

'Fitness standards have certainly dropped since I joined the Militsiya. I can't believe two adults couldn't catch them. We need their statements.'

'There are things you haven't considered,' said Yegor.

I gave him my fiercest glare. 'Your tone is verging on impudent, Lieutenant. What haven't I considered?'

'Trauma.' Yegor persisted.

'Elaborate.'

'Like Pronin said. The kids saw the body. It could mentally scar them for life.'

'True. Pronin, make sure Rita and Krill provide a full description of those kids. Finding them'll be next to impossible, but we've got to try.'

'Yes, Comrade Captain.' Pronin stepped over glittering shards of smashed vodka bottles, held out his hand in warning. 'Watch your step, comrades. Popular route for drunks, this. We've gathered pieces of glass near the crime scene. For forensics. But the place is littered with…well…litter. I reckon it's a pointless exercise.'

He was right. The area was strewn with all kinds of garbage, much of it slimy and fetid. 'That's it for witnesses?' I asked.

Pronin shrugged. 'Maybe there were more. Who knows? No one has come forward apart from the man who called it in.'

'Is it him?' I pushed branches aside as we edged ever closer to the murder scene.

Pronin stopped, eyebrows arched. 'Who?'

'You know who I mean. The missing student.'

'Hang on a second.' Pronin reached deep into his coat pocket. 'I found this near the body. He held out a dark green foreign passport. I went to take it, but he tightened his hold.

'Come on, man,' I growled. 'Give it to me.'

'Is the missing student a Nigerian, by any chance?'

'Stop playing games and hand it over.'

'Name of Aaron Adekanye? Date of birth 5th of January 1964?'

'Yes, damn you. I should have you sacked for such insolence.' Of course, that would never happen. Pronin was efficient, loyal and tough – one of the best officers I'd ever worked with.

Pronin released his grip and I snatched at the document, kept walking to where the path widened slightly to a small clearing. A quick scan of the passport confirmed what was until now a supposition.

Yegor stopped suddenly, grabbed my elbow. 'Captain, look.' I glanced in the direction his trembling index finger was pointing. I now saw what Rita Vasiliyeva had been staring at. 'Oh my god,' I mumbled. It was all I could do to not to throw up.

Revolution Day: Chapter Two

A MAN'S mutilated body hung limp from the bough. Higher up, strong gusts whistled through high-voltage power lines and support towers that marched across the parkland. Even this far into the woods, the wind punched through the bare, tightly bunched birch and larch trees. The corpse swayed almost imperceptibly in the wind, as if the man still had some life left in him.

    I stepped closer, a metre from the body. Simmering anger at the brutal treatment of the victim fought with my professional curiosity. For me, facing this kind of murder victim was unusual. The cases I deal with are mainly related to domestic violence. Women beaten to death by alcoholic husbands. Lovers knifed in fits of jealousy. Hit over the head with a rolling pin. Most cadavers I see are already at the morgue. I take people there to identify relatives. Accident victims. Drunk vagrants who passed out in the snow and died from hypothermia. Or drivers who refused to wear a seatbelt and ended their lives as human missiles flying through windscreens. Those dead souls looked at peace compared to the man on the end of the rope. His final moments would have been the stuff of nightmares. I tilted my head 45 degrees to the left.

'Any clearer at that angle, Captain Voloshin?' Yegor quipped over my shoulder.

'I hold my head like this when I'm concentrating.'

'Dogs do that when they're curious.'

'Are you comparing me to a dog, officer?'

'No, of course not, I...'

'I find it helps me determine the complexity of a problem. Figure out what's the best way forward.'

'Has it helped you now?'

'Not really.' I stood. 'This act is so heinous, I can't comprehend the mind of a human that would do this to another. Fucking monsters.'

Yegor scratched his cheek. 'That's an understatement. Not sure there's a precedent for this.'

'There is.'

'Really?'

'More than twenty years ago. A student from Ghana was found dead. Like this guy, in a forest.'

'You're kidding.'

'I'm serious. 1963 to be exact. It was a huge scandal. Embarrassing for the Soviet Union. There was plenty of press coverage abroad, but not here. Hushed up like you'd expect. There were even protests in Red Square. African students marched about with placards. They accused Moscow of being a city of racists, like Alabama in the USA.'

'Holy shit. Was the killer caught?'

'The official verdict was accidental death. The coroner declared the man drank too much, wandered into the forest, collapsed and froze to death.'

'Do you believe that version? Sounds way too convenient.'

I shook my head. 'To guarantee impartiality, a Ghanaian medical student attended the autopsy. To make sure there was no funny business.'

'But do you believe it was death by misadventure?'

'No. He was found far from his registered address. His institute was in another city altogether. The Ghanaian student could have been paid off, threatened. But it doesn't matter what I think. Whatever the truth, hundreds of Africans were pissed off, convinced the guy had been assassinated.'

'This man definitely was. I mean, it's not suicide.'

I gave a sharp nod, plucked a cigarette from a packet sporting the portrait of Laika, the first dog in space. I struck a match, cupped my hands. I hunched over and tried to disappear into my greatcoat. Cigarette lit, I emerged from the coat, expelled a cloud of smoke into the crisp morning air. 'Burov was right, the ramifications of this are massive.' I took a drag on the cigarette, the cheap tobacco tasted so foul it probably contained traces of Laika's fur. 'I'm nervous about what lies ahead.'

'Don't stress, Viktor Pavlovich. Remember, Burov said the CID would take over after we've completed the preliminary work.'

We both fell silent, refocusing on the victim. He was a big specimen; over two metres tall and broad in the shoulders.

'It must have taken a great deal of strength, numbers, or both to hoist the fellow up and secure the noose.'

'Got any theories about who might've done it?' Yegor shuffled his feet in the snow. 'Could it be someone involved in that incident you mentioned? Twenty-four years ago, but you never know. What if it was a relative of the real killer from 1963? Continuing the racist legacy.'

'Can you stop rambling?' I crushed the cigarette under my boot. 'Give me a few minutes to examine the scene before we embark on any speculation.'

'Sorry,' said Yegor. 'Just trying to help.'

'No. I'm sorry. I shouldn't have snapped like that.'

'That's OK, Viktor Pavlovich. Understandable given the circumstances. Not every day you're confronted by something like this.'

'Thankfully.'

A few metres from the victim's feet a wooden stool lay on its side. Those poor feet. Bits of toe and ankle bone protruded from the ruptured skin like gristle in bacon.

'They gave him a serious beating.'

'Unbelievable.' Yegor sniffed. 'Sick bastards.'

'The killers must've overpowered him or threatened him with a weapon. Then stood him on the chair and pulled it away. Left him there until he choked to death. I wonder why they didn't take the stool with them?'

'Maybe he was dead when they slipped the noose around his neck and the stool's got nothing to do with it. Could have been lying there the whole time.'

'Perhaps. The perps might've killed him first. But it's a lot harder lifting a dead man than a live one. I suspect he was still breathing before they strung him up.'

'Why harder?'

'Oh, for God's sake! Are you really that stupid?'

'Everyone knows you did a special KGB course. Learned some tricks.'

'Like someone asleep, a cadaver weighs no more than a live person. Basic physics. When you pick up a conscious man his centre of gravity shifts, weight distribution changes, muscles tense. Inadvertently, he helps you pick him up.'

'I hadn't thought of that.'

'If I try to lift my seven-year-old daughter after she's nodded off, it's like she weighs more than a refrigerator.'

Yegor rubbed his jaw. 'Maybe the killers beat him as he hung there.'

'Pointless if his neck was snapped. Perhaps they got perverse pleasure out of it. Anything's possible.'

'Fuckers.'

'Now, let me examine the scene thoroughly. I'm not standing around in the cold doing nothing waiting for forensics.'

'Of course.' He made two exaggerated steps to the left and a be-my-guest gesture with his hand.

'Have a poke around the woods for clues.'

'Will do, Comrade Captain.' Yegor marched off towards a well-worn side track.

Dark clouds threw a shadow over Adekanye's body, strung up like a sack of chaff. His face was a mass of bloody flesh around eyeballs swollen to the size of small potatoes, his head twisted at an unnatural angle, no doubt due to snapped vertebrae. His tongue lolled from his mouth, fat and long, his hands tied together behind his back with old rope. A wound – red, ragged and raw – framed the area where his genitals had been hacked off. Jesus, what kind of person would do this to another human being? Behind the body, his clothes lay in a disorganised pile: winter boots, thermal underwear, blue-and-white beanie, woollen jumper, gloves. Dressed for the outdoors. Most likely he hadn't been kidnapped from an indoor location. Poor bastard, out and about, living his life, suspecting nothing. A ragged Christian cross was carved into his back; a vertical line from the base of his neck to just above the coccyx. The horizontal line spanned his shoulder blades and looked to be a centimetre or two deep.

'Yegor, come back.' He turned and trotted back, splashing mud as he ran. 'Look at the cross.' I pointed to the wound.

'Jesus Christ!'

'In his honour, do you think?'

'What?'

'Not what. Who. Jesus.'

'Sorry. Didn't get your meaning. I'm an atheist, like most right-thinking citizens. But this is outright blasphemy whatever your beliefs.' Yegor doubled over like he was having an attack of appendicitis, took a couple of deep breaths. 'I mean…hell. What a thing to do to a man. Disgusting. And cutting off his dick and balls. Holy shit.'

Bile rose in my throat. 'There's symbolism attached to this.' I covered my mouth with my hand.

Yegor regained an upright posture, brought his breathing under control. 'Perhaps the killers were fanatical ultra-orthodox types and the cross means his existence was an offence to God.'

'And castrating a man is not an offence to God?' I shook my head.

'Hard-core racists believe black people are subhuman. Killing this guy would be of no more consequence than swatting a fly.'

I took a step back and marvelled at the outrageousness of the scene. Mahogany-coloured blood caked on the chest, stomach and legs. Again, my attention was drawn to the raspberry jam patch where his penis and testicles were supposed to be. Under him, more blood splatter – patches directly underneath, droplets of various sizes in a circular pattern around him.

I pulled a notebook from my coat pocket, made some quick notes and started to sketch the scene. I'd drawn a couple of lines when the crime scene photographer, Sergey Morozov, appeared from nowhere. He jumped about like a nervous rabbit, looked for the best spots to snap off a few shots.

'Excuse me, Viktor Pavlovich,' he stuttered, spittle flying through yellow teeth. 'May I take a picture from the front, right about where you're standing?' How fucking blasé could the man get? Had he no feelings? It was like we were at a model train exhibition rather than a murder scene.

'Wait a minute. I'm not finished drawing yet.'

Morozov frowned. 'You don't need to do that. My photographs will be good enough for the CID's investigation.'

'That's a matter of opinion.' I kept my eyes on my notebook. The little diagram was my form of insurance. Accidents occasionally happened in the dark room with film spoiling. Or negatives went missing. 'Come back when I'm done, okay? Then you can take all the pictures you want.' Morozov slinked off with a grimace, puffed away on a rancid papirosa cigarette. His black Zenit-19 camera bounced on his hip.

'We'll have to get the body down soon, Comrade Captain.' Yegor pointed to a pair of crows hopping about in the treetops. Two others squabbled on the ground nearby. Their cawing grew louder. The pallid sun peaked through the blanket of clouds momentarily before disappearing again.

'They sound hungry.' I jammed the notebook back in my pocket. 'And there's the man's dignity to consider. It's indecent to leave him there. We have to get the body to the morgue as quickly as possible. That was also Burov's directive. District Medical Examiner Ivanov's on standby for delivery, apparently.'

'Yes, Comrade Captain.' Colour was returning to Yegor's face.

'Where the hell are forensics, dammit? If they don't show in the next 15 minutes, I'm making the call for a truck to come and fetch the corpse.'

'Pronin, you combed the scene here before we arrived. I'm guessing no note was left claiming responsibility for this atrocity?'

'Sadly no.'

Wind gusted through the birch trees and I grabbed my hat to prevent it flying off. 'Maybe the killers did leave a message somewhere and it blew away in the wind.'

'With all due respect, I don't think we'll find anything apart from the stool, his clothes, the rope and more filthy trash. If they'd left a note, it would've been nailed to the tree he's dangling from or pinned to his person.'

'He's naked. How could they pin it to him?'

'Viktor Pavlovich, for a seasoned detective you are quite naïve at times.' Pronin had been at the station nearly as long as the dearly departed Peskov and wasn't afraid to voice his opinion to a senior officer. An insightful man, I was never offended by his directness the way others might be. 'People capable of doing this aren't going to baulk at pushing a safety pin through a man's flesh.'

My skin crawled. 'You're smarter than you look, Tolya. I can't understand why you haven't moved up in the ranks.'

'Never been one to aspire to your level, Comrade Captain. All that stress gives you wrinkles.'

I rubbed my forehead, feeling the network of furrows.

'Reckon we'll catch the killers?' Yegor squatted on his haunches like a peasant in a potato patch, patted his gloved hands together.

'Doubtful. Colonel Burov pulled me in for a briefing before we left the station. Said don't waste time on the matter if the body turned out to be the missing Nigerian. Gather evidence to hand over to CID and leave it at that.'

'Why?'

'He's the one who got me up to speed about the 1963 incident. Like you, I hadn't been aware of it.'

'Not exactly the kind of thing the Party would want taught in history classes, hey?'

'Indeed.' A light sleet swept across my eyes. 'Burov reckons there'll be massive pressure from the top to keep this case quiet. My opinion – they've already got to him.'

'What makes you say that?'

'Because this is clearly murder. If there was doubt about the cause of death 24 years ago, there is none here.'

'Surely Burov's interested in finding the culprits.'

'A repeat of the '63 protests is unthinkable with Perestroika and Glasnost in full swing. It might sound ironic, but the ideal of "openness" would be threatened by a public display of anger.'

'That doesn't make sense.'

'Think about it. Any protest today would be reported not just overseas, but here. Widely. Editors of the new liberal magazines would get an erection just thinking about publishing a story on protesting students. TV station executives, too. On the other hand you've got the old-school hardliners in the CPSU who'd claim all this openness has led to chaos. They'd say "We're not ready for it. We must return to the old ways." Bad publicity would put the entire program of reforms under imminent threat.'

'You can't believe what you're saying. A man's been murdered and the killers must be brought to justice. Simple as that.'

'I agree. But Burov said unless there's immediate and compelling evidence pointing to actual suspects, there'll be a quick autopsy and the body will be shipped back to Africa. In any event, we're to keep our investigations low-key.'

'Bloody hell.'

'He said there might be alternative scenarios. Internal squabbling or a black market deal gone wrong.'

'They may be plausible explanations, sure. We have to check all possibilities, right?'

'Of course. I reckon the insistence on discretion is to avoid spooking the foreign students. Averting public disorder is a worthy aim, I agree with that. This may turn out to be an isolated event.'

'I should bloody well hope so.'

'Burov's a good man at heart. If he tells us not to look hard for a racist motive, it's got to be pressure from above.'

'How high do you think? Politburo?'

'Possibly. The Ministry of Foreign Affairs would definitely have a vested interested in stalling our efforts. Then again, the victim's a student, meaning the Ministry of Education would be shitting bricks about adverse publicity. There's a ton of prestige attached to educating kids from the Third World. It's a matter of honour for the USSR. Besmirching that's gonna cost the country dearly.'

The distinct sound of marching boots sounded from down the path. Two Militsiya privates I didn't recognise emerged into the clearing. Probably seconded from another station; all our scant resources were either here at the crime scene or preparing for Revolution Day deployments.

One of the newcomers produced a hacksaw from a

vinyl duffel bag and gestured towards the victim. 'We've been ordered to take him to the morgue immediately.'

'Where the hell are the forensics team?'

'There's been a massive traffic accident outside Sheremetyevo Airport. Tourist bus cleaned up by a train at a level crossing. Mangled bodies everywhere.'

'Oh my God.' Reporting of a disaster like that would test the boundaries of Glasnost.

The man stared at me with pale grey eyes. 'Want us to cut him down now?'

'No, leave him there as a decoration for New Year's Eve. Of course cut him down, you idiot. Get him to the ground as gently as you can.'

One officer leap-frogged onto the shoulders of the other like a gymnast, and quickly sawed through the rope. The other chap stood flush against the cadaver, side on, wrapped a protective plastic sheet around the thighs, took a firm grip. Once the rope was cut, the man with the saw flung it to the ground. He snaked arms around the victim's neck to stop the body toppling forward. The first officer bent his knees, taking most of the weight of the body, while his companion dismounted from his mate's shoulders, never letting go of the neck. The two eased the dead man to the ground, stood to one side to let us take a closer look.

Morozov appeared again, snapped away from all angles. This time I said nothing until he'd used up the entire roll of film. He rewound the spool, popped it out and fished another from his pocket. I held up a hand. 'I think you've taken enough shots now.'

'But—'

'Enough, I said.' And, like mist, he was gone again.

On the ground the body seemed even bigger than when hung aloft. 'Bloating's a factor, but this is a larger-than-average human,' I said. 'At least two, maybe even three or more, were involved in his death. If it took these two strong lads to get him down, getting him up there would've been a struggle.'

'Sounds about right.' Yegor extracted a cigarette from his coat pocket. He offered me one and I took it. 'But who the hell did it?'

'That's what I'd like to find out.'

'So young.' Yegor shook his head as the shadows of the body and its two-man escort disappeared from view down the track. 'What was he doing in the USSR?'

'Medicine,' I said sharply. 'We know that.'

'Yeah, but was that all? We know foreign students are up to their eyeballs in illegal activities. Money changing, for example. Could be linked with that.'

'You're right. We have to rule things out before we rule things in. Let's talk to his classmates first. Break the bad news. And ask some questions.'

'What about interviewing babushka?'

'She can wait. Actually, I've got a better idea.' I waved to Rita Vasilyeva. She crabbed her way to me through slush and ice, probing sections of the path with the toes of her boots. 'Think you can get some useful information out of the old dear?'

'Doubt it, Comrade Captain. But I'll give it a try.'

'Take Pronin with you. Two is always better than one. Take notes and make sure to–'

'I can handle interviewing babushka,' she insisted gruffly. 'The old woman seemed to trust me when I took her home.'

'Sorry. We need more resources in this country to conduct investigations. The FBI would have put up crime scene tape all over the place. Squads of grunts in protective suits would be combing the area for clues, not to mention–'

'Yes,' said Yegor, a bit too curt for my liking. 'However we don't have their levels of violence.'

'Not yet.'

'We never will.'

'I hope you're right.' He wasn't. Violent crime was escalating in Moscow. Official statistics said otherwise, but government numbers were not to be trusted. In coming years the Militsiya would be found wanting when it came to fighting crime. Even now, our miserable rough-and-ready stockpile of equipment would make an American cop laugh his head off.

'Vasilyeva, you're a competent officer. Forgive me for questioning your abilities.'

She gave a nod and stared at the ground.

'Before you go, post Kozlov and Grigoriev by the tree. Morozov, too. He can be of use for a change.' There were thousands of trees all around, but everybody knew which one I meant.

Vasilyeva squared her shoulders. 'Yes, Comrade Captain.'

'Tell them to shoo away nosey parkers, forensics will be here shortly. I can't believe they weren't here before us. But I guess with that bad accident across town.'

'And it's extremely early, Comrade Captain,' Rita ventured. 'Extra manpower will free up soon.'

I nodded. 'Maybe. Anyway, all of us will chip in later to help Medical Examiner Ivanov conduct a methodical search. I suspect we'll have to wait until he's finished the autopsy.'

Disappointment clouded Pronin's face. 'That could take all day, Comrade Captain.'

'Do you have better things to do? More important than finding the sadistic pricks who tortured and murdered a man?'

'Well…'

'Didn't think so.'

'Stay here with the others until further notice.'

Pronin frowned.

'C'mon, Yegor. Let's get a move on. Do you know where the Gandhi University of Peace and Friendship is?'

'Of course. Not sure it's going to live up to its name, though.'

'Me either.'

Grab your copy…
vinci-books.com/revolution-day

About the Author

Blair Denholm is a born-and-bred Australian crime fiction writer whose previous jobs have been as varied as translator, debt collector, technology researcher, banking and insurance consultant, and even car-wash attendant. Over the years he has lived and worked in New York, Moscow, Munich, Abu Dhabi and Australia. His life-long love of sports is reflected in the plots of The Fighting Detective series.

Denholm's flagship series, The Fighting Detective, stars ex-boxer Detective Sergeant Jack Lisbon and is set in the steamy tropics of North Queensland, Australia. The series features heavy doses of noir crime with a vigilante justice twist. So far there are eight novels and one prequel novella in the series, with more in the pipeline.

Denholm's debut novel, *SOLD*, is the first in a noir trilogy featuring the detestable yet lovable one-man wrecking ball Gary Braswell. The book was long-listed for movie adaptation by Screen Queensland in 2019. The other books in this series are *Sold to the Devil* and *Sold Dirt Cheap*.

Denholm has also written two thriller novels set in Russia. Captain Viktor Voloshin is a hard-boiled investigator who has to fight the establishment in order for justice to be served in his own special way. The first in this series, *Revolution Day*, was published in 2021, with the follow-up, *The Defector*, released in 2024. One more book will round off this series.

In 2024, Denholm signed on with UK-based publisher Vinci Books.

Blair Denholm grew up in suburban Brisbane, Queensland. After two lengthy stints in Tasmania, he now resides in the relatively cooler climes of the Southern Downs region of Queensland with his partner, Sandra, and faithful dog, Bruno.

Acknowledgments

Thanks to my great Finnish friend, Mika, who introduced me to ice hockey many, many years ago. And, as always, to Sandra.

www.ingramcontent.com/pod-product-compliance
Ingram Content Group UK Ltd.
Pitfield, Milton Keynes, MK11 3LW, UK
UKHW040230220126
467235UK00004B/67